JUST SAY YES

MAXINE MORREY

Boldwood

First published in Great Britain in 2022 by Boldwood Books Ltd. This paperback edition first published in 2023.

1

Every effort has been made to obtain the necessary permissions with reference to copyright material, both illustrative and quoted. We apologise for any omissions in this respect and will be pleased to make the appropriate acknowledgements in any future edition.

A CIP catalogue record for this book is available from the British Library.

Paperback ISBN: 978-1-83518-815-6

Hardback ISBN 978-1-80162-640-8

Ebook ISBN 978-1-80162-644-6

Kindle ISBN 978-1-80162-643-9

Audio CD ISBN 978-1-80162-635-4

MP3 CD ISBN 978-1-80162-636-1

Digital audio download ISBN 978-1-80162-639-2

Large Print ISBN: 978-1-80162-642-2

Boldwood Books Ltd.

23 Bowerdean Street, London, SW6 3TN

www.boldwoodbooks.com

For Dad

Love you xx

PRONUNCIATION GUIDE

Brighid – Bree-ge (said in a similar way to 'breeze')
Eoghan – Owen
Fiadh – Fia
Roísín – Ro-sheen
Aoife – Ee-fah
Cillian – Killian
Siobhan – Shi-von (with a 'short' i)
Diarmaid – Dear-mad

1

Another deafening thunderclap boomed over the cottage, as lightning illuminated the dark day. The first rain in months fell heavily as the summer heatwave finally broke, sending that wonderful smell of petrichor drifting in through the open windows. Unfortunately, it didn't seem to be doing much to clear the humidity, and the air was still clammy as I listened to the steady drip drip drip from my leaking roof into the bucket I'd just emptied. The heat, although stifling, had at least been a respite from the emergency of a failing roof. That was the thing about old properties, they always held another surprise for you – and not always the good kind. My little cottage might look like the picture on a chocolate box but right now it was about as watertight as one. I crossed my fingers that today would help get me one step closer to changing that.

I glanced in the mirror, checking my appearance. I twisted my long auburn hair up and secured it neatly in a clip, keeping it off my neck in an attempt to stay cool, and then headed down the narrow stairs just as the brass doorbell clanged outside.

Pulling open the heavy front door revealed the epitome of a tall, dark, handsome – not to mention broad – stranger loitering there. From the emails I'd exchanged so far with the bride whose wedding I was being hired to plan, my initial thoughts were that she had great taste. Now seeing the man she was to marry, it seemed I was right.

He was looking around, striking dark blue eyes taking in the cluster of picturesque houses that hugged the village green, before his gaze returned to my own cottage. I was used to seeing this sense of wonder. I still got it myself at times when I came home, a feeling of surprise that this idyllic scene existed at all, let alone within easy access to London. I smiled, waiting patiently for the ensuing compliment.

'Jesus,' the soft Irish accent proclaimed. 'It's like something out of *Midsomer Murders*.'

I forced the smile to stay in place, mentally readjusting my earlier thoughts about the bride's taste. Clearing my throat, I stepped back from the door to indicate he should enter.

'Well, the police did find someone last month tied to the railway tracks in the model village with a toy train wedged in his mouth, but apart from that it's a perfectly lovely place to live. Would you like to come in?'

The man was staring at me.

'Don't worry. I promise it wasn't me. Do come in out of the rain.' I already had more than enough unwanted water coming into this house without standing here waiting for this rude man to let yet more in. His comment had irked me. It wasn't as if us villagers hadn't joked about the same thing ourselves, but there was something in the way he said it, as though he were laughing up his expensive sleeve at us, or would have been, had they not been rolled up to his elbows exposing tanned, muscular forearms. He stepped in and I took the black, old-fashioned umbrella with its beautiful, carved wooden handle from him and opened it to dry in the small boot room to the side of the front door. He might not have manners, but he did have good taste.

'Do you always invite strange men into your house without asking their name?' One coal-black brow rose, accompanying the softly spoken query.

'I'm afraid your accent gave you away and you are perfectly on time, Mr Kelly.'

'I'm not Mr Kelly,' the man replied, studying me, a hint of amusement showing at the corner of the just-full-enough lips.

A cool shiver trickled down my spine, despite the humidity of the day. The man's smile widened.

'Don't look so panicked. You're quite safe. I'm his best man, Lorcan O'Malley.' He held one large hand out. 'Pleased to meet you.'

I stuck out my own automatically, unsure what to make of this man other than the fact that he was probably one of the best-looking men I'd ever come across. Why did I only ever meet desirable men through work? I had a very strict policy about not mixing work with pleasure and right now work needed all the attention it could get. The pandemic had meant that my business, Hart's & Flowers, along with many like mine, had taken a big hit, so now I needed to find a way to recoup the losses I'd suffered. A lavish wedding for an American heiress could be the answer to, if not all my prayers, then at least some of them.

'Patrick should be here any minute. He's always late.'

'Oh dear. Hopefully he won't be late to the wedding,' I said, looking up at Lorcan.

'I guess that's my job to ensure he isn't.'

'Glad to hear you're already serious about your duties.' I smiled.

'I might not be a fan of weddings, or marriage, but I won't let Patrick down.'

'I see,' I replied, and made a mental note to keep an eye on him – not exactly the toughest of tasks when a man looked like he did.

'Would you like to come through to the kitchen? I must apologise – ordinarily I hold meetings in my garden office but the downpour has rather put paid to that today. I'm just waiting to have a path put in.'

In truth I was waiting for the money to be able to afford a path, but we didn't need to go into details.

'No problem.'

I led the way through into the airy kitchen. Thankfully, my cottage, though old, wasn't listed so I'd had leeway to make changes when I'd first moved in. Once dark and cramped, this room had been extended and it now opened out with patio doors to the well-tended garden beyond, flooding the kitchen with light. It was probably my favourite room in the house. A loud thunk caused me to spin around and I found Mr O'Malley rubbing his forehead and looking as if he was gritting back a choice word or two.

'Oh, my goodness, I'm so sorry! I should have warned you to mind your head. I'm not used to having people as tall as you in the house.'

'No problem,' he said again. 'So was that true, then? What you said about the model-village thing?'

As much as I would have loved to continue stringing this man along with the tale, I couldn't do it and a bubble of laughter burst from within me.

'Of course not, but you should have seen your face. I'm sorry. I couldn't resist the tease.'

He studied me for a moment then grinned, full wattage, and a tiny voice inside me whispered, *Wow*.

'Nicely done, Ms Hart.'

'Can I get you a drink or anything while we wait for the others? They should be here soon. And, please, call me Maddie.'

'I wouldn't count on it. As I said, Patrick is always late and his fiancée isn't much better.'

'Bad weather can play havoc with travel plans. I'd rather they were late than anything happen.' I turned back to face him as I said it, squashing the flash of memory that burst into my brain. Lorcan opened his mouth as if to say something but appeared to change his mind as his eyes met mine.

'Definitely,' he said. 'And a cold drink would be great, if it's not too much trouble.'

'I have some home-made lemonade or there's squash or water.'

'Lemonade sounds great, thanks.'

I moved to the fridge and pulled out a large glass jug. Taking two tall glasses from a cupboard, I poured the pale liquid into them before returning the jug to the fridge, popped a sprig of mint in each glass from the mini herb garden I kept on the windowsill and then handed one of the glasses to Lorcan. He took a sip.

'This is delicious. Home-made, you say?'

'I did.'

'By you?'

'You seem surprised.'

'Maybe,' he answered cryptically. 'I clearly haven't worked you out yet.'

I gave him a cool look. 'There's not a lot to work out.'

'See, that just makes me even more curious and think there's plenty to work out.' There was a dangerous half-smile on his lips that in other circumstances I might have acknowledged as being sexy.

2

The bell clanged again and I put down my glass, smoothed my hair quickly and went to open the door to my clients, only to find Betty, my next-door neighbour instead, with a plate full of pastries that smelled delicious.

'Hello, love,' she said, coming in as she usually did before I could say anything, bustling on through to the kitchen. 'I've just made these cheese straws and there's too many. If I leave them in the kitchen George will just eat them all and you know I'm trying to watch his weight. Oh, hello!' she said, coming to a halt as she saw Lorcan sitting at the kitchen table.

'I'm so sorry, dear.' She turned to me, her eyes shining with curiosity. 'I didn't realise you had company.'

'It's work,' I said quickly, before Betty jumped to any conclusions, although by the look on her face she already had.

'Oh.' The mischief disappeared from her kindly smile.

'The garden is too wet to get to the office so I'm having to hold my meeting in here.'

'Which is fine by me, if this is the service we get.' Lorcan smiled, eyeing the treats.

'Well, aren't you the charmer?' Betty laughed, holding out the plate towards him. 'Take two. Big lad like you.'

'Don't mind if I do, thank you.' He held out his hand. 'Lorcan O'Malley. It's nice to meet you.'

'And you, dear. I'm Betty. Betty Collins. George and I live next door.'

'It looks like a lovely village,' he said, catching my eye as he said so and I gave the tiniest brow raise acknowledging his earlier, slightly less flattering description of the place.

'It is, it is. So where's your lovely bride-to-be?'

'Oh, I'm not the lucky chap. I'm just the best man.'

'Ah, already tied the knot yourself, have you?' My neighbour couldn't have been more transparent if she'd been made of plate glass.

'No, not me. Still a bachelor, I'm afraid, Betty.'

'Is that so?' I saw the mischief slip back into her smile. 'We live in hope of hearing that Maddie's finally arranging her own wedding—'

'Thanks ever so much for the goodies, Betty,' I said, interrupting her, my face suddenly hot. 'That was very kind of you. I'll have to do an extra lap of the lake to burn those off.'

Betty waved my protestations away. 'Oh, hush. There's barely anything of you, is there, now, Mr O'Malley?'

Oh, Lord, the last thing I wanted was Lorcan O'Malley's opinion on my figure.

'Well, we'd better get on,' I said, gently hustling Betty away from Lorcan before he could reply. 'The bride and groom will be here any moment.'

'Oh! Yes, yes. Sorry, duck.'

'No, it's fine. Really. And thank you so much again for the treats. You really shouldn't have.'

'Got to feed you up a little bit, dear,' she said, touching my cheek gently. 'All this worrying about the business and the house repairs has done you no good at all.'

I smiled, ushering Betty to the front door before she revealed any more about my private life to my visitor. Closing the door behind her, I took a deep breath and returned to the kitchen.

'Sorry about that. Usually I don't answer as I'm in the office, so she just knows to leave stuff in the kitchen. I assumed it would be Patrick and Peyton.'

'They're going to be about another fifteen minutes,' Lorcan replied, looking up and waggling his phone. 'He just messaged me. I can only apologise for their appalling timekeeping. Have you got more appointments today?'

'No, it's fine. I cleared the afternoon for them.' The truth was the afternoon, and in fact the rest of the week, was far too clear for my liking.

He nodded. 'Betty seems nice.'

'She is.'

'Keen to hear news of you arranging your own wedding, by the sounds of it.'

'Yes, I think that would make her day.'

'No sign of that, then?'

I gave him a look.

He shrugged. 'Just making conversation.'

I remembered how badly I needed this job and pasted on a smile. 'Yes, I know. I'm sorry. I just prefer to keep my private life private, that's all.'

'Fair enough.' He finished the last of his lemonade and stood to take the glass to the sink.

'Just leave it there, it's fine.'

He washed it up anyway.

'Do you ever do anything you're told?'

He turned and gave me that smile again. 'Now that, Maddie, would depend entirely on the situation.'

I felt a flush tinge my cheeks as Lorcan's smile grew. God, he was infuriating... and way too sexy for his own good. And certainly my own good. Where were my clients?

'I see what you mean about needing a path,' Lorcan said, having now moved to the patio doors. His eyes took in the large muddy puddle that had once been the walkway to the garden office.

I sighed. 'Yes. I'm sorry about having to hold the meeting in here. I know it doesn't look the most professional.'

'Ah, don't be daft. It's perfectly lovely. Feels like a real home.'

I turned, and he met my eyes, holding the gaze.

'Thank you.'

'You're welcome.' There was a pause, then he rubbed his forehead. 'Doorways could do with being a bit higher though.'

I grinned. 'Yes, sorry. I should have warned you. Another reason it's better when the garden office is operational.' I peered a little closer. 'I'm afraid that's going to leave a bruise.'

'Don't worry about it. I'm sure I've had worse.'

'Walk into a lot of doorways, do you?'

'No, most people I know don't live in Hobbit houses.'

'Charming.'

'But I did used to be a bit of a scrapper when I was a nipper.'

'Why doesn't that surprise me?'

He turned more fully towards me. 'I don't know. Why doesn't it?' I looked up into his handsome face, that hint of trouble lingering in the dangerous smile. The silence stretched until it was broken by another enormous clap of thunder that made me physically jump. As it died away, another sound replaced it. A faint howling cry drifted through the smaller windows I'd left open that wouldn't let rain in.

'What is that sound?'

Lorcan was already moving towards the front door, pulling it open and heading back to his car. The rain was bucketing down and he was soaked through by the time he got to it, opening the door and attending to something inside. Grabbing his brolly, I rushed out after him, coming to a halt with the umbrella over both of us as he lifted out a little dog, cuddling it to his chest and making soothing noises as the rain beat heavily on the fabric above us.

'You left a dog in the car in a thunderstorm!' I glared at him.

'I didn't want to!' he snapped back. 'He had water and the windows were open so he had air and I was about to come check on him anyway.' I saw now there was plastic over the interior of the car and the windows were indeed open a little. But still, not many dogs were content in a thunderstorm and this one certainly didn't seem to be.

'What do you mean you didn't want to?' I reached out and gave the dog's caramel-coloured head a little stroke. It seemed content enough now, snuggled against the broad chest of his owner.

'Bod comes everywhere with me normally but Patrick said I wasn't to bring him into the meeting today. I didn't want to leave him at home because I didn't know how long I'd be and he was sleeping when I left him in here. The vet gave me some stuff to help calm him in storms but I guess it wore off.'

He fussed with the dog, kissing its soft, furry head and whispering that he was OK now.

'Come on, inside now, both of you. You should have just spoken to me about it. It's my house, not Patrick's.'

'You sure?'

'Of course, come on. You're already soaked.' I put my hand on his elbow and ushered them in as he briefly turned to beep the car locked and we hurried up the front path. Closing the door behind us, I took the umbrella through to the boot room again and set it dripping on the tiled floor before returning to my guest, who was also dripping.

'Stay there,' I said, before heading upstairs and rooting about in the back of the airing cupboard. Returning, I handed him a towel and a tee shirt and swapped them for the dog, whom I wrapped in a blanket. 'It might be a bit small.'

Lorcan rubbed his dark hair from sodden to merely damp with the towel. 'If it's yours, it's definitely going to be a bit small.' He had a point. A size eight shirt was not going to fit a six-foot-five man who was built like the proverbial brick outhouse.

'It's not mine.' I gave him a tight smile.

He held it out. It was definitely a man's tee shirt, and he raised one dark brow in question. I ignored him and instead took the dog through to the kitchen and popped him down on the floor while I knelt and made a makeshift bed from a big cosy blanket, leaving his owner to change his shirt in peace.

'I can hang your shirt in the airing cupboard if you—' My words dried up as I turned and saw Lorcan in the tee shirt I'd given him. To say it was snug was an understatement. The previous owner, although tall, had definitely not had this man's bulk. Not only was it stretched impossibly tight across his pecs, his biceps were almost bursting the seams and the too-short hem exposed the merest hint of a flat, tanned stomach and a line of dark hair leading to places I had no right even acknowledging, let alone thinking about.

3

'Fits perfectly, thanks.'

The laugh rippled out of me and his eyes crinkled as he joined in.

'I'm sorry. It's all I have, but you can't sit in that sodden shirt for the rest of the afternoon.'

'It's fine. As you say, it's dry at least.'

'Do you want me to hang the shirt somewhere?'

'No, but thanks. I'll sort it when I get home. You've done more than enough.'

'It's no trouble.'

He smiled down at where Bod was now snuggled into the blanket, his eyes closing as I drifted my hand over his soft fur.

'You're very kind, although if you have a bag or something I could put it in so it doesn't drip everywhere over your floor?'

'Give it here. I'll put it in the airing cupboard. It will hopefully dry off enough in there by the time we're done today.'

'Thanks again. You sure it's OK to bring him in? I hated leaving him out there.' His brow creased and I could see the decision hadn't been taken lightly.

'Yes, I can see that now. I'm sorry I told you off.'

'I know it was only out of concern for the dog.'

'I'm surprised you listened to your friend, though.'

'What's that supposed to mean?' There was a look of interest mixed with amusement on his lips.

'It's just that... well, you seem like a man who knows his own mind.'

'That's a tactful way of saying you think I can likely be a stubborn arse, isn't it?'

'Not at all.'

Maybe.

He gave me a disbelieving look.

'There was an unfortunate incident recently and Patrick got a bit uppity about it all. I've known Paddy since we were both tiny and he's not usually so tense but I think this wedding lark and the fact his fiancée's an heiress have made him feel a bit under pressure. As his best man, I'm supposed to make his life easier.' He gave a shrug.

'I think you're allowed to make your own decisions about your dog and his welfare. Anything else to do with the wedding, feel free to run by me.' I gave him a serious look that showed I was not to be messed with but all it did was make him smile.

'You look cute when you're trying to be serious.'

'I am not *trying* to be serious. I *am* serious.'

He gave that killer grin again. 'Then you look cute when you do that too.'

'Look. I'm happy to have your dog in here as he is clearly well behaved. If you're to stay, you need to be the same.'

Lorcan looked down at his dog, drifting off to sleep in his blanket nest. His eyelids were heavy but the odd rumble was still making itself known in the distance and he seemed reluctant to give in entirely.

'I'm more than happy to snuggle down there with him if you really want.'

'Oh, goodness. I can see I'm going to have to keep my eye on you.'

'Looks like there's going to be an upside in being involved in the planning of this wedding after all,' he replied, grinning.

'No,' I said, firmly. 'No upside.'

He gave a small head tilt.

I replayed the sentence back in my head. 'I mean, of course there is. It's all up. You get to be involved in helping your best friend plan the most beautiful day to begin his married life. But that's it. The sole upside.'

He shrugged, still with a hint of mischievous smile. 'Shame.'

'And don't think I won't be warning the bridesmaids about you either. The last thing I need is you upsetting that particular apple cart.'

'Are you always this severe on the best man?'

'Only when required.'

'Betty seemed to like me.'

'Then when we're done, I'll send you round to Betty's. Until then you need to behave.'

Moving past him, I double checked the table, making sure I had all I needed. Lorcan glanced down at my coloured sticky notes, pens, neatly lined-up pads (one for each person), and my main planner all organised on the table. His blue gaze then drifted to the fridge, where another colour-coded calendar was stuck with my schedule for the week. 'You really like to be organised, don't you?'

'It allows me to make the most efficient use of my time. I

like to plan and know exactly what's happening and what's coming.'

'It doesn't matter how much you plan, you don't know what life has in store.'

'Which is exactly the reason it's good to plan as much as possible so that you have as few surprises as possible.'

'Hate to say this, Maddie, but it doesn't work like that.'

I was the last person who needed telling that, but I wasn't about to go there now.

Lorcan's intense gaze was studying me and I felt as if he could see into where I kept all my secrets.

'Why do I get the feeling you know all that anyway?'

'How ridiculous!' I said, with a laugh that would get me thrown out of RADA.

Lorcan shrugged but all this did was make the tee shirt ride up and expose more stomach. 'And put that away,' I said, making a rough gesture around my own midriff as the bell outside clanged loudly, which hopefully signalled that this was, at last, my missing clients. Lorcan's low, deep chuckle followed me all the way to the door.

'Hi-i-i-i-i!' Peyton flashed a wide, very white, very straight-toothed smile at me as I hurried her and her fiancé in out of the weather and explained the situation about the office. 'Oh, that's fine. Oh, my gosh, your house is just so cute! It's like something out of an Agatha Christie movie. Who's that one I love, sweetie? The old lady?'

'Miss Marple,' Patrick said, shaking my hand.

'That's it. Miss Marple. Not that you're like an old lady, obviously.' Peyton looked momentarily flustered.

'I know what you mean and thank you. I like it.' *Apart from the leaking roof and the swimming pool where my garden used to be.* 'Do go through. Your best man is already here.' Peyton squeezed Patrick's hand, the wide smile still on her face as they walked through, and I followed.

'What did I say about that dog?' Patrick's face darkened as he finally saw Bod, now snoring quietly by Lorcan's chair.

'That was my decision,' I said quickly, in order to head off any disagreements. 'I told Lorcan to bring the dog inside. He did initially leave him in the car as you asked, but it wasn't fair on either of them. Lorcan was worried and Bod was scared. I'd rather the dog was safe and happy in here and he's no problem. He can come any time.' I glanced at Lorcan. 'I'm referring to the dog, of course.'

Patrick grinned. 'Glad to see Maddie's got the measure of you already, you big eejit.' His smile then faded a little. 'Are you sure, though?' Patrick asked, tilting his chin towards the ball of fluff on the blanket. 'Another planner we saw got very uppity about it.'

'Perhaps they were allergic? Or just not a fan of dogs?'

'No,' Lorcan interjected. 'She was just a sour...' He tailed off. 'She just made a big deal about how it wasn't in keeping with the tone of the wedding these two want. Like it had any connection at all! Ridiculous,' he mumbled.

'Bod really wasn't being any trouble,' Peyton added, sweetly.

'And he's no trouble here either and welcome any time. So, now that's settled shall we get on? Can I get you a drink to start?'

'I can thoroughly recommend the home-made lemonade,' Lorcan suggested.

'That sounds just perfect!' Peyton said.

'Great, thanks.' Patrick added, now staring at Lorcan, who stood up to help me with the lemonade. 'Mate, what on earth are you wearing?'

'Funny story. And in a way, it's all your fault.'

* * *

Two hours later we were making great progress and I was forming an even clearer idea in my mind, and on paper, about the wedding Patrick and Peyton wanted. I got the impression this was more Peyton's vision and that Patrick was just happy to give her whatever she wanted. Lorcan, so far, had mostly behaved himself although I'd seen him bite his tongue a couple of times when Peyton went particularly misty-eyed about the romance of the occasion.

'So when will you be able to go out and take a look at the venue?' Peyton asked, her eyes shining with excitement. 'Depending when it is, we might not be able to come but we can talk by video, right?'

'Oh... yes. Of course. I assumed you would want to be there but whatever works best for you.'

She exchanged a look with Patrick. 'There's actually something you should probably know.'

'Oh?' This sounded ominous. I glanced beside me at Lorcan, who was studying the grain in my lovingly worn and well-oiled oak table top.

Patrick picked up the conversation. 'An opportunity has come up for me to do a lecture term at Stanford University. The guy who was going to do it had to drop out and I really don't want to turn down the chance in case it doesn't come around again.' He looked at Peyton, who nodded and wrapped her arm around his biceps. 'Peyton is going to come with me so she can visit her family and friends on the way.'

'Also, I really don't want to be away from Patrick for that long. I mean, I know I could fly back and forth but it's not the same, is it?'

Ah, the benefits of never having to work for a living...

'No... it's not,' I said, a little bewildered. 'But you still want to get married at Christmas?'

'Absolutely,' Peyton confirmed. 'All the plans are to be kept as they are. I mean, as far as we have plans – which isn't much, thanks to our previous disaster.' Worry showed in her eyes and she scrunched her arm around Patrick's that little bit tighter. 'But I have my dress, so that's good, and the paperwork for getting married in Ireland is all done. The rest we thought, if you agree to it, we could do via video-conferencing and messaging. I know the time difference makes things a bit of a challenge but your references all said you could handle just about anything.'

'That's a bold claim to live up to,' Lorcan said, fixing me with a cool stare. To be fair, I had to give him kudos for almost pulling the serious look off in that outfit. The only reason I didn't crack up was because years of doing this job had had the benefit of enabling me to master my poker face. Also, I wasn't intimidated by people. Even six-five, rugby-player types who towered over me. To be fair, I don't think Lorcan was actually trying to intimidate me. He was sure of himself, and he wouldn't know romance if it whacked him across the face with a box of Milk Tray, but he didn't appear to be one of those idiots who tried to use their size as a weapon or tactic. Someone had tried that once and discovered, to their cost, it just meant my fist was perfectly placed to have them singing soprano for the next week.

'It is, but one I feel I can back up.' Admittedly planning a wedding almost from scratch without the bride or groom around was a new one on me but I didn't think they needed to know that.

'You have all my lists, and obviously we've talked things over on email and now today. Lorcan knows our tastes and preferences, so with all that we thought you two could kind of plan it together and then just run things past us before anything was locked in. You've already been great at picking up on all the things we want and suggesting perfect additions or alternatives. To be honest, after the last experience, I don't think I can deal with all the planning personally again now.' Peyton put a hand to her cheek and leant against Patrick, who wrapped his arm around her and dropped a kiss on her temple.

'It's all right, darlin'.'

She took a deep breath as though to calm herself. Lorcan rolled his eyes. Peyton was lovely but it did appear there was a touch of drama princess about her and I guessed that wasn't his type.

'Anyway,' Peyton continued with a brave smile, 'with Lorcan and Patrick being like peas in a pod, we just know that between you you'll make all the best choices. We didn't want to say anything until we had this meeting today but it's so clear it's going to work out perfectly.'

'Right,' I said, hauling up a smile and fixing it on my clients, agreeing enthusiastically, but hopefully just shy of the nodding-dog effect. 'Yes. That's great. Whatever, and however you want things done, we can make it work.' This was definitely not how I had foreseen the planning for this wedding proceeding, but I prided myself on being able to adjust to all manner of situations. My eyes drifted to the ever growing puddle in my garden cutting me off from my studio and I wondered how close the bucket upstairs was to full. This wedding was going to be perfect. It had to be!

4

'Lorcan has kindly offered to be available as often as you need him.'

'I'm sure I'll be able to do a good amount on my own, so hopefully I won't need to disturb you too much.'

'You won't be disturbing me.'

'Don't you have to work?'

'I do, but I run my own business and I have good people I can rely on. Plus they know this is going on and how important it is.' At this comment, Peyton beamed and turned to Patrick, who nodded down at her as he glanced at his friend, gratitude showing for a moment. I'd wondered about these two initially following Patrick's demand and ensuing reaction to the dog, but in that moment it was brilliantly clear that their bond was deep and didn't need to be spoken. It just was.

Lorcan continued. 'I've told the team I'll be less on hand than usual for a while, but I'm always at the end of the line if they need me.'

'It'll be great for Lorcan to take you to the venue too, as he knows the place so well.'

'You're familiar with the castle, then?' I tilted my head to meet Lorcan's eyes.

Peyton let out a tinkly laugh. 'Of course he is. It's his—'

'Friend's. It's my friend's place.'

'Oh, I see. That's handy.'

Patrick nodded and Peyton did the same. 'Very,' she added. I thought there was the hint of a frown about her features but as she was obviously a Botox fan it was hard to tell.

'So,' I said, wrapping up our meeting, 'it's obviously less time than we usually have to plan a wedding—'

Peyton's face fell and I automatically reached out, taking her hand. 'But as we already have a venue secured and you have your dress, that's two major items off the list. It will be fine. I promise, there's absolutely nothing to worry about.' Her bright smile returned and a perfectly manicured hand squeezed my less pampered one. Manicures had been one of the first things to go when money began getting tight.

Peyton turned her smile to Patrick and he took her free hand and kissed it. I smiled and glanced at Lorcan, who was just finishing another eye-roll at the sweet gesture. I narrowed my eyes at him briefly.

'And I'm sure, as the best man, Lorcan will be going above and beyond to ensure things go perfectly.' I gave him a big smile, topped with an innocent blink as all faces turned to his.

He gave a small, acknowledging tilt of his head and smiled. 'Of course.'

The other two looked at each other, caught up in the excitement of the moment, giving Lorcan enough time to fix me with a look that said he knew exactly what I was doing. I returned it with one of wide-eyed innocence and he shook his head. He might not be a fan of the institution of marriage and that was his prerogative, but he was going to be on board with this one – even if I had to tie him to the rigging myself.

* * *

Two weeks later, I realised that my kitchen wall had more interest in this wedding than Lorcan O'Malley, but luckily I was used to working alone. Peyton's suggestion that Lorcan and I plan the event together had admittedly horrified me so the fact I hadn't seen or heard anything from him since the initial meeting suited me just fine.

'So, we were talking about the theme and, although I know your basic theme is "Winter's Fairy Tale", are there any elements that you'd like to incorporate into the day that we haven't yet spoken about?'

We were sitting in a swanky restaurant in a tucked-away alley in London and I was looking forward to a relaxed meal and discussion with the bride and groom-to-be before they flew to the States tomorrow. As I sipped a glass of Cristal Peyton insisted I have, the door opened and, across the small room, I saw Lorcan fill its frame. Oh. Great. Patrick waved and, having handed over his coat and taken his time charming the pretty hostess, Lorcan eventually wandered over to the table and greeted Patrick with a clap on the shoulder and Peyton with a big hug and a kiss on the cheek.

'Maddie,' he said, taking the chair next to me, filling the space, his thigh inadvertently brushing mine as he did so. I quickly moved my legs further to the right.

'Pleasure to see you again.'

'Lorcan. I didn't realise you were coming this evening.'

'Oh, I never miss a campaign meeting.'

'We're planning a wedding, Lorcan, not a war,' I replied.

He made a slight movement of his head, while his gaze remained on me as he lifted the champagne glass to his lips. I gave a tight smile, turned away and downed the rest of my glass. Probably not the best idea but I was hoping the alcohol might make him a little less – whatever he was – and hopefully a little less good-looking.

'So, whose idea was it to marry in Ireland?' I asked, trying to dig deeper and see what details I could winkle out to make the day even more special for the couple.

'That was mine,' Peyton said, glancing at her fiancé. 'Patrick, darling that he is, was happy to marry anywhere but I've always dreamed of marrying there, in a beautiful setting, and connecting with my heritage.'

'Oh, you're Irish too?'

Lorcan made a snort, which both Peyton and I ignored, but Patrick's look buried his friend six feet under.

'Sorry. Went down the wrong way.' Lorcan pointed to the glass he'd just replaced on the table. I gave him a thump on the back a little harder than was strictly necessary.

'Is that better?' I asked sweetly.

'Much,' he said, eyes boring into me. Across the table, Patrick and Peyton were grinning.

'So,' I continued. 'You were saying that you have Irish ancestry too? Is that something you would like to incorporate into the wedding?'

This time Lorcan remained silent and Peyton explained her links to Ireland.

'I do have Irish connections, yes. Unfortunately, I haven't been able to find much during genealogy searches but I think that's likely to do with the fact that a lot of names got changed during emigration, either through choice or when the names were registered at Ellis Island.'

'Ah, I understand.'

'Or it could be because the so-called relatives were non-existent in the first place,' Lorcan mumbled under his breath.

'Lorcan!' Patrick snapped.

Peyton studied her beautiful engagement ring.

'I was just making a comment. Lots of people find out their ancestry isn't what they thought it was.'

Patrick's brow darkened even more and I sensed that this could escalate very quickly. I needed to keep this wedding on track and, by the looks of it, that meant keeping Lorcan O'Malley in check too.

'Perhaps that's something you could get a professional on to at some point, then, Peyton,' I said smoothly, 'but in the meantime this is your and Patrick's wedding, which means you can do and have whatever you want.' I gave Lorcan a pointed look as I made the statement, which he met, holding my gaze.

Peyton looked up, her face relaxing and smiling at me as Patrick wrapped his hand around hers.

'Lorcan is rather protective of being Irish and doesn't really like to share,' Peyton said in an uncharacteristic dig.

He opened his mouth to reply but I interrupted.

'I'm sure he didn't mean anything by it,' I said, grabbing his elbow beneath the table in warning, 'and I'm sure he'll be as helpful as it is possible to be in our quest to get you two the perfect wedding. Isn't that right?' I said, turning to Lorcan with a wide smile.

'Absolutely,' he said, turning a smile on me, his eyes sending a completely different message to his mouth.

We spent a while going over the things I'd already arranged for them, showing them the stationery I'd had designed and some ideas I'd put together for styling the castle, using the photos of it I'd seen online as a base.

'Well, it looks like we're in pretty good shape. Now, you said that you're using a local supplier for the cake, is that right?'

'Yes.' Peyton smiled widely. 'And they said they can fit you in any time for the tasting, so it's whatever suits you really.'

I pulled up my work calendar on my phone and glanced through the following week. There were a few items in it, but nowhere near as many as I would have hoped for, or as many as my roof needed to be in there. However, image was everything so I gave an umm and aah before advising that I could be pretty flexible and work around them. I felt Lorcan's eyes upon me, knowing he'd seen my too-empty calendar, and waited for the inevitable sarcastic comment. Instead, when I met his gaze, there was a look of understanding.

'So, what works best for you, Lorcan?' Peyton asked.

'I guess that depends on Miss Maddie here.'

'OK, we can discuss that shortly.'

'And we thought you'd probably have a list of preferred caterers and would know who was the best in the area, so felt it was better to leave it to you, especially with our travel plans now.'

'Yes. Of course. That's fine. I have your likes and dislikes and I'm sure we can work on a menu that will suit. And you're definitely happy for us to choose the cake too? I mean, it is your wedding cake.'

'Totally. I'm on a very strict diet at the moment so that I definitely fit into my beautiful gown.'

'You really don't have to taste very much,' I explained. 'Literally just a nibble, and Izzy can always make adjustments to your dress.'

Peyton looked horrified at this suggestion.

'I mean, not that I think she will have to,' I added and could see Lorcan trying not to smile at my back-pedalling. 'I'm just saying you don't have to starve yourself. And like I said, just a nibble of taste would be fine if you wanted to be involved in it.'

'Seems like a waste of good cake to me.'

Ignoring Lorcan's comment, although I did feel he had a valid point on this occasion, I continued addressing Peyton. 'Just a taste?'

'I couldn't possibly. My nutritionist has me on a restricted, and very particular, diet in order to cleanse my whole system and lift my energy and vitality. It's extremely important that I stick to the plan he's made for me. Unfortunately, that doesn't include cake, however small a piece.'

I stared at her for a moment and could practically hear Lorcan's eyes rolling in his skull.

"OK, then, yes, Lorcan and I can do that.'

'I have a few must-haves and must-avoids with the cake. Lorcan has his instructions.' Peyton glanced at him and gave him a small smile, then continued talking. 'So, to clarify, I don't want anything with fruit, or anything with cinnamon in it. Just in case I do have a tiny taste.' She pulled a disgusted face as she said the word cinnamon and I made a note on my pad in big letters that said 'no cinnamon', adding three exclamation marks for emphasis.

'Got it, and any preferences you do have? Like would you prefer chocolate, strawberry or vanilla?'

'To be honest, I doubt I'll be eating any of it anyway. I mean, we're going on honeymoon straight after so I still want to be looking my best, you know?'

I smiled over at Peyton and what looked like, to me, an already perfect figure, but I knew from previous history that if a bride, or a groom, wanted to diet before their wedding, then that was their prerogative. But I had to agree with Lorcan, that it did seem like a waste of a good cake opportunity.

'And we're not doing that smooshing of cake into each other's faces, either.' Peyton attempted another frown. 'I've never understood that. I mean, you go to all this effort to look amazing – hair, make-up, et cetera – then you ruin it all by smashing cake into each other's faces. I just don't get it.' She looked around at us with a horrified expression and we all nodded.

To be fair, I had to agree with her. I'd had brides pay thousands for top make-up and hair artists to create their perfect look only for it to be slathered a few hours later with cake and icing.

'So, OK, it's just me and Lorcan tasting?'

'Yes, does that work?'

'Of course. Just let me know where and when. It's good of them to come over here with the samples. That speaks well to their commitment to the event. Always a plus point.'

Suddenly the table fell silent and the others exchanged awkward glances with each other before focusing back on me.

'What have I missed?' I asked, feeling heat creep into my cheeks as I checked my notes, flipping pages back and forth. Peyton reached across for my hand. 'No, I'm so sorry. I think it was something we missed. Or, rather, forgot to tell you.'

5

'OK.' I smiled. How bad could it be? I'd dealt with plenty of crises in my time as a planner and whatever this was, I would fix it too.

'As you said, the supplier is local to the wedding. In the village that's adjacent to the castle, in fact.'

So far, so convenient.

'But they're not coming here for the tasting. We're going there. Or at least that was the original plan. Now you and Lorcan are going there.'

I stared at her for a moment while my voice refreshed its memory about how to form words. 'Going there.'

'Yes.'

'To Ireland?'

'Yes.'

'Next week.'

'Yes. That's OK, isn't it?'

The drip drip drip of my roof played in my brain. 'Yes, of course. Absolutely.'

'Wonderful!' Peyton gave a small, excited clap. 'Perfect. And

Lorcan can show you around the castle too while you're there so you can see the layout and go over the plans we've made from the photographs. It'll be great that you see it in person this soon, and I'm sure it will make it so much easier for you too.'

I realised I was still nodding like the head of a dashboard ornament someone had just flicked.

'Yes, yes. Good idea. Great.'

I turned to Lorcan. There was a bloody great grin on his face and this time it wasn't understanding I saw in those blue eyes. It was, unmistakeably, amusement.

'And don't you go breaking the hearts of any of Maddie's suppliers,' Peyton said, wagging her finger at Lorcan.

'I wouldn't dream of it.'

'I mean it!'

Lorcan drew a cross on his chest with his index finger. 'I promise.'

Peyton reached over and squeezed his hand. 'Thank you,' she said, before turning to me. 'There's a trail of broken hearts behind this one.'

'I can imagine.' And I could. The hostess he'd been chatting up when he got here had barely taken her eyes off him all evening, although he hadn't appeared to notice.

'Would going that soon be convenient for you?' I asked Lorcan.

'Sure. There's a couple of projects to check up on over in Ireland anyway so it works out just grand for me.' He smiled pleasantly but the mischief dancing in his eyes was obvious.

'Are you sure you can make it?' Peyton asked. There was a tenseness to her shoulders, despite the friendly confidence she was clearly doing her best to project.

'Of course.' I nodded. 'We'll make it happen.'

'Fantastic!' She did a mini clap, her smile wide and genuine, and I palpably sensed her relax.

'Do you want to make all the arrangements, Lorcan, so you're happy with everything, and liaise with Maddie?'

'Sure.'

'Just bill everything to Daddy,' she added.

'I'll pay for my own flight, but I can arrange for Madeline's to be on your dad's account if you like, save her having to add it onto your bill at the end.'

'If you're sure? I'm quite happy to pay for yours too.'

He smiled reassuringly. 'Positive. I'll make the arrangements, if Maddie's happy with that?' Everyone turned to face me.

'Sounds great.'

'Grand. I'm pretty sure I can sort something at short notice if you're available for a long weekend?'

'This weekend?'

'Yep.'

'Oh! Right, well, umm... hang on.' I knew there was nothing in either my work or social diary that couldn't be moved but, as Lorcan had already seen my too-empty work calendar, and laughed at my colour-coded diarising system, I didn't need him snooping at my similarly coded social life.

'This weekend looks doable,' I said, putting my phone back in my bag. 'If you're able to let me know the specifics as soon as possible, that would be great. I like to be organised and know what I'm doing when.'

'Is that so? You could have fooled me,' Lorcan replied.

'Lorcan...' Patrick cautioned, although even his mouth had a curve to it.

I didn't care. Organisation was wonderful. It meant you knew what was happening when and where and why, and that way you didn't get any nasty surprises. Or at the least you lowered the odds.

* * *

I waved Patrick and Peyton goodbye outside the restaurant, having exchanged hugs and kisses, and watched for a moment as they headed back to where Patrick had parked. They were driving to Heathrow tonight and flying off to the States tomorrow morning.

I was about to say a brief goodbye to Lorcan when he spoke first.

'My God, your face was a picture.'

I turned on my heel and then ruined my planned haughty flounce by almost twisting my ankle on the cobbled back street. My arms flailed momentarily like an over-zealous windmill before Lorcan reached out one strong arm, setting me back on my feet securely.

'Nice shoes but not perhaps the most practical for these streets.'

'Yes, well, I didn't know there were cobbles. Besides, had you not been taking up so much of the pavement,' I made a vague movement with my arms intimating his bulk and size, 'I wouldn't be standing in the gutter. But thank you for your sharply insightful comment.'

'You're welcome.'

'Goodnight, Lorcan.' I turned again, more carefully this time, and began to walk away. Before I'd gone three steps, his melodic tones stopped me.

'Don't you think we ought to talk?'

'About what?' I looked back over my shoulder. It was getting late and I was tired and, with rain forecast, I needed to make sure I had all my buckets emptied and back in place.

'About our little trip away together.'

We'd been the last ones in the restaurant and as he said this the hostess stepped out, having finished her shift. She glanced at me, shot a filthy look at Lorcan and strode off.

'I think you just lost a fan.'

He shrugged.

'I see now why Peyton warned you off the suppliers.' I turned back fully to face him. 'And it is not a "trip away together". It's a business trip.'

'I know that.'

'Just clarifying.'

He heaved what I assumed was meant to be a patient sigh but didn't quite nail it. 'So when's good for you? Your calendar looked pretty rammed.'

I looked up at him and he quirked an eyebrow.

'Very funny. You know, Patrick must have the patience of a saint to have been best friends with you for such a long time.'

'I'm sure I don't know what you mean. I'm perfectly delightful.'

'Is that so?'

'Completely.'

I turned to face him properly, taking a few steps until I was in front of him, still having to tip my chin up, despite the heels, to meet his eyes.

'We'll see about that.'

'The light's a little low but, if I'm not mistaken, there's doubt in those eyes.'

'You put it there.'

'And tell me just how I did that now?'

'I'm sure I can think of several examples, but most recently?'

'If you like?'

'Why the need to have a dig at Peyton about her Irish heritage? She's obviously excited and proud about it.'

'Because she doesn't have any.'

'How do you know? As she said, names often got changed so it's entirely possible that happened in her family's case too.'

'You, and she, are absolutely right. But the thing you said about getting a professional onto it?'

'Yes. Oh, wait. Don't tell me. You're a professional.' I gave him a look that I hoped conveyed the right amount of disbelief combined with haughtiness.

'Nope. But my sister is.'

'She is?'

'She is. It's what she does for a living. There's so much interest in genealogy these days. She set up her own business several years ago.'

'And?'

'And I asked her if she could trace Peyton's family.'

'Because you wanted to prove you were right?'

'No, because I thought getting my best friend's fiancée a family tree, which traced her roots back to Ireland, would be a nice thing to do.'

It really was and, for a moment, I was taken aback.

'It seems that I've given you the impression that I'm not the kind of person who does nice things.'

I opened my mouth to try and find a tactful way of saying, 'Well, I've had my doubts,' and closed it again when I couldn't. In the outer reaches of the puddle of light cast by a streetlamp, I saw the corners of Lorcan's mouth tilt upwards.

'I thought so.'

'I never said that.'

'No,' he said, still smiling. 'But your silence said so much more.'

I began to try and wriggle out of it, but he waved a large hand. 'Seriously, don't bother. I really don't give two figs about what most people think about me. If I don't know them, or I don't care about them, their opinion of me isn't generally something I worry about.'

That told me, then.

'So what happened?'

'My sister spent plenty of her own time putting together a tree for Peyton, and traced her ancestors back pretty far, but there's no link at all to Ireland. I mean, apart from the indigenous peoples, everyone in America is an immigrant if you go back far enough, so her family tree does go back to Europe, but no one in her lineage sailed from what they like to call The Old Country.'

'Does Peyton know this? That your sister did all this work?'

'No.'

I took a step back. 'What?'

'I didn't tell her.'

'So you have her whole ancestral history there and you haven't given it to her?'

'Nope.'

'May I ask why?'

'You may.'

I let out a sigh. 'Lorcan, why haven't you given the information to Peyton?'

'Because it's not what she wants to hear.'

'I don't understand. She wants to trace her lineage – which is something you've kindly had done for her. Why would you not give that to her?'

'Because she's not only in love with my best friend, she's in love with the idea of Irish blood running in her veins. If I gave her those documents, it would prove that she doesn't.'

'But you still made the dig about her not having that ancestry – and you know she doesn't.'

'Yeah, I know. It winds her up. I know I shouldn't but I've got three sisters so it comes naturally. But I did try and,' he glanced at me, 'tactfully bring it up a couple of time but she just ignores me, preferring to think it's because I'm somehow anti her having Irish descendants.'

'Are you?'

'No, of course not. I couldn't care less. But at least this way she gets to hold onto the illusion that she does have those roots rather than being told flat out she doesn't. It makes her happy to believe that, so...' He shrugged broad shoulders before leaning one against a rough wall of the sixteenth-century pub next to the restaurant.

'Could – and I mean no disrespect by this – but could your sister have been mistaken or missed something?'

'Not a chance. She's bloody good at what she does.'

'I'm sure. As I said, I didn't mean to imply—'

'I know you didn't. I'm not offended. It was a reasonable question.'

I looked back up at him and he looked back at me. 'And now you're trying to work out whether I'm an arse or a nice guy?'

'Or perhaps something in between.'

He laughed, rich, deep and throaty. 'I'm sure that, like most things, it depends who you ask.'

Something from earlier was prodding at my brain and, as much as I tried to ignore it, I couldn't.

'Thank you for arranging things with Peyton with regards to the flights.'

Lorcan shrugged as if he didn't know what I was referring to, but I'd already worked out he was way brighter than he let people believe. It wasn't just this man's cheekbones that were sharp.

'Shrug all you like but we both know I can't afford a trip anywhere at the moment, even if I get to claim it back. You saw the state of my garden and I'm pretty sure you heard the water dripping from my roof in the kitchen. You can give me that innocent look, but I noticed you conveniently close the door to the stairs, presumably to mask the sound of the leak. I wasn't sure if it was coincidence but your actions tonight show it wasn't. I don't like being beholden to anyone, but it would be rude of me not to thank you for making the arrangements in such a way that makes it easier on my bank account.'

'You don't owe me anything, Maddie. And you heard Peyton yourself say I was to bill it to her daddy.'

'I did.'

'So there you go. Nothing to thank me for or, God forbid, be beholden about.'

'Oh, for goodness' sake, can you not just accept a thank you?'

'I can, but you have a funny way of thanking people.'

'Excuse me? I most certainly do not.'

'Ah, yes, you do. You ever read any Jane Austen?'

'Of course. Have you?'

'Of course,' he shot back. 'You know when Darcy asks Elizabeth to marry him the first time, then mentions her terrible connections and recites a laundry list of objections?'

'Yes.'

'Your thank you was kind of like that.'

'Oh, it was not.'

Lorcan didn't answer, just looked down at me with those eyes, and that face and a ridiculously sexy curve of a smile.

'It was not!' I said again, turning away so that there was no chance of him seeing the flush I could feel on my cheeks.

'So, I guess you and I need to work out our long weekend to Ireland.'

'Perhaps you could refer to it as a business trip, as that's what it is? I'd hate anyone to get the wrong idea, should you mention it.'

'And who would I be mentioning it to?'

'I don't know. Anyone.'

'Are you trying to find out whether I have a girlfriend, Miss Madeleine?'

I let out a huff of air. 'Most certainly not.'

'Ahh, so there's someone your end you don't want getting the wrong idea?'

'No. That's not it, either. Not that that's any of your business. I just like to make sure everyone is on the same page.'

He scratched the day's growth now darkly shadowing his jawline. 'Oh, don't worry. Everything is crystal clear. I'll pick you up on Friday afternoon. I saw your calendar was free. We can fly back Monday. Sound good?'

'Excuse me. That was just my work calendar you saw. I do have a life outside work and that calendar is far more full.'

'Is it, now?'

The hint of disbelief in his tone infuriated me. 'Yes, it is. Look.' I pulled up the social calendar on my phone and thrust it in his face.

'That's a hell of a lot of colour coding. Also, don't you ever believe in having a day off? Leaving room for spontaneity or just simply doing nothing?'

'No, I don't. And I can rearrange things – I just didn't appreciate your disbelieving tone.'

'Why does it matter if I believe you or not?' He tilted his head in query.

'I... err...' I cleared my throat.

'It doesn't. Obviously. And yet you felt the need to thrust proof of your apparently thriving social life in my face. Interesting.'

'No, it's not. It's entirely uninteresting. I just—'

'Like to be right.'

'Look. This isn't getting us anywhere and really doesn't matter anyway. So you'll make the flight arrangements?'

'I will. I'll book you into the local pub. Comfy rooms and they do a grand breakfast.'

'I don't usually have breakfast.'

'I'll leave you to explain that to Brighid. She's very proud of her proper Irish breakfast.'

'I'm sure she'll understand. There'll be too much to do anyway. We have a lot to fit in this weekend.'

'Grand. I'll message you with a time tomorrow. I'm getting a cab home,' he said, looking up at the sky. The clouds had thickened and now hid the moon entirely, and the rain promised by the forecast was beginning to drizzle. 'Where can I drop you?'

'It's fine. I can walk from here to the Tube.'

'Nope,' he said, flagging down a black cab. 'Which station? We'll drop you. And before you try and argue again, it's not happening, even if I have to bundle you in myself. I have three sisters, not to mention a baby brother, and I'm used to making sure they have a safe trip home. If something happened to you, I'd then have to try and explain to Peyton and Patrick that they were once again planner-less. It's not worth the grief, so, please, Maddie, just do me a favour and get in the cab.'

I did as he asked and gave him the name of the station to pass on to the cabbie. 'I take it your car is at the other end?'

'Yes, it is.'

'Good. Message me when you're home.'

'I will do no such thing,' I replied, laughing.

'Yeah,' he said, turning to me, 'you will. Patrick gave me strict instructions to look after you and I take my responsibilities very seriously.'

'I'm sure he just meant in general, in Ireland.'

'It doesn't matter. Please. Just one word is enough. Whatever you choose that word to be is up to you.'

'Several come to mind.'

'Of that I have no doubt.' The killer grin was back.

I shook my head. 'Fine. Frankly I'm too tired to argue any longer.'

'Thank you.'

I glanced across at him and caught the smile. Turning away, I looked out of the window and onto the streets of London now shiny with rain, my mind buzzing with thoughts, ideas and to-do lists... and the best smile I'd seen in years.

6

'How's the roof?' Lorcan asked, meeting me halfway up the garden path and reaching out to take my suitcase.

'Thanks,' I said, passing it over to him. 'It's fine so long as it's not raining.'

'Going to be OK while you're away?'

'Tom's going to come by and check on it.'

'Tom?' He raised an enquiring eyebrow, which I pointedly ignored and walked past him towards the car.

'Morning, Maddie.'

I looked round. 'Morning, Tom,' I said, smiling. Tom was a few years older than me, with light brown hair and an easy smile on his handsome tanned face.

I practically heard Lorcan's ears prick up as I spoke.

'Ready for your trip?' Tom asked, still smiling and taking in the sleek and expensive car Lorcan had turned up in, as well as the man himself, to whom he gave a nod.

'Yes. Just about to head off to the airport. Thanks again for offering to keep an eye on the place. Betty volunteered but you're obviously a bit more informed as to how much longer the roof will hold if there's a downpour. I've emptied the two buckets upstairs so,' I looked up at the sky which was currently a beautiful, crisp blue. 'If it stays like this, it shouldn't be a worry.'

Tom's smile faded. 'Heavy rain forecast for tomorrow.'

'Seriously?'

'Afraid so.'

'Oh. Great. Well, I guess I just have to hope for the best.'

Tom glanced at Lorcan and then returned his gaze to me. 'You know I've said I'll fix it for you.'

'I know, Tom, and that really is so kind of you, but I just don't have the money to do it right now.'

'And as I said before,' Tom said, taking a step closer to me, his voice lowering a little, 'you don't have to pay right away. Just pay me when you have the money. It's no big deal.' He gave a shrug.

'I can't do that, Tom. I'd feel terrible.'

'I'd feel worse if your house flooded and I could have prevented it.'

'I know, and you're so kind to even offer. I just don't feel I can put you in that position. Besides, whatever would the rest of the village think? They'd all be after you for fix now, pay later deals.'

Tom shifted his weight, his eyes meeting mine, his expression more serious. 'I don't really care what the other villagers think. It's my business and how I run it is up to me, not them.'

'No, I know. I was just joking.' I smiled. 'But, fingers crossed, work seems to be picking up slowly again now so hopefully I'll be able to book something in with you before too long.'

Tom gave a short nod and a smile that didn't quite reach his eyes. 'So, going anywhere nice for your weekend away?'

'Ireland,' I replied.

'Nice. Hopefully the weather will be better there.'

A deep rich laugh came from the other side of the car as Lorcan straightened up from where he had now finished faffing about in the back seat with something. 'Not much chance of that,' he said, closing the door and coming back around to the pavement. 'This is Ireland we're talking about. It's not exactly known for its weather. At least, not in a good way. Lorcan O'Malley,' he said, holding his hand out towards Tom.

'Tom Harper,' Tom replied, shaking his hand.

'Pleased to meet you.' Lorcan smiled. 'So, you live in the village too?'

'I do.'

'And I understand you're being kind enough to look after Maddie's house for the weekend?'

Tom nodded.

'Well, we're both very grateful to you for that. It will be one less thing for her to worry about during our trip, won't it?' Lorcan looked down at me, mischief written all over his handsome face. It was clear he knew how village grapevines worked and had decided he'd have a bit of fun. That, however, was something I could soon fix. I opened my mouth to quickly clarify to Tom that the trip to Ireland was purely business but before I was able to do so, Lorcan spoke.

'We really ought to be making a move for the airport,' he said, flicking his wrist and checking the time on a square faced Tag Heuer watch. 'It was really nice to meet you, Tom.'

Tom nodded, his eyes shifting between me and Lorcan briefly as Lorcan walked back around the car and slid into the driver's seat, starting the engine so that a low throaty growl rumbled out in the quiet of the village morning.

'I'd better go,' I said, resting my hand briefly on Tom's arm. 'Thanks again for everything.'

'No problem,' he said. 'After all, that's what friends do for each other, isn't it?' He smiled. 'I'd better be on my way too.' He briefly lifted the paper that was folded in his hand. 'This paper won't read itself.'

'Thanks, Tom. I'll see you when I get back.'

'Yep. Great. Have a good time,' he said as I slid into the passenger side.

'Oh, it's a business thing.'

'Uh-huh.' Tom nodded, casting a glance at Lorcan as he did so. 'Take care,' he said before walking on.

I closed the door.

'That was awkward.' Lorcan grinned, pulling away smoothly and then heading towards the main part of the village. However, as that only consisted of a few essential but excellent shops and one pub, also excellent, it didn't take him long to see the sights.

'What was?'

'That.' He jerked a thumb back towards my house.

'Tom?'

'Yes, Tom.'

'No, it wasn't.'

He turned to me for a moment as he pulled up to a junction, checking it was clear. 'Seriously?'

'Yes. What? Well, apart from you trying to spread gossip around the village that I'm off on some romantic weekend away with you, which I've corrected now anyway. For a grown man, you can be terribly childish.'

'Being a grown-up isn't all it's cracked up to be.'

Hard to disagree with that.

We drove in silence for a while before he spoke again. 'So, how long did you go out with him for?'

I turned in my seat, frowning. 'Who?'

'Old Tom back there.'

My frown deepened. 'I didn't.'

'Aah.'

Don't ask. He's just trying to get a rise out of you. You're better than that.

'And what does "aah" mean precisely?'

Damn.

'It can mean a lot of things.'

I let out a sigh between my teeth. *Just let it go. He's trying to wind you up. Don't let him succeed.*

'And what, exactly, does it mean in this instance?'

Damn. Again.

'It means that explains the awkwardness.'

'Oh, for goodness' sake. I give up.'

'Funny. You don't strike me as a quitter.'

I gave him a sharp look and his smile got even wider.

'You know Tom's got a thing for you though, right?'

'Don't be ridiculous.'

'I'm not. I assumed you knew. By the way, you know he didn't buy that "it's just work" thing either, don't you?'

'No thanks to you. And it *is* just work and he doesn't have a thing for me. I've known him for ages.'

'Oh, darlin', he totally has a thing for you. Why do you think he's offering to do your roof for free?'

'He's not offering to do it for free. It's just until I can pay him.'

'Same difference.'

'No, it's not. It's completely different.'

'If you say so.'

'I do.' My brain was itching to follow this with *so there* but I managed to wrangle control just in time – I had several more days of Lorcan to go yet.

'Don't you like him, then?'

'That's not the point.'

'It's a relevant point.'

'But none of your business.'

'Maddie, we're going to be spending the next four days together. If you don't want to talk about anything other than Patrick's wedding, it's going to be a very quiet trip.'

'Good.' I sent him a meaningful glance. 'I like quiet.'

He gave a large, dramatic sigh. 'Great,' he muttered and drove on, thankfully, in silence.

* * *

Lorcan parked the car and I met him at the boot to retrieve my case. He hefted one out with each hand and placed them on the ground and I began wheeling mine along, scanning the surroundings for the lift to the terminal.

'Which airline did you—?' I stopped, realising that I was alone. Glancing back, I saw Lorcan was still at the car. I turned and walked back, pulling my weekend case behind me. It gave a quietly rhythmic squeak as I did so.

'You need to oil that,' he said, his head still inside the car.

'Annoyingly, my can of WD40 is in my other handbag.'

He gave me a tight smile as his head and shoulders and a fair bit of broad chest appeared back over the top of the car as he stood. 'Smart arse.'

'Takes one to know one.'

'I'm going to take that as a compliment.'

'It wasn't meant as one.'

'Too late,' he said, grabbing his case and walking towards me.

'What's that?'

Lorcan looked down at the pet carrier in his hand. 'Bod, of course.'

'You're bringing your dog?'

'No, I just thought he might enjoy a tour of the airport.'

I let out a huff and turned back towards the terminal entrance. Lorcan was beside me within a few strides.

'Problem?'

'No. I was just surprised.'

'My mam likes to see him, plus it looks like I'll be needing the company as you've sworn to not speak about anything other than the wedding, which, just for reference, I've already heard more than enough about for my liking.'

'I didn't say that at all. I merely advised I had no intention of talking about my love life with you.'

'So there is a story there with old Tom, then?'

'Ugh!' I tipped my head back momentarily. 'No. No story. No nothing with Tom.' I punched the lift button for the ground floor harder than I needed to and saw a pilot surreptitiously watching me, likely hoping I wasn't on his flight and being thankful for the locked-door policy. I turned and smiled at him. He smiled back but I was pretty sure the damage was already done.

'Why not? What's wrong with him?'

'Nothing, he's very nice.'

'And he's smitten with you.'

'He is not!'

'Oh, come on, you can't tell me you've never truly noticed.'

'We're friends.'

'Maddie, he looked like I'd kicked his puppy when he thought you were coming away on a weekend tryst with me.'

The lift arrived and we walked out, followed by the pilot striding purposefully away in the opposite direction.

I looked up at Lorcan, horrified. 'Don't talk about kicking puppies in front of Bod!' I whispered.

Lorcan stared at me for several beats then burst out laughing. And with that single action, his whole face, his whole demeanour changed. The cynical frown and questioning eyebrows were replaced by warmth and joy, which only enhanced his attractive features. Mean and moody was all well and good but its appeal was short-lived – at least for me. This version of Lorcan was far more approachable, and even more attractive, if that was possible. Oh crap.

'I promise not to do it again. And just for absolute clarity, I would never, ever kick a puppy, or any other animal.'

'I didn't think you would.'

'So Bod's saved my reputation.'

'I wouldn't go that far. He's excessively cute but I'm not sure he can work miracles. Now, which airline are we flying with?'

With a flurry of things to attend to at short notice, I'd been happy to let Lorcan make the arrangements as he'd suggested.

He named one of the north American lines and began moving off, apparently already knowing where to head without checking the signs.

'Really?' I asked, catching up with him and taking two steps in my heels to his one long-legged ones.

'Yep. Why?'

'I... I'm just surprised.'

'A lot of the regular European ones don't let animals in the cabin. I want Bod with me. This airline allows that. Hence, here we are,' he said as we approached the desk. He gave a winning smile to the attractive woman behind the desk, advising he'd already checked in online and going through the last items with her and confirming Bod's inclusion.

'Will he be all right for the flight?' I asked as we walked away.

'Yeah, he's an experienced flyer already.'

'No... I mean. His needs?'

Lorcan glanced at me. 'Don't worry. He won't wee on your expensive shoes.'

'I wasn't worried about me. I was thinking about him.' I stopped suddenly and Lorcan pulled up short beside me. 'Why do you always want to see the worst in people?' I snapped. 'You assumed Tom is after something with his kind offer and I just asked a perfectly reasonable question and you immediately jump to the worst possible reason for me asking it. Did it ever occur to you that I was concerned for your dog's comfort? I've never taken an animal on board a flight before so I don't know how that works.'

Lorcan was looking down at me. I'd worn heels but he still had quite the height advantage. He remained silent.

'I'm going to have a look around the shops. I'll catch up with you later.' He was still holding the boarding passes in his hand. I plucked them from his fingers, took mine, and handed the other back to him before heading off towards the security check.

7

I poked around the shops, squirted a few perfumes onto cardboard sticks and tried on a few pairs of designer sunglasses before wandering over to a coffee shop. Placing my order, I moved along, waiting for my drink. The barista put the hot chocolate and slice of cake down on a tray And I juggled it with one hand and my carry-on suitcase with the other, praying to any god that was listening not to let me send the whole tray flying in front of all these people.

Suddenly the tray was lifted from my hand. 'I can take that for you,' Lorcan said, looking down at me.

'Thank you,' I said, opting for gracious, and followed him to where two comfy chairs were pushed together, a small table in front of them, which already held a large black coffee and a piece of cake the same as I'd chosen. His case was next to one of the chairs and Bod, peering out from his pet carrier, was beside it. Lorcan unloaded my items for me and placed the empty tray to the side.

'You're welcome.'

I took a sip of the chocolate and felt it warming me from the inside as I cut off a piece of cake with the side of my fork. The zingyness of the lemon drizzle bounced around my taste buds.

'Not bad, eh?' Lorcan said, gesturing at his own piece of cake with his fork.

I gave a brief smile and nodded before leaning down to my bag to pull out my planner and go over what I needed to accomplish this weekend. Despite the faith Peyton had in me and my contacts book, what I hadn't liked to admit was that I didn't have any in this area of Ireland. I'd done a few weddings in Dublin and one in Belfast but none near the castle. I'd scanned the web to see what I could find and put out some feelers within my network but, so far, I wasn't having a lot of luck. That was definitely something I needed to sort this weekend. The cake-tasting had been arranged for tomorrow, which was good of the baker, allowing us to impinge on her weekend. From what I understood, it was a woman both Patrick and Lorcan had known for years, so I was sure that familiarity had helped grease those particular wheels. I sneaked a sideways look at Lorcan under my lashes. Surprisingly, and unlike about 95 per cent of the other customers in the coffee bar, he didn't have his nose stuck to his phone. He was just sitting, sipping strong black coffee and watching the world go by.

Suddenly he turned, as if sensing my eyes on him.

'I was just wondering how you two know the baker?' I said, before he could take a moment to think I'd been checking him out – which most certainly wasn't the case. Obviously. I'd already seen a couple of other women doing so but Lorcan didn't appear to have noticed.

'Primary school.'

'Really?' I asked, more interested than I wanted to be. 'I'm not in contact with anyone from primary school.' To be fair, I wasn't in contact with anyone from secondary school or university either, but I'd had my reasons at the time.

'I think it's probably easier if you come from a small village like ours. Some people move away but visit regularly, like Patrick and I, but some have lived their whole lives there. When there's only ten of you in the class, it's hard not to form a bond.'

'Ten?'

'Yep.'

'Wow.'

'More in yours, then?'

'About thirty odd.'

'Well, yeah, that would make it more difficult to bond like we all did.'

I nodded and looked down, an unexpected wash of emotion rolling over me. I jumped as one large hand touched my own. 'Maddie? Are you all right?' His words were soft, concerned. The gentle lilt of his accent wrapping around the deep voice felt as soothing as the hot chocolate had done a few moments ago. The noise around me receded and suddenly it felt as if it were just me and Lorcan. Alone. I looked up and met the intense eyes, felt the comforting weight of his hand on my wrist.

'I...'

He moved his head, leant a little closer, the line between his brows deepening as his frown grew.

A baby's piercing tired and hungry scream shattered the moment, and the world immediately zoomed back in on me. I dropped my gaze, focused for a moment on the warmth of his hand on my arm and then moved my hands, placing them together on my lap.

'Maddie?'

'Yes?' I asked, forcing normality into my voice as I locked

those memories back in the box they had momentarily escaped from.

'Where did you just go?' he asked, his voice still soft, his eyes locked on me.

I looked around and then back at him, confused. 'Nowhere.'

He lifted his hand and very gently touched my temple with his index finger. 'No, I mean where did you go in here?'

His navy eyes had an almost hypnotic quality and for a split second I nearly told him. But then I remembered where I was, and who he was.

'I don't know what you mean,' I said, forcing a small laugh into my voice. 'I was right here. You don't get rid of me that easily.' My eyes were now down, looking at the pages in front of me as I flipped onto the next day in my paper planner. 'So, we have the cake-tasting at ten o'clock tomorrow morning and then, if it's convenient, we could go to have a look round the castle straight from there. That way I can get a real idea of the space and liaise with Patrick and Peyton. I gather the photographer is someone they know too. Do you know anything about them? Are they local?' I asked as I lifted my hot chocolate and gave a glance Lorcan's way.

Our eyes met and he held the gaze for a moment before giving the tiniest headshake and lifting his mug to drain the last of his coffee.

'No, I don't. I don't think Patrick knows too much about him either. Someone Peyton knows from back home apparently. I guess she knows what she's doing.'

'Hmm.' I tapped my pen against my lip. 'I always like to meet the contractors prior to the wedding if at all possible. Still, we can make it work, I'm sure. Do you know if he's been over to visit the location at all?'

Lorcan shrugged and bent down to check on Bod.

'OK. I'll ask Peyton. If he hasn't, I wonder if there's any way we could get him one of these 360-degree videos? I mean, I assume he's going to be coming over a few days prior to the wedding to check out the location in person. At least, I hope he is.' I made another note on my planner.

I was talking to myself more than Lorcan, which was just as well as he clearly wasn't listening. Bod was now on his lap, surveying the surrounding area much as his owner had been doing a short time ago. The dog looked so tiny sitting there.

'How much bigger will he get?'

Lorcan's eyes remained on Bod as his hand gently and lazily stroked over the dog, almost covering his entire body each time.

'A little, but he's almost there.'

'He's fully grown?'

'Yep.'

'He's a poodle, yes? He's very small.'

'Size isn't everything, Maddie.' Lorcan looked up as I let out a sigh.

'You know, for someone so large you have an incredible ability to act like a small child.'

'Well, everyone has a talent, so they say. And Bod's a toy poodle. Come on, ask it, then.'

'Ask what?'

'The question that's practically falling out of those scarlet-red lips.'

'OK,' I said, slightly unnerved by the fact that this was the second time a man I hardly knew seemed to have the ability to read my mind. I squashed the thought from my brain. Lucky guess, I told myself. 'If I were to pick a dog for you, it wouldn't have been the tiniest one in the window, so to speak.'

Lorcan shrugged his broad shoulders, the movement

causing Bod to look up at him momentarily, assess the situation and then go back to people-watching.

'I guess that's a fair comment, and you're not the first one to have made that observation. But not everything can be planned. You fall in love with who you fall in love with.'

'I like his name. It suits him.'

Lorcan looked down, tilted his head so that he could see the dog's face more, at which point Bod looked up and bopped his nose against his owner's face, making him laugh, and I watched as once again that transformation spread across him. 'It does,' he agreed.

I waited for more. When nothing else was said I prompted him. 'So?'

'So what?'

'How did you end up with Bod?'

'Ah, I was seeing a girl who works at Battersea dogs home. Bod's mum was found wandering the streets, heavily pregnant and in a bad way. My girlfriend-at-the-time had volunteered to do a shift watching her. The vet was concerned about how she would cope with the pregnancy and whether the puppies would even survive, bearing in mind she'd clearly been living on the streets. She was just this tiny little thing. Anyway, we had plans, which she obviously had to cancel, so I offered to go along on her shift with my girlfriend. Bod's mum went into labour about two hours after we got there and there were these two tiny, weenie bundles of fluff. I guess it was love at first sight.'

I reached over and scratched under Bod's chin. When I stopped he nudged my hand to continue, making me laugh.

'I can see how easy that would be.' I looked up and met Lorcan's warm blue gaze.

'Yep. You don't know it's happening till it's happened. And

there you are, totally and utterly in love.' He gave a smile, not the usual mischievous one with a hint of sarcasm. This was genuine, soft and way too attractive. 'And why are you looking me like that now?' The smile was still there but this time there was humour in his eyes.

'Like what?' I asked, dropping my gaze immediately and fiddling with Bod's ears as he stood up on his master's lap and put his tiny paws on one solid thigh, stretching his head towards me for more fussing.

'I don't know. Sometimes I can read you like a book and sometimes you're like a diary with the key turned, locking your thoughts away,' Lorcan said, lifting up the dog with one hand and placing him on my lap. 'And don't worry, he's not going to wee on you.'

'That wasn't what I was worried about,' I said quietly, cuddling the little ball of fur to me. 'I didn't know how flying with pets worked and I was concerned about him having to cross his legs for the next however long.'

'I know,' Lorcan said quietly. 'I realise that now, and I'm sorry that I snapped at you earlier.'

'So why did you?' I turned to face him, still cuddling the dog to me. I wasn't angry any more, or upset – just curious. From the little I'd been able to figure out of Lorcan O'Malley so far, he could be cynical and blunt but also incredibly kind. The effort he had gone to to try and find Peyton's Irish ancestors, for example. And not minding that his date had to cancel on him in order to watch over a poorly dog, instead sitting with her and then falling in love with a tiny ball of fluff. Lorcan was like an onion – only with more layers.

'It doesn't matter,' I said easily, smiling to show him that I meant it.

'No, it does matter. The whole thing about Patrick telling

me not to bring the dog to our first meeting?'

'Yes, I did wonder about that. He must know how attached you are to him.'

'A while ago Bod was sitting on Peyton's lap in, apparently, a very expensive dress. Peyton, that is, not the dog.' He flashed that grin and I couldn't help but giggle. 'He's really good. He housetrained super quickly. But this night he began to get fidgety and it wasn't like him, so I decided to take him home. As I lifted him up he...' he leant over and put his big hands over the dog's ears, which effectively hid Bod's entire head '... had a little accident. Peyton was actually fine about it, considering, which was good of her, but I did feel awful. Patrick's not really a dog person and kind of went off the deep end. We didn't talk for two days, which is unheard of for us. He never used to be this uptight. I think this bloody wedding is freaking him out more than he lets on.'

'Are you sure that's what it is? Maybe it's something to do with work.'

'No, he'd have told me if it was.' There was an air of finality about his reply that prevented me from saying anything more. 'Anyway, turned out the little man had an infection so he wasn't his normal self. I apologised again to Peyton the next day after we'd been to the vet and she really was sweet about it, more concerned for the dog than anything else. But I guess I'm a bit touchy about the whole thing and I took that out on you, for which I'm very sorry.'

'Apology accepted.'

Lorcan gave a glance at his watch. 'I should think the gate number is up now, so we could make a move if you're ready.'

I nodded and returned my things to my bag as he packed Bod back into his pet carrier and we headed off to the departure gate.

8

'I booked you the window seat, but you can swap if you don't want it. I'm not fussed.'

'No, that's fine, if you don't mind?'

'Not at all,' he said, taking my case off me and hefting it up into the overhead locker with little effort, quickly followed by his own. Taking his own seat, he placed Bod's carrier on the floor and fastened his seat belt.

'Is this where we fight over the armrest?'

'You're taking up part of my seat, so I think I already lost that battle.'

He gave me a look, half frown, half smile. 'I got us premium seats. The only other option is for me to sit out on the wing.'

I turned and looked out of the window, tapping my finger on my chin.

'Oh, very funny. Besides, you're not using all yours anyway.'

I spread my petite frame out as far as I could. 'Yes, I am. And I need that armrest too.'

The deep laugh rumbled in his chest as the grin spread

across his face. 'You know, you're pretty fun when you're not trying to control everything.'

I pulled myself back up into a more elegant position, calmly lifted my current novel from my bag and turned to the correct page.

'Now what did I do?'

'You didn't do anything.'

'I must have. One minute you're all relaxed and fun, and the next you've shut down and acting like you're got a ramrod stuck up your—'

'Ladies and gentlemen, this is your captain speaking.'

'Maddie?'

'Shoosh.' I held my finger to my lips. 'I want to listen.'

Lorcan gave me a long, studied look, let out a hiss of breath through his teeth, tipped his head back against his seat and closed his eyes. I snuck a glance and saw that his jaw was tight and his hands were still bunched into fists, something I'd noticed he did whenever he got frustrated. He literally had no clue about tact. No wonder he was single.

* * *

As the plane lurched, I vehemently regretted the hot chocolate and cake I'd eaten earlier.

'Oh!'

Lorcan had been asleep within minutes of us taking to the sky, which suited me perfectly, but at the jolt his eyes flew open and he leant forward a little to check on Bod. As he did so, he caught sight of my face and made the wise choice of pulling out the sick bag from his side and handing it to me before attending to the dog, which, as it turned out, was an excellent decision as I immediately made use of it.

'Not a good traveller, eh?'

I didn't reply, misery surrounding me, wrapped within an outer casing of embarrassment.

The plane bounced some more and Lorcan pulled another bag from in front of me, deftly opening it as I fumbled. Moving his hand to my hair, he held it back with one hand, gently rubbing my back with his other.

'There you go. You'll feel better now.' His words were soft, the gentle lilt calming my senses, which was just as well as the plane continued to bounce about and the captain advised us we would be experiencing some turbulence. No shit, Sherlock. A member of the cabin crew appeared at Lorcan's side and he discreetly handed him the two bags I'd made use of, asking for some more in case, just as subtly.

'I think I'm done.'

The captain's voice came over the tannoy again. 'I'm sorry about this, folks, but it's going to be a little bumpy for a bit.'

My eyes widened. 'That wasn't bumpy?' I croaked.

Lorcan pulled a sympathetic face as the captain continued. 'Cabin crew, please take your seats.'

The man from earlier reappeared at Lorcan's side, gave him a handful of sick bags and me a sympathetic look, before heading off to buckle up himself.

'Is Bod OK?'

'Yeah.' Lorcan nodded. 'He's grand. A seasoned traveller.'

The plane lurched again and a few people let out shrieks and sounds of what could have been surprise or terror. In my case, it was a mixture of both.

'Nothing to worry about,' Lorcan said.

I shot him a disbelieving look.

'It's fine. Happens all the time. We'll be there soon and you can have some proper food to settle your stomach.'

I snatched one of the bags and emptied the remainder of my stomach contents into it.

* * *

After a while the weather calmed until we broke through the clouds in preparation for landing. According to the captain, a storm was rolling in off the Atlantic and, I quote, it 'might get a bit bumpy again' as we came in to land.

I turned to Lorcan. 'It might get a bit bumpy? It's already been bumpy. Surely that's more than enough bumpiness for one short flight?'

He shrugged his shoulders as rain began pelting the windows of the plane and once again we began to jolt around. I've never been afraid of flying but this was the roughest flight I'd ever been on, despite being one of the shortest. My hands gripped the armrests – Lorcan having wisely relinquished any claim – my knuckles showing white before I closed my eyes. We tilted to the side sharply as a gust of wind caught one of the wings. My eyes flew open and I whipped my head round to look at Lorcan. He laid one large hand over mine on the armrest in response. The plane continued to fight against the weather as we descended towards the airport. I risked a glance out of the window but could see little as heavy rain streaked across the oval glass panel.

'We're close to the airport now,' Lorcan said, his voice calm and soothing. 'It will be over soon.'

I squeezed my eyes shut even tighter. 'One way or the other,' I ground out between gritted teeth.

The next thing I knew my hand was being peeled from the armrest. 'No!' Opening my eyes quickly, I met Lorcan's. 'I need to hold on.'

'It's OK,' he said, his gaze trained on mine as his warm hands folded around mine. 'I've got you. I promise.'

Without thinking, I gripped his hand. The plane moved back and forth as it caught in the crosswind and all the time Lorcan whispered soothing words into my ear, his other hand stroking mine gently. We finally landed, the left wheel slightly before the right, but then we were down and the reverse thrusters went into operation, slowing the aircraft on the runway.

I risked opening one eye. 'Is that it?'

'That's it,' Lorcan confirmed softly, the large warm hand still wrapped around mine. I glanced down and his gaze followed as I took a few deep breaths. Carefully I began to slide my hand out from his.

'Sorry about that.'

'No problem.'

'And earlier the whole... you know.'

'Don't even think about it. Happens to the best of us.'

I leant my head back against the headrest. 'Somehow I doubt you've ever thrown up on a flight.'

'Well, then, you'd be wrong.'

'Really?' I rolled my head tentatively to look at him.

He nodded.

'Are you going to tell me about it?'

'Will it make you feel better?'

Right now I couldn't think of anything that would make me feel better but it was worth a shot.

'It might do.'

'Fine,' he condescended. 'But remember I'm only telling you this because of exceptional circumstances.'

'Duly noted. So what happened? Turbulence?'

'No, I'm afraid not. You at least have that excuse. I have none other than drinking far too much, knowing I had drunk far too much, and still getting on the plane.'

'I think we've all done things like that when we were young.'

'That is true. Unfortunately I don't have that excuse either. I was definitely old enough to know better at this point.'

Calmer now as we taxied into our gate, I studied him. I had been about to ask more about the circumstances but there was something in his eyes that halted me. I got the feeling that his aeroplane episode wasn't simply the result of a night out on the lash with the boys. There was something more to it and I didn't want to pry further than I already had.

'Thank you,' I said.

'Did it make you feel better?'

'I'm not sure. But I appreciate the effort. Thank you.'

'You're welcome,' he said, looking forward, as he repeatedly stretched his left hand out, then balled it into a fist.

'Is everything OK?' I asked, looking at his hand before raising my eyes to his face.

'Everything's grand. You just have quite the grip for a wee thing.'

'Oh, God. Sorry.'

'No problem.'

'Were you really not worried?'

'Jesus. Absolutely terrified!'

'Really?' My voice jumped an octave. Attractive, Maddie.

The laughter was back. 'I'm teasing you.'

Admittedly his laughter had taken my stress levels down another notch, which I guessed had been his intention.

'And no. Not particularly and I'm sure the flight back will be far less eventful. The storm should have passed through by then.'

'I hope so.'

Lorcan looked down at his hand, flexing the long fingers. 'I hope so too,' he replied before giving me a mischievous grin and bending down to lift Bod's carrier up onto his lap, ready for disembarkation.

* * *

A short time later, we were through the airport and waiting at the hire-car area to collect the vehicle Lorcan had already arranged. Bod had been taken out of his carrier and was now investigating on the end of his lead while his master sorted out the paperwork for the car. The little dog seemed no worse for wear despite our adventurous trip over and happily sniffed around and watered various bits of the surrounding area until Lorcan reappeared from the building and Bod lurched for him as though he'd been gone years.

9

'How are you feeling now?' Lorcan asked as we left Dublin behind and headed west. He'd produced a bottle of cold water from somewhere before we'd even left the plane and I'd been sipping it ever since. My heartbeat was now somewhere back around its normal rate but I wasn't sure if my stomach would ever be the same again.

'Better, thanks.'

He glanced over. 'You still look a little green around the gills.'

'I feel it, to be honest. I'm sure I just need a rest and I'll be right as rain.'

'That's the spirit.'

'How long is it until we get there?'

He glanced at the clock on the centre console where the satnav displayed our route.

'We should be there in about an hour and a half, traffic permitting. It's not showing any hold-ups en route at the moment but this weather isn't doing us any favours.'

The storm the pilot had mentioned had the windscreen

wipers working double time to keep it free from rain, and every so often Lorcan would correct the steering as the wind whipped the car off course.

'Is there not an airport closer to the actual village?'

'Yeah, there's a few but not all of them have direct flights and it's not easy to find airlines that let you take your dog on board in Europe.'

'I suppose he'd have to go cargo?'

'Yep. And that's not happening.'

I looked down at the little bundle of fluff now happily curled up in my lap, snoozing contentedly, and understood Lorcan's view completely.

* * *

When I looked out of the window again, the rain was less ferocious and the sky was darkening into early evening. Bod was now sitting on a small blanket on the back seat, strapped into a seat belt, and Lorcan's coat had been laid over me like a blanket.

'Good nap?'

'Umm... Yeah. Sorry, I never fall asleep in cars.' I looked down at the coat. 'Did we stop?'

'Only briefly. You needed the rest and I didn't want you to wake up.'

'Thanks. You should have woken me though.'

'No need.'

'Not exactly great company for the drive.'

'No worries. You weren't exactly great company on the plane either but...' He let the words drift off as I gave him a cold and icy glare.

'It was hardly my fault.'

'I didn't say it was. I was just trying to make a joke. Don't take life so seriously.'

'I'm sorry. It was just an unpleasant and embarrassing experience.'

'I didn't mean anything by it. Don't take it so personally.'

'It's rather hard not to when I was the one throwing up.'

Lorcan didn't reply. He just let out a sigh, gave a quick glance at the side window before focusing back on the road as we continued the rest of the journey in silence. Maybe I had overreacted but I was embarrassed and I'd been surprised by the feeling of being taken care of – especially by this man I hardly knew. I'd felt warm and comforted and the whole thing had just felt 'right' – and that had unnerved me more than anything.

Thankfully it wasn't long until we were pulling into a small village, the lights of it welcoming after what felt like miles of darkness. After a short distance Lorcan swung the car into the entranceway of a pub, its roof low, as though hunkered down against the harsh Atlantic weather that blew in from the nearby ocean. Yellow-tinged lights spilled from the windows. A couple entered as we got out of the car and the sound of laughter and music poured out momentarily before silence reigned again as the heavy wooden door closed behind them.

'This is you,' Lorcan said, scooping Bod up with one hand and opening the door with the other.

'Are you not staying here too?' I asked, following him out and heading towards the boot to retrieve my luggage.

'Nope.'

I waited for him to elaborate but he didn't so I pulled the handle up on my suitcase and belted my coat back around my waist.

'Right. Goodnight, then.'

'I'll see you in.'

I remembered back to what he'd said the night of the restaurant meal about always ensuring his sisters got home safe and tempered my reply. 'Thank you, but I'm sure I'll be OK walking from here to the door.'

Lorcan shut the boot of the car and took a step towards me. I could feel the warmth of his body despite the chill evening air. He tilted his head down as I looked up, meeting his eyes, cool as the air around us. 'I said,' his voice low and with a rough edge of tiredness to it, 'I'll see you in.' His body was almost touching mine, his eyes lingering on me a second longer as he leant towards me a little more. I felt my heart speed up despite my brain yelling at it to fall back into line. That hint of smile tempted his lips as he moved closer again. 'I'll take this.' His words brushed my ear as he took the handle of my suitcase, turned and, forgoing the wheels, carried it towards the pub.

I let out a breath, angry with myself and at him – but mostly myself. If we managed to survive the weekend without me pushing him off one of those steep, brooding cliffs I'd seen catching the moonlight as we approached the village, it would be a miracle. I turned on my heel and followed him towards my abode for the weekend.

Lorcan pushed open the heavy door and the noise we'd heard earlier almost bowled me over. It was a total cacophony of laughter, music and chat. The pub was completely jammed and I hesitated for a moment at the door.

'In you go,' Lorcan said, holding the door for me to go first. 'They won't bite.'

I twisted my head to look at him and gave him a glare before moving forward, very slowly through the pub towards the bar. Once I'd managed that particular hurdle, trying to get the attention of someone to attend to me was the next. I glanced over my shoulder but Lorcan was further back in the pub, laughing with a small group of people, his whole demeanour entirely changed now that he was out of my company. I turned back to the bar and made another attempt to check in. Finally, I got someone's attention.

'Hello. I've got a room booked here for the next three nights.'

'No, sorry, love. We're full.'

'No.' I waved my hand and began to try explaining again, having to practically shout to get myself heard above the very lively Friday-night crowd. It hadn't seemed like a very big village as we'd driven through it, but from the looks of it absolutely everyone who lived in it was here tonight.

'I have a room booked already.'

'Here?'

'Yes, here. Tonight. Three nights.' I held up my fingers for emphasis.

'Ah now. Why didn't you say so?'

I smiled patiently and waited as the man reached below the bar and pulled out a ledger that he put down onto the surface with a heavy thump.

'And what would your name be?'

'Madeline Hart.'

The man ran a meaty finger down one page, then flicked back to the previous one and did the same again, before returning to the first page.

'Nope. No booking under that name. Sorry.'

A shiver of insecurity ran through me before I caught it. I'd dealt with worse problems than this before. It was obviously an error. 'I'm sorry, but there must be. Please would you mind checking again?'

He shrugged his shoulders genially and did as I asked, coming up with the same answer.

'I can give you the name of a few hotels. They're all a bit of a drive from here. I'm guessing you have a car?'

'No, I don't have a car. I got a lift. And I know for certain the room was booked for me. There must be some mistake.'

'Not that I can see. Sorry I can't be more helpful.' His manner was still friendly and I was trying my best to see this from his point of view. But I'd also had an incredibly shit day and really just wanted to have a wash and go to bed.

'I don't know what to tell you, love. I wish I could help.'

'But it must—'

'I booked the room, Gerald. Maybe Brighid put it under my name.'

'Aah, Lorcan, lad,' the man said, extending his hand over the bar to shake Lorcan's. 'Good to see you again. Let me just have a look. Oh, yes, here we are. One double room as requested.' His eyes darted between me and Lorcan. 'Sorry about the confusion there, miss.'

'Not to worry. It's sorted now, that's the main thing.'

He nodded and gave a wide, friendly smile before turning around and lifting the last remaining key from a small board behind him.

'Here you go,' he said, handing the key to Lorcan. 'You know where everything is.'

'Oh! It's my room, actually.'

The landlord looked at me and Lorcan took the key off him. 'It's her room, as she says.' Then, turning to me, 'Come on, I'll show you up. Gerry's got enough on his hands here.'

'Thanks. That's grand, Lorcan, and welcome to Ballalee, miss. I hope you enjoy your stay.'

I nodded in thanks, my throat already sore from my in-air

exploits and then shouting over the noise of the bar. I'd rather not have had Lorcan O'Malley showing me to my room, but it seemed it was going to be the quickest way of getting there so I went along with it. As I reached for my case, he lifted it by the handle, then took my hand with his free one.

'Hold on.' With that, he headed back into the crowd, making a pathway with his broad shoulders. I gratefully followed in his wake until we got to the other side of the pub and the bottom of some narrow stairs.

'Ladies first.' He quirked a brow as I glanced up at him, his face still inscrutable, the smile he'd had for his friends – and earlier for me – now nowhere to be seen. The man he'd been on the plane, kind, patient and calming, had disappeared behind a distant exterior. I knew I was probably partly responsible for that but I couldn't help it. I was tired, embarrassed and out of my comfort zone with the feelings his platonic attention had caused and unfortunately Lorcan had got the brunt of my reaction earlier in the car.

The stairs creaked and groaned as I mounted them, looking at the old black and white pictures decorating the walls as I did so. Images of the village centuries ago showed that, from what I'd seen on the drive in, it had changed very little in all that time.

'Sorry,' I said, realising I was probably keeping Lorcan from his friends.

'No problem.'

I continued up the stairs. I could look at the rest of them tomorrow when I didn't have an unnerving Irishman behind me.

'This is you,' he said, pointing to a door at the end of a corridor so narrow I had to flatten myself against the wall as Lorcan stepped forward. He was already having to stoop. These places certainly weren't built for men of his size. He unlocked the door and pushed it open, signalling for me to go in first before following me in.

'It's beautiful,' I said, looking around, unable to stop the smile I turned to Lorcan with. The room was in a cosy cottage style, with an overstuffed armchair in one corner, an inviting-looking bed dressed with a handmade quilt, all lit with a soft glow from the single bedside lamp the owners had left on. It felt welcoming, homely and perfect.

Lorcan merely nodded and I reined in my own smile. 'Well, thank you for bringing the case up. You should go back to your friends now.'

He took a step towards me, his eyes locked onto mine, dark in the intimately lit room. His hand reached out and gently took my arm, sliding down until his hand circled my wrist. I wanted to pull away, tell him his Irish charm might work on everyone else in the village, from the reactions I'd seen so far, but I was immune to it. But I couldn't. Images of him being so attentive on the plane, holding my hair, rubbing my back, telling me I was safe, swam around my traitorous mind. His hand momentarily tightened around my wrist and my heart sped up, before he continued, taking my hand tenderly in his. He bent, close to my ear, his warm breath sending sparks of fire throughout my body.

'This is yours,' he whispered as I felt cold, hard metal in my hand. The key.

Lorcan stood back straight, only able to do so in the middle of the room where the pitch was highest. He gave a wicked smile as if he could read my thoughts and I could have kicked myself. But only after I'd kicked him first. At least once.

'Thank you,' I said, pretending he'd had no effect whatsoever and, by the look on his face, utterly failing. 'If you don't mind leaving now, I'd like to get some rest. Goodnight.'

'Goodnight, Maddie.'

I was already turning away and attending to my luggage when the door closed and I sank down onto the bed, giving my heart rate time to return to normal once again. Lorcan O'Malley was good-looking – that was, unfortunately, undisputable. But I needed this job – with no complications. Especially not in the form of dark, dangerously sexy Irishmen.

10

I shook my head, as if to shake out the ridiculous feelings that had flooded my body at his touch, and unzipped my suitcase. Having packed light, I was organised, showered and in my pyjamas fifteen minutes later. The noise of the pub drifted up through the rafters, but I didn't mind. There was something soothing about it, rather than annoying. Grabbing my hairbrush, I began to sort out the tangles my hair had accumulated whipping in the wind as we'd gone to collect the hire car. A few ouches and winces later, I'd got them all out and the brush glided through the hair I'd carefully straightened after my shower this morning. Suddenly that all seemed such a long time ago. Perhaps I was more tired than I thought. The day had certainly had its trying moments. I sat down on the bed and sank back into its wonderfully soft comfort just as my stomach gave a loud growl. I'd only had a juice for breakfast and then ruined my good intentions by the hot chocolate and slice of cake but, as it was, that hadn't stayed in my system all that long anyway so I reckoned I could probably discount those calories. Suddenly I was starving but, glancing at the time on my phone,

I knew the kitchen would be closed, plus there was the small fact I was now wearing Snoopy pyjamas and it wasn't exactly the sort of place that did room service. My stomach let out another loud, complaining grumble and I curled up into a ball, hoping to be able to ignore the pangs long enough to get to sleep.

A knock at the door made me jump and I stared at it for a moment before reaching out for the light, pushing myself back up from the bed and padding over to the door. I turned the key and pulled it open a crack to find Lorcan on the other side.

'I thought you might be hungry.' He indicated the plate he held in one hand that had the most mouth-watering-looking sandwich on it.

'Oh!' Manners kicked in. 'Thank you.' I pulled the door open further, hiding myself behind it as he entered, putting the sandwich and a large, steaming mug on the desk that stood to one side of the window. 'There's a chamomile tea there too. Soothes the nerves and should help you sleep.'

See? This was what was so damn annoying about the man. One minute he was a teasing, full-of-himself pain in the arse and the next minute he did something thoughtful and caring.

'Thank you. That was very kind.'

'I've also changed the cake-tasting to the afternoon. I didn't think, after today, you'd much feel like doing that at ten o'clock in the morning. Calum is going to meet us at the castle on Sunday now we're not rushing.'

This exact thought had been spiralling around in my mind for hours but I hadn't mentioned it. Lorcan had an uncanny way of knowing what I was thinking. For someone like me, who very much kept themselves to themselves, it was extremely unnerving and I wasn't at all sure that I liked it.

'You didn't have to do that.'

'Well, it's done now so you can have a lie-in.'

'I don't do lie-ins.'

He stopped on his way to the door. 'Come again?'

'I don't do lie-ins. It's a waste of the day.'

'What if you don't have any plans?'

'I always have plans.'

'Not from what I saw on your calendar.'

'That was work. That's different. There's always something to do.'

'No, there isn't. Sometimes there's nothing to do at all.'

I stood straighter. 'Perhaps for you. But I like to make use of my time.'

'As do I. Doing nothing is a perfectly good use of time.'

'We'll have to agree to disagree on that point, I'm afraid.'

He gave an incline of his head and moved to the door, one hand on the dark gold of the solid oak.

'See you tomorrow.'

I nodded briefly and began to close the door.

'Nice jammies, by the way. Always was a fan of Snoopy.'

I closed the door with a solid thunk and ignored the deep chuckle I heard from the other side of it.

* * *

Turning over in the deliciously comfortable bed, I noticed tendrils of sunlight dancing and swaying on the thick rug beside it as they escaped from under the curtains. I slid my hand over to the bedside and looked at my phone. After Lorcan had left last night, I'd pounced on the sandwich, which had turned out to be made just perfectly, with home-made bread, thick slices of roasted ham, not like the wafer-thin sheets I got from the supermarket, and just the right amount of mustard.

The tea, as Lorcan had promised, had indeed been soothing and, once tucked into the cosy bed with a full tummy, I'd been asleep within minutes. Blurry eyes focused on the phone: 10.10 a.m. I bolted upright, rubbed my eyes and looked again: 10.11 a.m. With everything else that had happened yesterday, I'd forgotten to set an alarm! Oh my God! Half the day was already gone!

Within ten minutes, I'd washed, dressed and was downstairs in the bar area. I was sure breakfast would be over by now but if I could get a cup of tea, that would at least be something. I looked around, and headed towards where I heard voices coming from the bar.

'Well, good morning there, miss. Did you sleep well?' Gerald's friendly face beamed at me from where he was sitting at a table as a woman I assumed to be his wife bustled up to me.

'Too well, I'm afraid. I'm so sorry. I don't normally sleep this late. Never, actually.'

The woman patted my arm. 'That'll be the fresh air for you. Don't you worry. Now, what would you like for breakfast? The full Irish? Do you like black pudding? How would you like your eggs? Toast or fried bread?'

'Let the poor girl speak, Brighid.' Her husband pronounced the name like breeze, with a soft g, laughing as he did so.

She laughed along with him, patting my arm and guiding me to a table by the window that looked out onto an enclosed area that was currently scattered with chickens of differing colours tottering about and pecking at the ground, their fluffy bloomer legs making me smile. Beyond it stretched fields so lush and green, they looked like something from a CGI film. I laid the coat I'd brought down with me over an empty chair, planning to head straight out after breakfast and scout the village for suppliers.

'So, the full breakfast, then?' Brighid asked again.

'Oh, no. I'm fine, really. I don't tend to eat breakfast anyway and it's my fault I missed the sitting. I don't want to put you to any trouble, but a cup of tea would be lovely, if that's possible?'

'No breakfast? Nonsense. Most important meal of the day and it's no trouble at all. So, black pudding or no?'

I enjoyed food but I also tried to be healthy, but somehow I had the feeling I was in a losing battle here and this couple seemed so lovely and friendly, I really didn't want to offend them. After all, it was just the one day – I'd arrange something different tomorrow. Also, despite the huge and delicious sandwich Lorcan had brought me last night, I was somehow starving.

'No black pudding, thank you.'

'Right you are, then. And a big pot of tea, of course. Perfect. Be with you in a while. You just take it easy there and watch the girls,' she said, pointing to the chickens. 'Time wasters, so they are, but lovely ones.'

'I can imagine,' I said, smiling at their busyness and laughing as one seemed to notice us and turned her black, beady eyes on us.

'That's our Helen. Helen of Troy, she's named after. Thinks she's the most beautiful creature.'

'She is rather.'

'That she is, but don't you be telling her or we'll never hear the end of it.'

I laughed again, loving the way Brighid talked about the animals and their personalities.

'Are they all different? I mean in character?'

'Oh, absolutely! Just as people are. Have you never had chickens?'

'I've... umm... never actually had a pet at all.'

'Well, there. Now that's a shame. I'll take you out to meet them after you've finished your breakfast if you like. Introduce you properly.'

'Oh, that's very kind but I really should be getting on.'

'Mornin' there, sleepyhead.'

I looked away from the yard to see Lorcan walking through from behind the bar, Bod toddling behind him. When the little dog noticed me, he sped over, resting his paws up against the chair. Automatically I reached down and plopped him on my lap. 'Slept well, I take it,' his owner continued. There was a teasing note to his voice and a glint to his eye. 'Good to have a lie-in, isn't it?'

Ugh.

'And we've nothing to do until two o'clock this afternoon so there's plenty of time to enjoy a leisurely breakfast and then go out and meet the girls.'

'Perfect.' Brighid squeezed my shoulder and bustled off back towards where Lorcan had come from, followed by Gerry. Lorcan came to stand by my table.

'May I?' he asked, hooking his gaze onto mine.

Gerry was still hovering by the bar, checking on the optics, and I didn't want to appear rude in front of him so, despite irritation fizzing through me at his smart-alec comment about having a lie-in, I gave a brief movement of my head that was neither yes or no. Lorcan took it as a yes. Shocker.

'You look rested.'

'Hardly surprising,' I said, still a little annoyed at wasting several hours of the day but keeping my eyes fixed outside.

'You obviously needed it. You have to listen to your body sometimes.'

I thought about what my body had been saying last night as Lorcan's had moved closer to mine and decided that I would most definitely not be following that advice.

'I have a lot to do.'

'There's nothing to do until the cake-tasting at two.'

'You may have nothing to do, but I have plenty.'

'Such as?' he asked, leaning back in the chair and crossing his arms over his broad chest.

'There's more that goes into a wedding than just cake.'

'Believe me, I'm entirely aware of that.' There was something in the way he said it that caught my attention, a flicker behind his eyes, before his face became impassive once again.

'I need to find local suppliers for the flowers and the catering for a start, and the area's not exactly swimming with choices from what I can see.'

'There's enough.'

'And how would you know?'

'Because, as much as I'm not a fan of weddings, I've heard about very little else from my best friend since this all began and even more after the first wedding planner upped and left, leaving me with a hysterical bride and panicking groom when they found out she hadn't arranged anything at all. None of the catering, band, venue – nothing.'

'She hadn't done anything? That seems unusual.'

'Unusual isn't the word I'd use for her, but whatever.'

'How did they find out?'

'Peyton rang the venue to ask something when she couldn't get hold of the planner one day. They had no booking for their wedding. Cue a bridal meltdown as Patrick rang more of the providers and got the same response.'

'That's awful!'

'Yeah, it wasn't great. The poor girl had her heart set on this country house in Dublin that goes all out for weddings.'

'And, of course, they then had no availability.'

'Not for the next two years.'

Our conversation was interrupted by Brighid bringing me my breakfast and a huge pot of tea.

'Oh, wow! That looks incredible. Thank you so much!'

'Ah, you're more than welcome. I've brought a cup for you too, Lorcan. Did you want anything to eat?'

'No, thanks, Brighid, I'm grand.'

'I'll leave you two to it, then. Enjoy.'

11

'Thank you,' I called as she bustled off back towards the kitchen before turning wide eyes on Lorcan. 'Oh my God, this is huge!' I whispered, picking up my cutlery but not knowing where to start. Thankfully there was no black pudding, but there were fried eggs, bacon done just to the perfect point of crispiness, sausages, beans, fried bread, mushrooms, fried tomatoes and a couple of things I wasn't sure of.

'Is this some sort of pancake?'

'Potato farl. Delicious.'

'And this?'

'White pudding.'

'White pudding?'

'Yeah. Like black pudding but better for the more squeamish amongst us. No blood.'

I looked back down at my plate.

'Try it.'

I remained unconvinced. 'Maybe in a bit. How on earth am I going to eat all this?'

'I can give you a hand with this,' he said, reaching over and swiping a piece of fried bread. I bit into the other piece so he couldn't nick that one. It tasted heavenly.

'Oh God,' I said, my hand over my full mouth.

The mischievous blue eyes sparkled. 'Good, eh?'

'So good,' I said, feeling the delight spread across my face.

'That'll be the butter.'

'Hmm?' I asked as I reloaded my fork.

'The butter. None of that olive or sunflower oil around here. Good old Irish butter it's fried in. You can't beat it.'

I swallowed my mouthful. 'I think I can hear my arteries revolting as we speak.'

'Nah, they'll be loving it, and, if not, you'll die well fed at least.'

I flicked a glance at him. 'One way to look at it, I suppose.'

'The only way to look at it. You have to enjoy life.'

'Yes, but you can't enjoy one of these every day otherwise it will be a short one.'

'Fair enough. But you can't beat it on a lazy Sunday morning.'

'I will agree with that.' Having tasted Brighid's cooking, it was hard not to. 'However, this is neither Sunday nor going to be lazy.'

'So you say. Still, fill yourself up now it's there because you can't tell me you're not enjoying it when your face looks like that.' He flashed a grin and stole a piece of toast.

'It really is heavenly.'

'I'll leave you to enjoy your breakfast.' He began to rise from his chair but something made me stop him.

'Don't you want a cup of tea? She brought two cups after all, and I certainly won't be able to drink all that.' I nodded my head at the family-sized teapot Brighid had placed between us.

'Unless you have somewhere to be, of course. Sorry. I'm sure that you do.'

Lorcan sat back down. 'No, I don't have any plans at all.' He flashed me a teasing look. 'And that would be very nice, thank you.'

'I'm not sure I'm going to have any room for cake later.'

'We can work it off you, don't worry.'

My head snapped up and his gaze rose slowly to meet mine. 'I was going to show you the area a bit before heading to the bakery. I hope you brought shoes sturdier than those ones you were wearing yesterday.'

I nodded.

'What did you think I meant?'

'Nothing!' I said, far too quickly, and made a point of carefully loading another forkful, then looking out at the chickens as I lifted it to my mouth. Everywhere, essentially, other than at Lorcan.

'Lorcan, love. Could you come give Gerry a hand with something? He's insisting on doing it himself and I know he's going to put his back out again.'

'Sure.' He drained his cup, placed it carefully back in the saucer and rose from the table. 'Enjoy the rest of your breakfast. I'll be waiting for you when you're done. But no rush. You're in Ireland now, don't forget.'

'Oh, time works differently here, does it?'

'It can do, yeah. If you let it.' He gave me a cheeky wink and headed off in the direction of the kitchen, crossing the room quickly with long, relaxed strides until he disappeared through the door to the back. Bod looked up from where he'd been curled up on my feet since my food had arrived, considered his options and trotted hurriedly after his master. I ate the rest of my breakfast and sat contentedly with several cups of tea, watching the chickens bustle about, trying to pick out the characters their owner had told me about.

'And where have you been all my life?' A tall, broad man dressed for the weather in a thick jumper and jeans smiled cheekily at me, removing the woollen hat he'd been wearing as he did so.

'Avoiding you, like any sensible woman should, Liam.' Lorcan replied for me as he re-entered the room, flashing a grin at the newcomer.

'Aye, I should have known with a woman this gorgeous around, you wouldn't be far behind, you eejit,' the man said, laughing as he shook hands warmly with Lorcan. 'I'd have warned you off him,' the man said, turning back to me, 'but it looks like I'm too late.'

'No, not at all. Our connection is purely work. Lorcan's not at all my type.'

The man let loose a roaring laugh. 'Now, there's something I bet you don't hear too much, O'Malley. I like this one.'

'You would. What are you doing here anyway, apart from making the place look untidy?'

'I've just come over to see the folks and see what's for lunch.'

'Some people have only just had their breakfast...' Lorcan eyed me, his unfortunately tempting mouth tilted in a provocative smile.

'Ah, that's all right. That's what the weekend's for, isn't it?'

Before I could say much else Liam's mum came back into the room and began fussing around me. Having eventually been persuaded that I was more than full enough and had drunk enough tea to float a battleship, she began to clear the breakfast away, roping in Liam to help her.

'Right, where should I meet you for the cake-tasting this afternoon? You did say two o'clock, didn't you?'

'I did. And where are you hurrying off to? I thought we were going sightseeing.'

'As lovely as that might be, as I said before, I have things to do.'

'Such as?'

'I already told you,' I replied, tilting my head to meet his eyes as I tried to work out whether he was winding me up or if he truly did not comprehend the full situation.

He folded his arms across his chest, stretching the fabric of the black tee shirt he wore over the faded jeans that I'd noticed fitted his bum just perfectly. Not that I'd been purposely looking, of course. What can I say? It's part of my job to take note of details.

'I'm trying to plan a wedding practically from scratch in very little time, and we're not exactly in London.' I raised an arm to encompass the view from the window.

'Your point?'

'My point is, as I said, suppliers aren't exactly abundant and I'm having to search out new ones as my network doesn't cover this far west.'

'Are you saying you're out of your depth?' he asked, taking a seat back at the table.

I narrowed my eyes at him. 'No,' I said, slowly. 'Merely that, unlike some people this weekend, I need to work.'

'I'm working this afternoon and tomorrow. And I'm not even getting paid for it.' He shrugged solid, square shoulders.

'I wouldn't say helping out your best friend is work, and, if you object that much, you can wait somewhere else while I tour the venue tomorrow.'

'As much as that appeals, I have strict instructions to accompany you.'

I gave a disbelieving snort. 'Like you've ever followed a strict instruction in your life.'

'Well, that always depends on what it is, and who's issuing it.' He waggled his eyebrows.

'You're incorrigible,' I replied, doing my best not to give in to the smile and failing, picking up my phone, holding it up, down, to one side and then the other. 'Is there any signal here?'

'Patchy at best.'

'Wi-Fi?'

'Sure. We're not backwards.'

'I wasn't suggesting you were. I don't suppose you happen to know the password?'

'The password is freewifi, no capitals. What is it exactly you're after?'

A patient sigh escaped my teeth as I typed it in. OK, perhaps not that patient. 'Caterers, a florist, music, glassware suppliers, cutlery suppliers, crockery—'

'Suppliers,' he finished for me. 'I get it.' He pushed his chair back, wood scraping against the floorboard as he held out his hand. 'Come with me.'

'Lorcan, I really don't have—'

'Come with me.'

I stayed where I was for a moment, challenging him with my eyes. He remained impassive.

'Ugh. You're impossible.'

'You do say the nicest things, Miss Madeleine.'

'It's Ms.'

'Yes, ma'am,' he noted, helping me on with my coat. His hands moved to my belt, one holding one end, the other holding its opposite and gently pulled, the action turning me around to face him. Deep blue eyes looked down, locking onto mine for a moment before his gaze dropped to the belt, which he fastened around me securely. 'Chillier than it looks out there today.' His voice was soft and that rolling lilt only enhanced the gentleness of the words. I took a step closer so that there was barely an inch of space between us and stood up on my tiptoes, even then still only reaching his jaw, rough with the shadow of dark stubble, with my temple.

'You're forgetting something,' I whispered.

'What's that?' I could hear the faint rasp in his words, underlying the deep, smooth tones.

'Your charms don't work on me.' I made to step back but his hand quickly caught mine, making me stop and look up.

His eyes fixed on me and I couldn't help but look back, part of me wanting to stay there, locked in that moment, and part of me wanting to push away. What felt like ages probably lasted only a beat before Lorcan spoke again.

'Come with me.' And without waiting for an answer, he took my hand and led me with long-legged strides out of the room.

'I need my planner!' I huffed out, a little breathless from keeping up.

'Got it,' he said, holding it up in his other hand. 'God forbid we should go anywhere without it.'

12

'Where are we going?' I asked as we strode down the small pavement of what seemed to be the central street of the village.

'You'll see.'

'Where's Bod?'

'Staying with Brighid for a bit to be thoroughly spoiled.'

'I don't think you need to hold my hand.'

'Got to keep up, Maddie.' Lorcan stopped without warning and I came to a sudden halt. 'After all, we have a lot of work to do.' He gave a quick wink as he tossed my words back at me before starting off again.

I swore under my breath.

'Any more of that and we'll have to make an extra stop at the church for someone to take confession.'

'You know, you're not as funny as you think you are,' I said, taking two to three steps to his one, determined not to fall behind.

'That's what I like about you, Maddie. You keep a man grounded.'

I opened my mouth with a riposte when Lorcan halted,

rapping on a glass door with the back of his knuckles. Swallowing my retort, I looked properly at the place we had stopped at. It was a double-fronted premises set in what appeared to have once been a large house. The roof and paintwork were both new but the door gave nothing away. To the side of it, however, was a small sign.

Ur

'It means "Fresh" in Gaelic,' Lorcan explained, following my eyeline just as the door opened and a tall, rangy man with striking green eyes and a shock of red hair tied back in a short ponytail appeared.

'I was just wondering where you'd all got to.' The man smiled, shaking Lorcan's hand enthusiastically, before switching to me.

'Sorry. We would have been earlier. Someone overslept. Not used to all this fresh country air,' Lorcan explained with a grin. My mouth fell open and I felt the blush from forehead to toes.

'No problem at all. Pleased to meet you. You must be Madeleine.'

'I... yes, I am,' I replied, feeling at a loss as I willed the blush to subside.

'I'm Eoghan. And I hear you have a wedding to plan for our Patrick.'

'Yes. Yes, that's right. At the castle.'

'And you're in need of a caterer?'

My eyes widened as I looked round at Lorcan. He gave the merest hint of a shrug. 'Yes! Yes, we are.'

'Eoghan here's your man.'

'Hold it there, now, Lorcan. I'm sure Madeleine, if she's as

good a planner as I've heard her talked about, will be wanting
to try some samples before she books anyone.'

I'd been talked about?

'That would be wonderful, if you're able to? Are you aware
of the size of the wedding and the short time scale?'

'I am.'

'I see. Then, yes. A tasting would be great.' I took my
planner back from Lorcan and tucked it under my arm before
pulling up the calendar on my phone. 'When would be a good
time for that?'

Eoghan pulled a face, looking from me to Lorcan and then
back again. 'That's what I understood you were coming here
today for.'

'Oh! Oh, I see! Right. Yes, that would be perfect. Are you
sure?'

'Absolutely. Take a seat and I'll be back in a bit.'

'You had this planned?' I whispered quickly once Eoghan
disappeared through a door I guessed led to the kitchens, 'And
you didn't think to tell me?'

'It wasn't confirmed until last night in the pub.' Lorcan
shrugged as if he couldn't understand the problem.

'Then you should have rung me so that we weren't late!'

'We weren't that late and, besides, you were enjoying your
breakfast and watching the chickens. You looked relaxed. For
once. It seemed a shame to ruin it.'

'I am relaxed! I do relax. All the time. And you should have
told me.'

'Noted. And no, you don't. From what I've seen you plan
and cram everything you possibly can into your life.'

I looked away.

'Sometimes you just have to let life happen.'

Do not cry. Do not cry.

I studied the menu on the table and the simple, classical décor of the room and focused on the task.

Lorcan's hand was cool as it covered mine, his voice softer now. 'Shit. Maddie, what did I say?'

'Nothing!' I said, making a small performance of pulling a tissue from my pocket and dabbing at my eye with it, looking up at the ceiling. 'I have an eyelash in my eye.'

His chair scraped and the next moment he was crouched in front of me, taking the tissue gently and touching my face more softly than I thought anyone ever could. 'If that's the case, then you must have one in both eyes.' He blotted away all the tear traces and handed me back the tissue, just as the kitchen door swung open. Lorcan's eyes remained on me. 'Whatever it was,' he whispered, 'I'm sorry.' Straightening, he retook his seat and turned his attention to his friend, who was expertly carrying a full tray on each arm, which he then proceeded to put in front of us. Oh, bloody hell. I really shouldn't have had that massive breakfast.

Some time later when we had both tried various starters, mains and puddings – and, incredibly, come to the same conclusion about which we thought would be best for the wedding – I sent Peyton a message and asked her to call me when she could. I knew they were travelling, and didn't want to wake them if they were still sleeping. Moments later, my phone vibrated and I answered the video call from her.

'Hi, Maddie,' she said, slinging a small towel around her neck, clearly having just finished a workout.

'Hi, Peyton. I didn't like to call straight away in case it was early.'

She gave her tinkling laugh. 'Oh, it is early, but I have to keep in shape.'

'You are in perfect shape, woman. Now come back to bed

like a normal human being.' Patrick's voice, off camera, was thick with sleep.

'Too much to do, sweetie! You should be up too.'

There was some more grumbling and a word we'd have had to bleep out if we'd been broadcasting but Peyton seemed unperturbed. 'How's Ireland? Isn't the village gorgeous? Have you been to the castle yet?' She fired questions at me and Lorcan shook his head. I nudged him with my knee.

'Ireland is lovely, and yes, it's a beautiful village. We're going to tour the castle tomorrow. Right now, we're at the caterers.'

'You found one?' She squealed with excitement and there was another pained groan from Patrick.

'Lorcan did, actually.' I turned the camera towards him momentarily and he gave a small wave before I turned it back, catching the look he gave me as I did so. 'It's a restaurant in the village so everything is sourced locally. They were kind enough to see us today and we've just tasted a selection.'

'Oh, that's wonderful!' Peyton clapped her hands excitedly. 'And what do you think?'

'I'm going to send you the menu that we think might work, having discussed it with Lorcan and Eoghan, who owns the restaurant, together with a photo of each dish to see what you think. If you want something different, or feel it's not what you want, just come back to me and we'll work something out.'

'That sounds perfect. Thank you! I can't believe you found someone so quickly.'

'Well, as I said, it's thanks to Lorcan entirely.'

'Tell him I owe him a big hug.'

'I will,' I said, smiling widely at him as he gave me a long-suffering look. However, I had a feeling it was more for show than anything else. The fact that he'd gone to all this effort to arrange today showed there were cracks in his put-upon-best-man-who-doesn't-even-like-weddings act. 'He's looking forward to it.' I smiled back at Peyton. Lorcan's knee nudged me back and I turned the smile on him. 'Hang on, let me send you the info and you can look with Patrick and get back to me.'

'OK.'

I gave a quick wave and hung up, then sent over pictures I'd taken of the dishes we were considering before we'd tucked in, and, with help from Eoghan, explained what was in them. He then busied himself making tea and coffee while we waited for Patrick and Peyton's decision.

'Just for future reference, I'm more than happy for you to take all the credit,' Lorcan said.

'Credit where credit's due,' I replied without looking up, making some notes in my planner.

'I'd just prefer if you kept me out of it in the future.'

I closed my planner and turned towards him. 'What exactly is your problem?'

'I don't have a problem.'

'Clearly you do.'

'I just don't want to be dragged into all this wedding malarkey further than I need to be.'

'I hate to tell you that you're already in this up to your neck, especially with Patrick and Peyton out of the country. Believe me, if I could do this alone, I would. But right now, both of us will just have to put up with things we're not thrilled about because all this...' I made a circle with my hand around my planner. 'This is not about you or me. It's about Patrick and Peyton. I want them to be happy and have what they want, and you can help with that, so we each just have to put up with our own inconveniences and get on with things.'

'And I'm your biggest inconvenience, I suppose?'

'I never said that. You're currently extremely helpful as a local contact.'

'Good to know I have my uses.'

I gave him a brief side glance, and watched as he spread his hands on the table and studied them for a moment, his mind clearly somewhere else.

'What happened to you?' I asked, my voice soft.

A small, humourless smile lifted the corners of his mouth, before he turned towards me.

'Nothing.'

'You're a terrible liar.'

'Am I now?'

'Yes.'

'Maybe that's true. But I'm not the only one keeping secrets, am I?' His gaze pinned me where I was, and I felt my breath quicken, sure that for a moment he could see deep into my soul where I kept everything stored safely. Hidden but not forgotten. Never forgotten.

13

'Here we are!' Eoghan backed out of the kitchen door carrying a huge tray of tea and coffee as well as a cheese course. 'I thought I'd bring a few of these to try to see which you preferred,' he said, pointing at them as I helped him unload the tray onto the table.

'That's great! Thanks. Do you mind if I just excuse myself for a moment?'

'No problem. Go to the end of the room, then turn left.'

'Thanks,' I said, without looking at Lorcan, and headed to the ladies to regain the composure he'd unexpectedly dislodged.

As I walked back to the table, Peyton's number buzzed on my phone. I answered the video call and Peyton was now showered and dressed immaculately. A still sleepy-looking Patrick ducked his head in and waved.

'All right, Maddie. That eejit, Lorcan, behaving himself?'

'I'm right here, thank you. Eejit yourself, you are.'

I turned the camera around to where the two men were

sitting at the table. 'Ah, so you are. Hey there, Eoghan. How you doing?'

'Good, thanks, Paddy. And yourself?'

'Ah, good. Crazy busy but good. Thanks for agreeing to do the food. I know it's late notice. I didn't think you normally did outside catering.'

'I don't normally but when Lorcan rang and explained the situation. Well, you have to change the rules for a pal and his beautiful bride. Lord knows why she's marrying you though.' Eoghan winked before laughing with Lorcan, and I guessed that Patrick had made a gesture.

'Right. I'll hand you back to my beautiful bride and Maddie.' The two men waved and I spun the camera again. 'Thanks, Maddie,' Patrick said. 'I've got some prep work to do so I'll leave you with Peyton. Speak to you soon,' and with that he disappeared from the shot.

'So, what did you both think?' I asked Peyton as I retook my seat at the table and mouthed a thank you to our host as he poured me a cup of tea into a beautiful bone-china Limoges cup.

'The dishes look amazing. And if both you and Lorcan think they taste as good as they look, we're happy.'

'They definitely do,' I confirmed, glancing at Lorcan, who was nodding, but not turning the camera to him this time.

'Let's go for it, then. Can I leave you to set it all up? They can definitely do the date and the amount of guests?'

'Yes. I've double-checked and we're all good.'

'Perfect! Oh, yay! I'm so excited. Thank you both for this. I knew you'd work brilliantly together.'

I fixed on a smile, pretty sure that neither I nor Lorcan would agree on that front while doing my best to hide the fact that we were nowhere near done with arranging this wedding and the clock was ticking – loudly!

'Great.'

'OK. I'll talk to you later.' Peyton waved, blew a kiss at the screen and was gone.

'She seems nice,' Eoghan said, taking a sip of tea as Lorcan crunched down on a handmade oat biscuit.

'Wow, these are grand,' Lorcan said, munching away.

'She is,' I said, picking up on our host's comment. 'That's why I really want this to come together for them.'

'Not to mention you want to get paid,' Lorcan added, not looking at me.

'Everybody likes to get paid,' his friend batted back. 'Even you, when you get around to sending a bill.' Eoghan turned to me. 'Lorcan helped me out when I wanted to redevelop this place into a restaurant. I didn't know where to start but it's turned out exactly how I pictured it in my mind.'

'That's fabulous. Lorcan didn't tell me that's how he knew you. You've all certainly done a wonderful job. It's beautiful in here and complements your food perfectly.'

'Ah, I've known Lorcan since school and most of us have moved around but we all know our old friends are there if we need them. It's grand.'

'It must be lovely to have that bond of friendship and history.'

'Aye, it is. Even though it does make it difficult to try and get your mate to ever send you a bill for all the effort and time he put in.'

'I was busy,' Lorcan said, studying a menu.

'Too busy to collect the money you were owed. We know you do well, mate, but you're not using a gold-plated loo seat just yet. You've got to treat everyone the same and let us pay what we owe when you're owed.'

'Quit your whingeing. You paid, didn't you?'

Eoghan turned to me. 'Eighteen months it took me to get a bill out of him. Eighteen months.' He shook his head and bit down on a cracker. Lorcan continued to study the menu and I worked on trying to figure out just who this man was. Why did he try to act so nonchalant and casual, when it was becoming clearer that there was a heart of solid gold in that hard and muscled chest? My eyes drifted down to it and I found myself wondering what it looked like without the tee shirt. I'd already had a glimpse of a toned stomach and I could only imagine— No! I couldn't imagine! I mean, I really could, which was the problem! I shouldn't. I mustn't. Lorcan O'Malley was too laid-back in a lot of ways and too complicated in others. A romance would be a disaster. And against my rules. And just...

'Maddie?'

'Nothing!'

A smile began to tease Lorcan's lips. 'You OK, there?'

'Yes. Just... thinking of... stuff. For the wedding. Obviously.' I tapped my planner with my nail for emphasis. 'Yep. All about the wedding.' Oh, God, Eoghan must think I was an idiot. 'Sorry.' I turned to him. 'It's just kind of an important wedding. I mean, not that all of them aren't but... you know. It's a biggie.'

'Yep. All our sort of businesses certainly took a hit, didn't they? Don't worry. It's going to be great.'

I smiled at his reassurance and felt the flush of colour fading from my cheeks. Ireland was having a very strange effect on me. So far I'd slept in, which I hadn't done for fifteen years, I'd eaten a massive cooked breakfast, which again was a rarity, and now I was having inappropriate thoughts about a man who, although admittedly good-looking, was completely wrong for me and had only ever shown interest in me when it gave him an opportunity to wind me up. Had it not been against my own rules to date anyone I'd met through the business, Lorcan O'Malley was not someone I'd consider anyway. He was gorgeous – but trouble. Peyton's comment about the trail of broken hearts scattered behind him was enough to keep me warned off. The sooner I got back to the safety of my own house, the better, even if it did leak like a sieve. At least there my mind didn't drift off into hot daydreams about Lorcan O' bloody Malley!

'OK, do you want me to meet up with you in a bit?' I asked as we left the restaurant. 'We have some time before the cake-tasting, thank goodness,' I said, patting my tummy, 'so if you want to go off and do something, that's fine.'

'What's next on your list?' he asked.

'A few things but that's OK. I thought I could ask Brighid for some tips on places around here. You've done more than enough already.'

'And how are you going to get to them if Brighid recommends somewhere?'

'I'm sure there's a taxi firm.'

'There is. But, let's just say, he tends to work to his own timetable.'

'Which means?'

'Which means whether you get one is hit and miss.'

'Well, then, I'll use a different one.'

A curl of amusement slid onto Lorcan's face. 'This isn't Surrey, Maddie. Pete's is the only taxi service for a distance around here.'

'I'll walk, then.'

He looked down at my shoes as we strode back the short way to the pub, stopping at the hire car we'd collected yesterday. The heels were only two inches high as opposed to the four-inch ones I wore as a rule, but admittedly perhaps not ideal for tramping about a village like this in.

'So,' he said languidly, leaning on the roof of the car, arms crossed, 'I'll ask again. What's next on that list of yours?'

'A florist.'

'Right. In you get, then.'

One part of me really wanted to sort this out for myself but he'd inarguably come up trumps with the catering and he certainly had local knowledge. Practicality – and my sad bank balance – won out.

'As you asked so nicely...' I said, opening the door, not missing the flicker of amusement on the handsome face before I disappeared inside.

'Fiadh's family have had this business for years, but she's the one that's really brought it on and dragged it into the twenty-first century. To be honest, I don't think it would still be going if it wasn't for her innovations and ideas.'

'Sounds great. So you've known the family a long time?'

'Forever. Fiadh was a few years below me in school. Here we are,' Lorcan said, pulling up.

'We could have walked that.'

'Did you not notice the dirty great splash pool we drove through back there? I didn't think you'd fancy mucking up your nice shoes wading through that and I'm sure as hell not going to carry you.'

'And I sure as hell wouldn't let you,' I returned with a tight smile. 'But thank you for thinking of my shoes. I assume this is it?' I said, pointing at the shop in front of us and exiting the car before he could say anything else.

That distinctive scent of flower shops wafted over me as I stepped through the door, a small bell chiming as I did so.

Greenery mixed with a myriad of different flowers and a hint of damp. Everywhere I looked, the blooms were perfect. From the outside it had looked like a typical village shop but inside it transformed into a stylish city boutique.

'Morning. Is there anything I can help you with?'

'You have a beautiful shop here.'

'Thank you.' The woman smiled. Her voice had the same soft lilt I was quickly getting accustomed to and what my mother would have described as kind eyes. They were bright blue and contrasted with the dark hair she had tied messily, but chicly, into a loose chignon at the nape of her neck, accessorised with a sunshine-yellow triangle headscarf. 'Is there anything particular you're looking... for?' She faltered on the last words as behind me I heard the doorbell tinkle again. 'Lorcan O'Malley, as I live and breathe.' Her smile widened as she came around the counter and towards him, accepting the hug he offered.

'Fiadh, my girl. How are you?' He stepped back, holding onto her hands as he did so. 'You look great.'

She glanced at me. 'Always did have the right lines.'

I smiled and turned back to the flowers.

'Are you together?' she asked. 'O'Malley, is there something you're wanting to tell me?'

'Oh! No. We're definitely not together,' I filled in quickly before Lorcan could say anything. 'Well. We are, but not in that way. I'm planning Patrick Kelly's wedding and Mr O'Malley is kindly helping out with some local contacts.'

'I see,' she said, smiling widely at Lorcan. 'I've heard all about the wedding. I thought they were doing it over in Dublin though? Isn't he marrying some rich American?'

'He is,' Lorcan informed her, leaning on the counter as I continued to study the flowers, feeling the velvety touch of rose petals and inhaling the intoxicating scent of lilies. 'But the wedding planner let them down and the venue was gone.'

'Oh...' Fiadh's eyes drifted to me.

'No!' Lorcan realised her thoughts at the same time. 'Maddie wasn't that planner. She's the one that's stepped in to try and rescue it all, thank God.'

I smiled, a little shocked at the compliment but feeling a warm rush of pleasure at the note of appreciation in his tone.

'Lord. Picking up the pieces someone else dropped and trying to fit them all together for the same date can't be the easiest job you've ever had, I'm sure?'

'Definitely not,' I said, grateful for her understanding. I already liked this woman. I wasn't into anything like astrology or fate, but I had a sense for people – well, except for Lorcan, who refused to be sussed out – and I had a good feeling about Fiadh.

'But if anyone can help Maddie do it, it's you, Fiadh.'

She turned to me. 'He's a silver tongue, but it's generally speaking the truth. Do you want to come back to the office? I'll get us a cup of tea and let's see if we can't get Patrick and his bride their flowers.'

'That'd be great! Thank you.'

'Let me know when you're done. I'll come pick you up,' Lorcan said, straightening from where he'd been leaning.

'You off to your ma's?' his friend asked.

'I am. She's wanting to see the dog and I need to collect him from the pub and make sure Brighid's not feeding him every tidbit going and making him oversize to qualify for carry-on luggage.'

Fiadh stepped back towards him. 'It's good to see you, Lorcan. Your visits are too fly by night. She misses you, you know. They all do.'

'I know. You know how it is.'

'I do,' she said, taking his hand gently. The look of under-standing that passed between them in that moment was so inti-mate, and spoke of so much history, that I felt like an intruder. Turning my back, and in lieu of being able to actually melt through the floor, I made an intense effort to study the intrica-cies of an unusual orchid.

'Good to see you, Fiadh. Shaun's a lucky man, so he is.'

'As I remind him every day. Take care of yourself,' she said, hugging him tightly.

'I will. When you're ready, Maddie.'

I turned, as if I'd been pulled out of a reverie. 'Oh! Right, yes. Thanks.'

He nodded and left the shop, the door jangling in the quiet. Fiadh turned towards me. 'Right. Time to make tea and a plan of attack.'

An hour later and we'd had plenty of the first and a brilliant one of the second. 'This is just fabulous. Thank you so much. I know the flowers are going to be beautiful. And that bouquet design? Wow. Well, you heard Peyton yourself on the video call!'

'I think the whole village did!' Fiadh said, laughing. 'Hon-estly, I'm thrilled she likes it, and we'll do all we can to make everything as perfect as she wants it to be. I've done a few weddings at the castle now so I know the layout pretty well, but I'll arrange a snoop next week just to get some final thoughts down and send them over to you.'

'Sounds perfect. Right, well, I guess I'd better head back for the cake-tasting.'

'Ooh, the best part. It's a shame the bride and groom aren't able to do it themselves.'

'Having had a full Irish breakfast and done a full menu-tasting today as well, my stomach would definitely agree.'

'Aah,' she said, laughing, 'there's always room for cake. Are you going to call Lorcan?'

'No, it's fine. The pub's only up the road. Lorcan made this big thing of me having to navigate a puddle – he enjoys winding me up.' I gave her a quick eye-roll.

'He's got a good heart though, that one. It's just hidden away more than it used to be.' She held the door for me. 'Hard to blame him.' A sad smile flitted across her face before turning back to her regular, cheerful one and I was once again left wondering what Lorcan had closed away in that heart. 'Lovely to meet you and we'll talk again soon. Enjoy the cake!'

The puddle looked far bigger on foot than it had in the car. Perhaps Lorcan had been onto something when he'd referred to it as a splash pool. But still, there was a pavement, by the looks. I could just tiptoe through this bit and... Arghh!

14

'Jesus, what happened to you?' Lorcan was, of course, the first one I saw as I walked through the door to the pub because the universe clearly liked a good laugh. It would have been too much to ask for him to have still been at his mother's, thereby giving me the chance to sneak in and avoid having to explain that I'd fallen face first into the puddle he'd warned me about. Which was, as he'd rightly determined, definitely larger and deeper than average – by quite some way. How was that even possible? Was it legal to have a hole that deep on a main road?

'I tripped.'

'Into the Irish sea?'

I squelched across the floor in my ruined shoes, heading for the stairs, leaving a dripping trail behind me.

'I told you to call me.'

'Oh, for God's sake, could you just not, for one time in your life?' I snapped, although the full force of my attack was somewhat muted by the fact my teeth were chattering and therefore the words came out in a far more stuttered manner than I'd hoped for. Lorcan strode towards me and took my arm, which I immediately, and unsuccessfully, tried to snatch back as he folded his long legs and crouched before me.

'What are you—?'

'You're bleeding.'

'I'm not. I'm just... Oh! Oh, bloody hell.'

'Oh, my dear!' Brighid bustled in, coming to a halt at the sight of me standing dripping, chattering and apparently bleeding from the gash on my leg all over her floor.

'I'm so sorry. I'm making a mess.'

'Don't be daft. Sure you'll freeze to death if you don't get out of those clothes. Whatever happened?'

'I... tripped.'

'That bloody huge pothole down the road, I bet? Why on earth didn't you drive her, Lorcan? What were you thinking?'

He opened his mouth, looked over the landlady's head at me and appeared to change his mind. 'She's cut her leg too.'

'You have?' Brighid bent, hands on thighs, and took a look. 'Oh, Lord. That's going to need stitches. Right. Lorcan, you call Frank and in the meantime we'll get her warmed up.'

'I'm sure just a plaster will be fine.'

'I've had five children, my dear, and if I say it's going to need stitches, it's going to need stitches. Now, up you go.'

* * *

'Oh dear, now that's going to need stitches,' Frank McGinty, the local doctor, confirmed a short time later when I was clean, warm and nursing a hot whiskey between my hands. 'Do you want to pop down to the surgery and we can get it done?'

I looked at the whiskey.

'Knock it back, woman. You're in Ireland now,' Lorcan said.

I glared at him. I could see him waiting for me to tackle the glass, knowing I wouldn't. Something else he'd be right about. I wasn't a whiskey drinker. But I wasn't a quitter either. I downed it in one and, for a minute, lost the ability to speak entirely.

'That's more like it.' He grinned. Rising from his chair, he hooked one of my arms around his shoulders and hoisted me up.

'I can walk on my own.'

'You can, but you're going to bleed all over Brighid's clean floor.'

'Oh, Brighid, I'm so sorry. I'll pay, obviously...' I wasn't sure with what. Until I got paid for this job, things were squeakily tight already.

'He's pulling your leg, so he is. And, believe me, I've cleared up a lot worse than that.' That I did believe and I gave Lorcan a prod in the ribs for the tease while trying to release myself.

'Stop wriggling.'

'You're too tall. My arm's coming out of its socket!'

He stopped and gently took my arm from his neck. 'Jesus, woman, do you ever do anything but complain?' With that, he swept an arm under my knees and, with the other around my back, strode out of the pub towards the car.

'Lorcan, put me down!'

'When we get to the car.'

'It's just a cut. I'm fine.'

'You need sewing together. And here we are.' He beeped the remote and bent slightly to open the door before gently releasing my legs and helping me into the car. Once I was in, he walked round the front and slid in the other side.

'I didn't need carrying.'

'You're welcome.'

'You're impossible.'

'So I've been told,' he said, not looking at me as he concentrated on pulling out of the car park and onto the road.

'Where's the surgery?'

'Other end of the village. Why? Is it bleeding more?' His eyes, concerned, flicked momentarily to me, his forehead furrowed.

'No, it's fine.'

'I'm pretty sure it's not fine, but you're doing a good job of making it look like it is.'

'Everyone is making far too much fuss.'

'Maddie, a qualified doctor said you need stitches. A little concern is allowed.'

I looked out of the window, unable to think of a good riposte.

'You're really not one for being taken care of, are you?'

'Not when it's unnecessary.'

'And when do you deem it necessary?'

I didn't have a good answer for that either, so I said nothing.

'That's what I thought.'

'Do you think he's going to be able to do this within twenty minutes?' I asked, checking the time on my phone.

'I've no idea. Why?'

'Because we have the cake-tasting in just under half an hour.'

Lorcan swung the car into the empty car park of a newish-looking building on the edge of the village, parking in front of the doors. The sign declared it to be Ballalee Health Centre.

'You really think that's important right now?'

I looked round at him as I undid the seat belt. 'Of course!'

'You once asked what happened to me,' he said, his voice soft, his eyes intense. 'Now I'm going to ask you the same question.'

'Me? Nothing. Why?'

'Because, like I said before, I don't think I'm the only one keeping secrets.'

'You are, however, the only one keeping us from our appointment. Come on, out you get.' I gave him an instructive push, before getting out my side and doing my best to keep the pain off my face as I put weight on my leg.

'Good try,' Lorcan said. 'I can still see it hurts like hell.'

I ignored him and instead returned the wave Dr McGinty gave us through the glass doors as he unlocked them for us. 'In you come. Here, take my arm and let's get the weight off it a bit,' he said, offering his arm for me, which I duly took. 'Honestly, Lorcan. The poor girl is bleeding here. You could have carried her, big lad like you.' The doctor turned back to me. 'They say chivalry is dead. I never like to believe that, but the more I see, the more I wonder. Here we go. Let's get you up here,' he said, helping me onto a bed in a room equipped for small procedures. 'Lorcan, give me a hand here, will you? Make yourself useful now, at least. There we go, good lad.' As he helped me settle onto the couch, I met Lorcan's eyes. Amusement danced within them.

'I knew you were going to be trouble,' he whispered.

A short time later I had four neat stitches in my shin. I'd busied myself with looking around the room while the doctor performed his needlework and thankfully, between him and Lorcan, the chat was continual, which helped keep my mind off the fact a man was sewing a part of my body back together. At one point, Lorcan caught my eye and gave a wink before taking up the conversation again and I realised he was keeping the flow of chatter going for my benefit. Perhaps, as Fiadh had said, underneath the sometimes scratchy exterior there was a good heart. I'd seen flashes of it but then it would disappear again beneath the cool carapace making me doubt what I'd momentarily thought. But there was no doubt here and I was grateful to him for his kindness and concern. He'd been right. I wasn't used to being fussed over whereas, coming from what sounded like a large family, it came far more naturally to him.

'Now, I've used traditional stitches as I think that's best with this wound. They're a little stronger but you'll need to get them removed in about seven to ten days. How long are you staying with us?' Dr McGinty asked.

'Only for the weekend.'

'Then you'll need to see your own GP for that. If there's any problem in the meantime, just give me a call. After that, contact your local surgery, or A & E. Lorcan, I want you to keep an eye on her. Can you do that?'

'I can try.'

'I'm really fine,' I said, standing cautiously and finding it didn't hurt anywhere near as much as it had before. 'See, it's feeling better already.'

'That's because the local anaesthetic is still doing its job at the moment. Try and rest it for a few days.'

'Oh, that's not possible.'

'But she's going to do her best, aren't you, Maddie?' Lorcan caught my gaze and widened his eyes meaningfully.

'Yes! Yes. Absolutely. Of course.' I smiled at the doctor, nodding for emphasis. 'Thank you so much for all your help.'

He smiled back, seemingly satisfied. 'You're welcome. I've been on at the powers that be to get that bit of road and kerb repaired for ages. Would you be all right with me using the photos I took of your injury to help further the case?'

'Of course. I definitely wouldn't want anyone else hurting themselves. It could be someone more elderly and be a lot more serious next time.'

'Exactly.'

'If you'd have just called me like I told you to, you wouldn't have hurt yourself either.'

'That's not the point.' Doctor McGinty and I responded at the same time and Lorcan held up his hands in surrender.

'I was just saying.'

'Well, stop just saying and make yourself useful and help Miss Hart here back to the car.'

'Yes, Doc.'

'And take those painkillers once the anaesthetic starts to wear off. It's going to be a bit sore for a while. Two every four hours but not more than eight in a twenty-four-hour period. They may make you sleepy though, so no driving, or operating machinery, so no JCB driving for a few days.'

'Oh, drat,' I replied, laughing. 'And I had several holes to dig this afternoon. I guess they'll have to wait now.'

The doc patted my arm, his kind brown eyes crinkling with amusement. 'Good girl. Now, come on, Lorcan. Help her back to the car.'

Lorcan stepped closer as Dr McGinty crossed the room to open the door, momentarily distracted as his phone rang. 'If you don't let me carry you now, it's going to be all over the village what a selfish eejit I am, letting an injured woman struggle alone.'

'I'm not struggling!' I whispered back.

He shook his head. 'That is entirely beside the point. It makes a good story.'

'And you want to be seen as the hero, I suppose?'

'Not at all. I don't care what most people think. I'd just rather my mam didn't get to hear that I'd been acting like the opposite.'

'Your mum?'

'Yeah.'

'Right, here we go. Sorry about that,' the doctor said, opening the door.

Lorcan looked at me, a question in his eyes. Something about him not wanting to upset his mum slid under my defences and I gave him the tiniest nod. His eyes crinkled momentarily with the brief smile he returned. It was honest, genuine and beautiful and I suddenly had second thoughts about the wisdom of what I'd just agreed to.

Lorcan slid one arm around me and the other swept gently under my legs, as he took care not to bump the injured one. 'Comfy?'

'Yes. Thank you.'

His smile sent its own thanks right back. The last thing I wanted was to come across like some damsel in distress. I'd looked after myself for long enough to know that I was more than capable of doing so in pretty much any situation but the look in Lorcan's eyes was enough. He wanted to be his best for his mum and her good opinion, just because she was his mum. And that won over everything.

'Oh, God, the time!' I said, looking at my phone as Lorcan folded his tall frame back behind the steering wheel of the hire car, having ensured I was in and comfortable. 'We're so late!'

'I messaged and rearranged it when the doc was sewing you back together.'

'You did?'

'I did.'

'Were they OK?'

'Yep, no bother.'

'Wow.'

'What?'

'Just that quite a few of the suppliers I've worked with

wouldn't have been impressed at me messing them about at the last minute.'

'It's business. They're not likely to kick up a stink if they might lose the business.'

'Good people always have other clients to fall back on.'

'No. Good people understand that sometimes life doesn't go to plan and you have to reschedule.'

He had a point.

'You are right, of course. Life definitely doesn't always go to plan.'

'Says the woman who plans everything she possibly can.'

I looked out of the window, mentally sweeping my unwanted emotions back into the corner of my mind where they had begun to spill out from.

'Did I say something wrong?' Lorcan's hand touched my leg lightly. 'I didn't mean anything by it. I wasn't being an arse – for once.'

I turned to look back at him, his self-deprecation tugging me from the past. 'For once,' I said, trying not to smile.

'Don't worry. I won't make a habit of it.'

'Now that I don't doubt. Thank you for rearranging the appointment. I was a little distracted. I do appreciate it.'

'You had every right to be distracted, and you're welcome. They're going to drop the samples off at the castle tomorrow afternoon. Although I'm not sure how that's going to work as the doc said you're supposed to be resting that leg as much as possible.'

'I'll be fine. Honestly, it's not as bad as it looks.'

15

'Oh, my good God!' I gripped the bedsheets as pain seared through my leg. 'Shit, shit, shit!' My teeth were gritted and every muscle in my body was clenched in agony. When Lorcan had dropped me back at the pub and done his he-man bit again, depositing me on the bed in my room, I'd reassured him I was all right and got back to work, answering a few emails. Slowly but thankfully, the work was beginning to trickle in – at least, the enquiries were, which was a start – and I didn't want to give anyone the chance to hire someone else by not being responsive. After a couple of hours, I'd felt a bit tired and decided a power nap would perk me up and so, pulling off my skirt and blouse, I'd changed into my jammies and lain down on the bed. Some time between then and now my leg had woken up from the anaesthetic, decided it really wasn't happy and was currently making me grit my teeth so hard I could double up as a nutcracker.

'Anyone in?' Lorcan's deep, melodic voice followed the knock at the door.

I attempted a yes but it came out as a sound more akin to a cat being strangled.

'Can I come in?'

'Open,' I forced out the word.

Lorcan stepped through, ducking beneath the low beam of the door. He took one look at me and grimaced sympathetically. 'Anaesthetic wore off, then?'

I nodded, in too much pain to come up with a smart reply.

'Did you take any of those pills the doc gave you?'

I shook my head. 'Not yet.'

Lorcan took them from the dressing table and read the label. 'You ought to have some food with these,' he said, shaking two into his hand before undoing the top of the water bottle that had been standing next to them. 'What do you want to eat?'

I took the pills and knocked them back with the water. 'Thanks. I really don't think I could eat anything. Apart from that, I don't think I can face getting down those stairs, especially as it means I'd have to change again and I don't have the energy.'

'That's fine. I can understand not wanting company right now.'

'I don't mean to be rude. They're lovely people.'

He gave a smile. 'I knew what you meant. Don't worry. Those pills should kick in soon, but you do need to eat. Let me get you something.'

'That's kind, but I'm sure you have far better things to do with your Saturday night than wait on me.'

'You'd think I would, wouldn't you?' He really did have a killer smile, even when he just let a glimmer of it show as he did now. 'Now, what do you feel like eating? Brighid has got fish pie on the menu tonight that I can tell you from experience is hard to beat. Good, home-cooked comfort food – just what you need.'

I pulled a face.

'You don't like fish pie?'

'No, I do. But I hate prawns. Bad experience many years ago. Do you know if there are prawns in it?'

'Nope. Prawns in fish pie is plain wrong anyway. It's supposed to be fish pie, not seafood pie. Two entirely different things.'

'Exactly!' I said, flinging my hand out, glad that someone else clearly understood this important distinction.

'So fish pie it is, then?'

'Sounds great,' I said, wincing as another sear of pain raced up my leg. 'Thank you. And thank you for everything today. I really am grateful, although you might not believe it.'

The soft smile lasted for a moment before Lorcan stood from where he'd sat next to me on the bed. 'Come on, rest back a bit now while I go and sort it out.' Lorcan moved and leant behind me, fluffing the downy pillows before straightening the blanket and laying it gently back over me. The faintest hint of woody aftershave drifted around me, lingering briefly before dissipating as he moved back. It had been a very long time since anyone had fluffed my pillows and something deep in my heart tightened painfully. I closed my eyes against the memory.

'It'll get better soon,' he soothed, the words as soft as the touch of his hand momentarily on my cheek. 'Just rest now.'

Keeping my eyes closed, I nodded and it wasn't until I heard the door close behind him that I let the tears trickle down onto the soft Irish linen of the pillow.

* * *

'Up you come.' Lorcan's arms wrapped around me and helped me into the sitting position I'd been flailing about trying to get into for the last ten seconds. Suddenly his face was close to mine and I studied it as he faffed about behind me with the pillows.

'You're very handsome, you know. Like classically. You have the whole strong jaw thing going on and gre-e-e-eat cheekbones. And then there's your eyes.'

'That's kind of you to say so. I see the painkillers have kicked in.'

I automatically looked down at my leg and headbutted him. 'Oops. Sorry.' I patted his head, safe in the knowledge that this would make it better. He pulled away, rubbing his forehead.

'Now. Here's your food. You all right with it there? You comfy?' he asked, placing a bed table across my legs.

'Lovely, thank you. Mmm! Smells yummy!' I said and dipped down to get the full effect of the delicious aromas. 'Ouch. Hot,' I said, bringing my head up again, which somehow appeared to have doubled in density since this afternoon, mashed potato now on the end of my nose. 'Closer than I thought.' I swiped at the spud and missed not only that, but my entire face.

'Here,' Lorcan said, sitting on the side of the bed, taking the napkin from me and wiping the food from my face. 'Try eating rather than wearing it now.'

I nodded with my too-heavy head and scooped up a forkful. 'Mmmmm. Delicious,' I stated with my mouth full.

'Good. I'll be back in a bit to collect your plate. Just ring me if you need anything, OK?'

'You're going?'

'Just downstairs.'

'Oh... OK.' I turned back to my food and loaded up another

forkful, this time with a little less enthusiasm although I wasn't sure why. Lorcan hadn't been kidding when he said Brighid's fish pie took some beating.

'You all right?'

'Mm-hmm.'

'Would you rather I stayed?'

I shook my head but the word 'Yes' somehow fell out of my lips. 'It's nice to have company for dinner.'

'I can bring my food up here, if you like.'

I nodded before letting my gaze, which also felt heavier than usual, reach up to meet his. 'That would be nice.'

'Yes,' he replied. 'It would. I have Bod here. You OK for me to bring him too?'

'Yes. I so love Bod. He's wonderful. You're very lucky. Although I think he is too. It's clearly a love match.' I grinned and Lorcan gave a half-smile.

'It is that.'

'I've always wanted a dog. It's just so hard with my job so I love getting to spend time with Bod when I see you.' I started giggling. 'Bod is a funny name. I like it.'

Lorcan watched me for a moment, the smile still there. 'I'm glad to hear it. I'll be back in a few minutes. Eat your dinner.' With that, he took a couple of long strides across the room, ducked out of the door and closed it behind him. The pub was still quiet and the silence settled around me as I waited for his return.

* * *

'I've eaten too much!' I said, flopping down on the bed as Lorcan removed the tray along with an empty bowl that had once held an enormous portion of sticky toffee pudding with thick home-made custard. 'I'm going to burst.'

'I'd rather you didn't. These jeans are new and it'd be a hell of a job for Brighid to clean up.'

'It'd be your fault.'

'That seems to be a pattern when it comes to you.'

'True. It was delicious though. Will you thank her for me?'

'I will. How's the leg?'

'Not so bad, actually.' I lifted it and stared.

Lorcan gently wrapped one large hand around my ankle and lowered it. 'That's good but probably best not to be flinging it around just yet.' He sat on the end of the bed, his hand resting on my feet. 'Pills are doing their job, then. That's good.'

'I guess. Or maybe the pain's just going off?'

He straightened a bed sock that was creeping off my foot, the toe hanging over the end. 'Maybe, but I'm putting my money on the pills for the moment.'

'Do you think?'

'Pretty sure.'

'Are you going now?' I looked at his empty plates, and then down at Bod, who had made himself a little nest in the duvet in the vicinity of my lap.

'Do you want me to?'

'Not really.'

'Then I'll stay. What would you like to do?'

'Well, apparently I'm not allowed to drive heavy machinery so I guess that's out.'

His laugh was rich and deep and wrapped itself around me, warming me from inside. But maybe that was the pills too.

'I guess we'll have to think of something else, then,' he said, giving me a wink.

16

'You are such a cheat!'

'I am not. You're just a sore loser.'

'You said he didn't have glasses.'

'No. I said he did have glasses.'

'If you'd said that, why did I flip over all the faces that don't have glasses?'

'What goes on in that brain of yours is for better men than me to explain. But the end result is that you lose. Again.'

'Only because you cheated.'

'Hand it over.'

'No.'

'Don't make me come and get it.'

'You wouldn't dare.'

He gave me a look that, even in my groggy state, told me he'd do exactly that, so I reached over and gave him the last square of chocolate. He took it, popped it in his mouth and began making noises of enjoyment. 'Mmm, so good.'

'Oh, shut up,' I said, swiping at him with a cushion and by pure luck scoring a direct hit.

'Hey, it's not my fault you're terrible at Guess Who?.'

'You're clearly a ringer. And a cheat. A ringing cheat.'

He tipped the game boards so all the little faces were down and put them back in the box. 'You need to get some rest.'

'I'm not tired.'

'Tell that to your eyes. They can hardly stay open. And the next set of pills will be kicking in soon. That will help. How's the leg?'

I gave a shrug. 'Hurts a bit.'

'By a bit, do you mean a lot?'

'That too.'

'Thought so. Come on, scoot down.'

'I need to clean my teeth.'

'God won't mind one night.'

'God won't wake up with fish breath. I will.'

'Good point. Come on, then.' He helped guide me to the bathroom, supporting my weight on the injured side, and sat me down on the closed toilet seat, leaving me to do my ablutions. When I was done, we did the return journey and he held the duvet up as I crawled under and flopped down.

'Comfy?' he asked, fluffing the pillows again and straightening the covers.

'You're good at this,' I replied quietly.

'What's that now?'

'Being kind. Making someone feel safe and looked after.'

'I didn't think you went in for all that stuff.'

'Everyone should be kind. And I think we all want to feel looked after from time to time.'

'I'd agree. Maybe you ought to let people do it for you now and then. Now, get some sleep.' He clicked the light off beside me, allowing the beams of the full moon to shine through the open curtains and bathe the room in a peaceful, heavenly light. 'Do you want these closed?'

I shook my head. 'I like the moon.'

'Me too.'

I returned his soft, moonlit smile and snuggled down, realising he'd been right about my eyes. They were doing their utmost to shut all by themselves.

'Goodnight, Maddie,' he said, turning, one hand on the door catch.

''Night, Lorcan.'

The door clicked behind him.

'Lorcan!'

'What's wrong?' he asked, returning immediately, concern shadowing the blue of his eyes.

'Thank you.'

This time the smile was full-wattage but I only got a glimpse as my eyes closed. The words 'you're welcome' drifted around in my mind for a moment before everything faded to black.

* * *

The next morning found me, still sore, but sitting in the window seat of the pub tucking into another of Brighid's amazing breakfasts with her fussing around me like one of the mother hens outside the window. After my attempts to kindly stop her doing so, Gerry had paused by my table, bent and whispered, 'Just let her, love. It makes her happy.' Patting my hand, he'd then ambled back on his way. So I had. As unfamiliar as it felt, it was also wonderful. I'd stayed at plenty of hotels in my time, including some of the best five stars in the world, with very attentive staff, but this was nothing like any of them. This felt like a home, and Brighid's fussings were almost familial, because, as Gerry had said, she did it because she really cared. It wasn't just a gimmick to try and bring the money in.

'And what are you up to today?' she asked as she came over and began pouring me another cup of tea from the enormous pot. 'Not too much, I hope. Dr McGinty said you're to rest for a couple of days when you can.'

'Not many secrets around here, are there?' I said, laughing as I thanked her for the tea.

'Ah, no. That's for sure.'

'I do have to go and check out the castle though. Make sure I know what I'm working with.'

'And I assume young Lorcan is coming to get you?'

'I think so,' I said, having only very vague memories of last night. Whatever the doc had given me was good stuff. I'd settled for paracetamol this morning as I needed to be able to remember what I saw at the venue. 'I'm not entirely sure what we discussed, if I'm honest. The painkillers were rather strong.'

'He'll show up. For all his bravado, he's a good lad. Do anything for anyone.'

'Really?'

'Oh, yes,' she said, clearing away my main plate and pushing one full of hot, buttered toast towards me. 'He never used to have that tough exterior, of course.'

'Oh?' I asked, biting into a piece of toast and closing my eyes momentarily in bliss. Lorcan had been right about the butter.

'No. But life can do that to you, can't it?'

I had to agree.

'But we all know he's the same old Lorcan underneath and

nobody stands for his messing here anyway,' she added, laughing.

'Maybe he's just worried about his mum finding out,' I added, thinking back to what he'd said at the health centre.

'There's that too.' Brighid laughed. 'But he's a good boy in here, so he is,' she said, tapping her heart with her hand, 'and that's where it matters.'

I smiled through a mouthful of toast and she went on her way.

'There she is,' Lorcan said, closing the door behind him. The weather was brighter today but colder and part of me would have been happy just to sit in the cosy pub reading a book and drinking tea all day. Which was odd as that was definitely not me. I didn't do sitting still if I could help it. And yet, here I was wanting to while away the day by disappearing into a book. As much as I loved the Ireland I had so far experienced, the sooner I got home, the better. Its laid-back charm was far too seductive and already doing its best to rub its magic off on me. Not to mention the wonderful food I was eating. Staying here much longer would lead to none of my waistbands being friends with me when I got home, and not only had I invested a good deal of money in my work wardrobe, right now I didn't have the finances to replace anything.

'Hi,' I said, grabbing my bag and pushing myself up from the chair, still careful not to put much weight on the bad leg but also attempting to hide that fact from Lorcan.

'Ready to go?'

'I am. Where's Bod?'

'Being treated like God at my mam's. Don't worry. He's in good hands.'

'Oh! I didn't mean—'

'I know you didn't. How you feeling?'

'OK. A little groggy first thing but an enormous breakfast and a family-sized pot of tea seems to have sorted that out.'

'I'm not surprised. You were high as a kite last night on those painkillers. I had to tie a string to your ankle to stop you floating out the window.'

'I was not,' I said, stepping through the door as he held it open for me.

'Yeah, you were.' He followed, laughter in his words. 'I think I got to see the real Madeleine last night. Quite a lot of her, as it turned out. I might see the doc and see if we can get you some more of those pills.'

I gave him a steady look as I reached the car. 'You're hilarious. I may have been a little woozy but I do remember keeping my clothes on, so your infantile teasing isn't going to get a rise out of me.'

'A little woozy. Is that what you call it?' he continued, grinning as he slid into the driver's seat, having closed my door for me.

'I do.'

'Darlin', you were a total space cadet. It was great.'

I let out a sigh and opened my planner as we pulled out onto the quiet road. 'I'm glad you enjoyed yourself.'

'I did, actually,' he replied, his voice sounding carefree and honest, missing that teasing note his words were so often wrapped in. I risked a glance at him. His eyes were still on the road and his whole body had a loose, relaxed feeling to it. I turned back to the window, watching as we passed impossibly green rolling hills dotted with fluffy clouds of sheep. Old drystone walls divided some of the fields, the narrow road winding between them. My thoughts drifted back to last night. Hazy memories of laughter and easy conversation floated into my mind and a feeling of lightness that I wanted to attribute entirely to the drugs but had the niggling feeling there might have been more to it than that.

'Thank you for your help and kindness yesterday. I do appreciate it. I'm sure you had much better ways to spend a rare Saturday night back home than keeping me company. In normal circumstances, I wouldn't have asked you, so I apologise for putting you on the spot.'

The shadow of a smile flitted momentarily across his handsome features. 'Then I'm glad it wasn't normal circumstances. We both enjoyed the craic so let's leave it at that.'

We rode the rest of the way in silence and I took pleasure in the countryside around me, almost deserted apart from the sheep and a farmer in a tractor.

'Most people are at church, if that's what you're wondering,' Lorcan said after a while, as though reading my thoughts.

'Oh, I see. And am I stopping you from attending?'

'Nope. Much to the chagrin of Mammy but there we are.'

'Do Brighid and Gerry not go either?'

'Most people have a lie-in on a Sunday so they go to the early service. Liam hangs about if there's any requests for an unsociably early breakfast.'

'He's another non-conformer like you, is he?'

Lorcan glanced towards me and gave me a patient smile before turning his eyes back to the road, following a bend before taking a small turning on the left. 'Here we are.'

'Oh!'

I felt his eyes on me as we travelled up the driveway. 'Is that a good oh or a bad oh?'

'It's a good oh,' I confirmed, beaming at him before returning my gaze to the view in front of me. 'Definitely a good oh. It's incredible! No wonder Peyton wants the wedding here. You can practically feel the history washing over you.'

'Yep, she was pretty excited about it when they came to take a look.'

'I can imagine. I'd have liked to have seen that.'

He huffed out a laugh. 'She doesn't hold back when she's enthusiastic about something. That's for sure.'

'I don't think that's a bad trait.'

'No, I agree. It wouldn't do for us all to be reserved.'

His words bounced around in my head. Was that aimed at me? I certainly got enthusiastic about things, but I did try and keep it all within a professional realm and, if I was honest, that characteristic might have morphed into my private life far more than I intended it to. And now that it was there, it was hard to remove it without suddenly seeming fake. Inside I knew I was excited and enthusiastic about things but did the people who should know realise that?

'Come on, space cadet,' he said, pulling on the handbrake. 'Let's take a look inside. Calum's already here, by the looks.' He nodded at a small, bright green car.

'Gosh! You wouldn't miss that coming towards you, would you?'

'No. And Calum is much the same,' Lorcan said, opening one of the heavy front doors. 'Ladies first.'

'Thank you,' I said, my eyes already scanning the surroundings as I did my best not to hobble too much. Thank God I'd packed some flat shoes.

'Here.' Lorcan offered his arm. 'Just to help with the weight, like the doc said. The longer you go against his directions, the longer it will take to heal.'

He had a point, so I took his arm and continued taking in the scene around me. 'This is amazing!'

'Glad you like it. Think you can do something with it?'

I turned to him, the laughter in my eyes matching his. 'I'm pretty sure I'll manage.'

'Good to hear,' he said, squeezing my arm gently with the tease.

'Lorcan! Darling! There you are. And this must be the gorgeous Madeleine everyone is talking about.'

'They are?' I glanced up worriedly at Lorcan but he merely shrugged and gave one of those enigmatic half-smiles he was so good at, which at this point was entirely unhelpful. 'I mean... umm, yes.' Calum was barrelling towards us in black trousers and a beautifully embroidered, fuchsia-pink waistcoat over a white shirt. 'Hello. Pleased to meet you. Madeleine Hart,' I said, holding out my hand to shake his. My actual feet might be on the ground, but my mental ones were sliding all over place as I tried to get a grip and regain my composure following Calum's disclosure I was the talk of the village.

'Calum O'Shea. So good to meet you. I've heard so much about you.'

'You have?'

'Oh, yes. Peyton and Patrick were raving about you the last time we spoke and, of course, Lorcan here.'

'I see. Well, feel free to believe my clients but please take whatever Lorcan says with a pinch of salt. We don't always see eye to eye.'

'Is that so?' Calum raised an eyebrow so groomed I had serious brow envy, and cast a glance at Lorcan and me. 'And what's happened here?' he said, looking down at my leg.

'I tripped yesterday and I'm supposed to take care of it for a couple of days but I'm too busy, so this is the compromise.'

'Oh, no! Here, let me get you a chair. Lorcan, why didn't you say? Honestly.'

'No, really. This is good. I'm happy to get on with things.'

'Are you sure?' Calum asked, laying his hand on my free arm.

'Perfectly. But thank you.'

'No problem. Any time you need to stop or sit down, you just say so, love.'

'I will. I promise.'

'Right. So, what's Lorcan told you already about the place?'

'Umm.' I glanced up at him. 'Nothing.'

'Oh.' Calum threw him a questioning look. 'Right, so this is obviously the main entrance hall. We have photographs of previous weddings that I can show you to illustrate how we've set them up, but we can pretty much do whatever you like. Especially as it's for Patrick's wedding. Lorcan's already told us we have to bend over backwards for this one. Not that we wouldn't have anyway, but you know.'

I felt Lorcan's body tense beside me. 'As Calum said, Paddy's from the village so we're all just doing what we can to make the day what they want, especially as the original plans fell through.'

'Which,' Calum picked up the conversation, 'Stressful as that's been for darling Peyton, I think is probably for the best.

Why they were having their wedding all the way over there anyway when there's this sat on the doorstep I'll never know. So,' he said, moving off, 'through here leads to the main reception area and...' We trailed behind Calum on his tour, me pausing to take photos with my phone and note down all my thoughts, questions and ideas and Lorcan surreptitiously keeping an eye on me.

'So, this is what we call our "Winter Garden" and is where we hold the weddings.' Calum leaned in conspiratorially. 'Basically it's like a big old conservatory, but we've stuck with the original name as it sounds posher.'

'I think you made the right decision.' I grinned back, before looking around more. 'It really is the most beautiful room.'

Three sides of the stone-walled room were almost entirely made up of windows, flooding the area with natural light and looking out onto the bucolic scenes beyond. Various grouped pots of towering, lush-leaved houseplants added softness and lent a slightly tropical feel, contrasting but somehow still working with the setting.

'We could wind fairy lights through all these plants. Would that be OK?'

'Anything you want. It'll look fab.'

'Great.' I made a note to order more lights. Calum led me up the aisle to where a carved table painted in the softest white stood to one side at the front, a thick, pale rug of the same hue underneath it.

'This is where we have the couple sign the register, and pose for photos,' Calum explained. 'And obviously the bride will come in from the back, and up this aisle.' His hands made the motions and I half expected him to start telling me where the exits were and how to put my life jacket on. Suddenly he looked over and giggled. 'I used to be cabin crew. I need to work on my presentation here more!'

I joined him in the giggles. 'That explains things, but it's fine. Always good to know where the exits are anyway. And could I have the chicken?'

Calum burst into another fit of giggles and linked his arm through mine, looking over to Lorcan, who had taken a seat on one of the chairs from the rows that faced the front. 'We have to keep her. She's adorable.'

Lorcan gave a small tilt of his head. 'She is that,' he replied as his eyes met mine. Calum squeezed my arm, gave another chuckle and bustled us down the aisle, as fast as I was able, to take in the view from the back.

'We've more chairs if we need them, although I understand the ceremony is smaller than the reception and obviously you already saw the ballroom can hold more than enough for that.'

'No, this is perfect. The light is beautiful. We can swathe the chairs with sashes in the wedding colours.'

'She's having white and wine, isn't she?'

'Yes, exactly. So the fabric can pick up the colour of the bridesmaids' dresses, and then all the flowers are going to be white and scented. It's going to look amazing here, and, with all those flowers, smell wonderful.'

'Are you giving out hayfever medicine as wedding favours?' Lorcan said, having turned in the chair, his chin now resting on his hands, elbows on knees.

'Oh, shush, you. Just because you're not romantic.'

'I can be romantic.'

Both Calum and I waited for more.

Lorcan shrugged. 'I'm just saying. Romance isn't all about flowers. There's more to it.'

'Stealth romance.' I cocked an eyebrow at him.

'Maybe,' he said, beginning to smile at the description.

'I see. Well, my job requires it to be a little more on show. Why don't you go and do something else if you're bored? I'm fine here,' I said, snapping a few more shots with my phone of the setting.

'I'm all right. How's the leg?'

'Can hardly feel it.' OK, bit of a fib but I didn't want him fussing any more. Lorcan met my gaze and I knew he'd seen straight through me. The truth was the bloody thing was throbbing.

'Why don't we take a break for a bit?'

'Oh, that's a good idea. I'll bring the cake through for you to try and sort some refreshments out. Do you want to take Madeleine to the snug?'

Lorcan nodded and offered his arm to me.

'That's very chivalrous but not necessary. I've been scooting about without support for the last hour.'

'Which is exactly why you need to take some weight off it now.'

I looked up to see his brows drawn together, the blue eyes serious.

'Are you going to sulk if I don't?'

'I don't sulk, but let's just say I'd be happier if you did.'

I took his arm and let him lead me gently into the room Calum had mentioned. I was beginning to think that this wedding was one of the most enjoyable I'd ever planned, especially when it came to the people I was working with.

Calum and I had been chatting back and forth the whole time as though we'd known each other forever. This was a new experience for me. I was sociable but none of my friendships really ran deeply, which was mostly down to me. Friendships took nurture and time and my diary was always so full with things I wanted to achieve that I didn't have a lot of the second to devote to the first.

I met people for coffee, I did Pilates, took classes in things that interested me and met friends for dinner but there wasn't anyone I'd call especially close. No one with whom I could totally be myself. Not for a long time. That was until last night with Lorcan – but admittedly that had probably been due to the painkillers.

This morning though, at breakfast, chatting to Brighid had felt natural and easy, and now Calum, although rather than the cliché of the laid-back Irish persona he was the very opposite of that. Calum was like a jack-in-the-box who'd been stored too long and was now dancing about on his spring with abandon – and thoroughly enjoying it, trailing that joy like a train of glitter as he went.

'You seem to be getting on well with Calum.'

'He's wonderful!' I said, laughing as Lorcan placed a foot-stool in front of the sofa where we'd settled for a rest. Calum was still off rustling up refreshments.

'He is. Perfect for the manager's job here. Everybody loves him and I'm sure a lot of the bookings are purely down to him and his blarney.'

'So long as it's followed up by great service and everything the couple want, that seems like an ideal combination.'

'It is. There, that comfy?'

'Yes, thank you. I'm fine though. You really do need to stop fussing.'

'Ah, shush, woman.'

'Did you just tell me to shush?'

'I did. And I'll tell you again if you don't.' A sparkle of mischief danced in his eyes. I met them levelly and did my best to keep any hint of smile off my face, which, oddly, was proving harder than it once had.

'Ha. Well, don't expect me to take any notice.'

'I don't. I was just living in hope.'

'Very funny.' I leant out over the arm of the sofa in the direction Calum had gone and, seeing no sign of him, turned to Lorcan. 'What was that he was saying about everyone talking about me?'

Lorcan took a seat next to me on the dusty pink, squashy, overfilled and delightfully comfy sofa. The windows in this room were dressed with thick, padded velvet curtains in a pale, cloudy blue and, beyond them, deep green fields stretched down and away as far as you could see, broken only by dry-stone walls and magnificent trees, their leaves just beginning to turn and dot the view with gold and yellow. In amongst this, sheep stood about, munching at the lush grass, seemingly content with their simple lives.

'Nothing.'

'It must be something.'

'Nothing for you to worry about. You're a new face in a small village so people talk,' Lorcan replied, shrugging his shoulders.

'I'm not keen on people talking about me,' I said, pulling back as my plait caught behind me.

'That's not really something any of us have much control over.' Lorcan reached out and leant me forward a little, gently freeing my hair and laying it over my shoulder. 'Don't worry about the gossip. No one means anything by it. I know it can be a pain in the arse, but they mean well here. You're a novelty, shipping in from the big smoke.'

'I don't live in the big smoke.'

'Close enough, and compared to here...'

'So is Calum local too? He seems nice.'

'He is. A great bloke and a brilliant manager. He's had it tough at times. Being gay in rural Ireland isn't the easiest card to be dealt but he's had people who care about him on his side and now no one really pays it any mind.'

'I get the feeling you're among those who were on his side during difficult times.'

'We're good friends.'

'He's being modest,' Calum said, coming back into the room. 'You can't talk about me without my radar picking it up. I've got the ears of a bat when it comes to gossip,' he said, an infectious bubble of laughter bursting from him as he did so. 'Lorcan here's had more than a few fights on my behalf over the years.'

Lorcan turned his attention to the tray Calum had put down in front of us.

'He's my hero,' Calum continued, fluttering his eyelashes at me, and placing a hand on his chest, all the while looking adoringly at his friend.

'Knock it off, you eejit,' Lorcan returned, laughing now.

'He loves me really.'

Of that, I had no doubt. There was a feeling about this village that was already winding itself into my consciousness without invitation. A part of me welcomed it, albeit cautiously. Everyone knew each other, which, in some circumstances, could be awkward but here they seemed to harness that power for good. And certainly for the good of this wedding. From the hints that Peyton had dropped, getting hold of this castle for the dates they'd already arranged with friends and family was all down to Lorcan. Whatever strings he had pulled at such short notice for such a fabulous venue were obviously strong ones, but I'd had no luck so far in discovering what they were.

There was clearly more to Lorcan O'Malley than he showed to the outside world. Here, in his own domain, there was something different about him. And, annoying as it was, and as he could be – on that front, I was pretty sure he felt the same about me – it still intrigued me.

18

'Have you done many weddings here?'

'Oh, God, yeah. We love a good wedding, don't we?' He caught Lorcan in his gaze and the expression returned indicated disagreement. 'Well, some of us do, anyway.'

I looked across at Lorcan but he kept his eyes averted, concentrating instead on the large slice of cake Calum had put before him.

''This is the chocolate cake. There's three others to try yet, so don't fill up on that one.' He rapped Lorcan's knuckles lightly with a spoon. 'I've never seen such big cake samples. You're lucky lovely Caitlin forgave you for breaking her heart.'

'I didn't break her heart,' Lorcan said. 'Besides, it was years ago.'

'Is there anyone in the village you haven't gone out with?' I asked, eyeing him over the edge of my teacup. During our flower planning, Fiadh had told me her and Lorcan had also dated years ago.

He eyed me back before forking up the third choice of cake.

His eyes widened. 'That one,' he said, swallowing the mouthful. 'Try it.' He loaded up a fork and passed it to me.

'Nice change of subject.'

'I don't know what you're talking about. I'm just helping you make decisions as instructed.'

'Of course you are,' I said, popping in the cake. 'Oh my God!' I exclaimed, my hand over my mouth to help cover my poor manners. 'You're right. That's bloody delicious.'

'Great minds think alike, then,' Lorcan returned.

'It would appear so.'

Calum watched us both for a moment, gave a grin and then dived in to try the cake of choice before Lorcan finished it all.

'Do you want to see some of the previous weddings we've hosted?' he asked as we sat reclining on the overstuffed furniture, letting our refreshments go down.

'That would be great, thanks. Peyton and Patrick are going for a Winter's Fairy Tale theme—' Lorcan gave a snort and we both gave him a sharp look. I continued. 'I can see this is going to be the perfect setting for it.'

'It totally is. Look.' He produced a beautiful leather-bound album. 'I know lots of places do this on tablets but we like to stick to the old ways here when we can. There's something lovely about being able to hand this to a bride and groom and watch them turn the pages. We do, of course, have the information digitally too for those who absolutely can't cope with anything that doesn't involve technology.'

'I've never thought about it that way,' I said, turning a page myself. 'I can definitely see what you mean. Oh, this is just stunning!'

'Isn't it though?' Calum said, laying a hand on my arm. 'Honestly, the whole day was just a dream.'

'That!' I said, pointing at him. 'That feeling is exactly what we want for Patrick and Peyton.'

'Just so long as they don't wake up to a nightmare.' Lorcan mumbled the comment low under his breath and Calum didn't even react, seemingly prepared to let it go again, but my patience was worn thinner. Or perhaps I didn't have enough experience of the man. As much as I thought there were more layers to him, I wasn't sure I actually had the patience to peel enough of them away.

'What exactly is your problem?'

Lorcan stretched his long legs out and forked up another helping of cake, despite the fact we'd already made our choice. 'I don't have a problem.'

'Clearly you do, judging by all the snarky sounds and comments when it comes to talking about wedding plans. While I do appreciate your help in sourcing and liaising with suppliers this weekend, you don't need to stay here for this. I'm sure Calum and I can work it between us, and you'd obviously rather be somewhere else.'

He chewed his cake, raising his cool blue gaze to meet my controlled one. 'No place else to be.'

'That is a shame. Then perhaps you'd be kind enough to keep any unhelpful comments and noises to yourself while we do our jobs and arrange a perfect wedding for *your* best friend and his fiancée.'

'Nothing's perfect.'

God, this man was impossible.

'While that may be true, it's my job to make this wedding as close as possible to it and I'm sure it would be appreciated by Patrick and Peyton if you could get fully on board with that. It would certainly be appreciated by me, considering they have given you a responsibility which should be an honour and which you're treating as a burden. You may not believe in any of this but what you and I think about love, weddings and marriage is irrelevant. It's what they want. And if they mean anything to you at all, which they clearly do, it should be what you want for them too.'

Lorcan just stared at me, the silence thickening around us with every second that passed.

'Oh, boy, she told you!' Calum broke the uncomfortable hush with a cackle of delight. He tucked his arm around mine. 'I like this one.'

Lorcan shifted his gaze back to the tray and poured another cup of coffee for himself. 'Of course you do,' he grumped, causing Calum to laugh even more.

'Now, where were we?'

* * *

'There's a wonderful view out over the sea from that side of the grounds,' Calum said, pointing to the west. 'But I've strict instructions not to take you too far with your poorly leg.'

I glanced back at where we'd left Lorcan dozing as we crept off to have another look around a couple of areas I wanted to revisit.

'Ooh, is there' I asked, peering in the direction Calum had pointed.

'Yeah. It's stunning. All dark and moody cliffs sweeping down into the deep, untamed waters of the Atlantic,' he said in a dreamy voice as we both stood at the window, looking out across the beautiful, well-tended gardens of the castle, still full with seasonal colour.

The weather was chilly but it was one of those beautifully bright early autumn days and the picture Calum painted was one I was now desperate to see. I could imagine the sunshine glinting and shimmering on the depths of the dark ocean waters crashing against the cliffs, just as they had for centuries.

'Let's go,' I whispered. 'He'll never know.'

'Never know what?' The voice was deep, sleep-roughened and incredibly close, making both of us let out a squeal of surprise as we turned.

'Jesus, what are you thinking of, creeping around like that?' Calum gave Lorcan a surprisingly forceful punch on his arm. Something told me he'd learned the skill from the friend who was now rubbing his arm and possibly regretting giving those lessons. 'You frightened the bejeezus out of us both.'

'What are you up to?' Lorcan asked, his eyes taking in the view and then landing squarely back on me. He knew exactly what we were up to.

'Oh, nothing,' Calum said, flapping his hands a little, doing his best to radiate innocence and failing as his cheeks coloured and his hands fidgeted until he shoved them in his trouser pockets.

'Actually, Calum was just going to show me the view. I understand there's a beautiful one to the west.' I tilted my chin in defiance.

'There's a beautiful one in every direction, but yes, that is a particularly lovely one. But I believe Calum had been told you aren't to go romping around the place right now with that leg.'

'I wasn't planning to romp anywhere.'

'Now that's a shame.' Lorcan's eyes sparkled and Calum immediately turned his laughter into a poorly executed cough. There didn't seem to be any form of fibbing he excelled at, which was sweet but not helpful in this exact moment.

I gave a sigh to show how unimpressed I was with Lorcan's infantile humour before continuing. 'But I would like to see the view.'

'That's a shame. It's currently closed to visitors.'

'Calum was about to show me, so it's obviously not, and I'm pretty sure he knows more about this place, and has more authority than you do over who sees what.'

'Umm...' Calum began but I was on a roll.

'So if I want to see it, which I do, then I should be able to. Not to mention it's my responsibility to know as much as possible about the venue so that I can do my job to the best of my ability.'

'Is that so now?'

'It is,' I said, standing as tall as I could and cursing my injury and my consequent lack of heels, which would have reduced the amount that Lorcan O'Malley with his dark, brooding looks could tower above me. He bent a little closer until his mouth was close to my ear and I could feel the warmth of his breath as his voice, soft, deep and lilting in my ear, whispered.

'And here I was thinking you were just being nosy.' He grinned as he stood back to his full six feet five.

'You're such a—'

'I have no doubt that I am whatever you're about to call me,' he interrupted as he took my hand. 'Come on.'

'Where?'

'You want to see the view or not?'

'It would be helpful, yes.'

'But I thought you said I couldn't take her?' Calum said.

'Only because she's not supposed to be tramping about on that leg and if you did this, she might thump you, and I reckon she's probably got a good left hook.'

'Did what?'

'This,' Lorcan said, sweeping me up against his chest, this time without asking.

'Lorcan! Put me down,' I said, pushing at his shoulder and giving it a frustrated punch when he wouldn't.

'See what I mean?' he stated, before turning his head to meet mine. Up at his level, our faces were suddenly close and I noticed the scar above his right eyebrow and a deeper one to the side of his mouth that was hidden when he smiled. Right now though, his face was serious and focused fully on mine. 'Now, do you want to see the views or not?'

I glared at him in reply. 'Put. Me. Down.' My teeth were gritted but the words were clear.

'If you do want to see them, I'll take you. If you don't, then I'll put you down and we can go back to the pub, assuming your business here is concluded for the day.'

'I'm not letting you carry me all the way out there!'

'Jesus, woman. I'm not planning to! I'll be needing to see the doc myself if I do that.'

'Oi!' I gave him another thump, this time with more feeling.

'To be fair, you deserved that one,' Calum said, his arms folded across his chest.

'Look. We're all getting older by the minute here. What do you want to do?'

What I wanted to do was walk out with some dignity, preferably over an unconscious Lorcan O'Malley, but clearly that wasn't going to happen.

'The views are beautiful,' Calum added. 'It'd be a shame to miss them as you're here and it's such a good day. Believe me, people have stayed for a fortnight and not had one day as beautiful as today.'

I took a deep breath and then nodded.

'Was that a "yes, please, Lorcan"?'

I glared at him under my lashes.

'I'll take that.'

19

Five minutes later, I'd been deposited in a golf buggy with the name of the castle written on the front and Lorcan was driving us around the grounds.

'How come you didn't just suggest this to Calum? We could have taken our time and left you to your afternoon snooze and kept everyone happy.'

'Who said I'm not happy?'

'Without being rude, you rarely look happy when you're in my company and it's no secret you'd rather not have anything to do with this wedding for whatever reason. Calum, on the other hand, is enthusiastic about the plans, as it's his job. And even if it wasn't his job I get the feeling he still would be.' I shifted in my seat. 'I know Patrick gave you instructions about making choices by proxy, but I have a pretty good idea what they want and this is what I do for a living. I'm good at it. You really don't need to shadow me around the whole time when it's obvious you'd rather be anywhere else – and understandably so.'

'Me being here has nothing to do with questioning how

good a planner you are. Just because the last experience of one blew up in our faces doesn't mean I think you'll be the same or that I don't trust you to do a great job for them.'

'So why are you here?'

'Maybe I enjoy it.'

'I think we both know that's not true.'

He turned briefly, a small smile playing around the corners of his mouth. There was something in that moment, a lowering of shields, even temporarily, that caused me to return the smile, his own widening as I did so.

'Here we are. The best view is from down near that bench,' he said as he came around to the side of the buggy. 'I'd rather you were off that leg entirely but perhaps we can come to a compromise?' He offered his arm.

The waves were crashing below, out of sight, and Lorcan had to raise his voice a little to make himself heard as the wind off the ocean whipped away some of his words, but I got the idea and nodded, taking his arm as I exited the vehicle, careful to put most of the weight on my good leg and Lorcan's arm.

'Ready?'

'Yes, thank you.'

We headed a little closer to the edge before turning right and coming to three wide stone steps that led into a beautifully tended area of garden, a few late summer blooms still hanging on, surrounded by bursts of early autumn colour. A large oak tree stood sentinel over all of it, and a freshly white painted Lutyens-style bench was placed under it, facing out towards the sea.

'This is beautiful,' I said, navigating the steps carefully one at a time. As I lifted my head, I caught Lorcan's anxious, studious face watching my feet with every step.

'I'm fine.'

'I know,' he said, still watching.

'You're dying to do the romantic-hero thing again, aren't you?'

The smile was wider this time when he looked at me, more on a level now as he was already a couple of steps below me.

'Is it that obvious?'

'I think it's probably the setting. I'm sure you'll come to your senses in a moment.'

'I expect you're right. I'm not sure I'm the romantic-hero type, to be honest.'

Tall, dark and solid as a rock with a face that was made for things most of the people in church this morning were regularly warned against, I was disinclined to agree.

'I guess we each have our own definition of romance.'

Lorcan led me to the bench and waited while I sat before taking a spot next to me.

'I guess,' he said after a while. His eyes focused out on the ocean, but his mind seemed to be somewhere completely different. Part of me wanted to ask him about it but something stopped me. I'd have liked to have said it was my professionalism – don't get involved, don't get personal – but sometimes you had to get personal. Marriage was a personal thing, it was full of emotions and sometimes those spilled out and it was up to me to try and contain them in a way that kept things on track. I'd worked for a corporate planning company before setting up on my own and I'd always felt as though there was something missing. One day, an hour before the ceremony, with a bride sobbing on my shoulder that she couldn't do this because her mum wasn't there to see her or hold her hand, I threw out the company rule book and the sensible, scripted responses I'd been taught and just talked to her, telling her that her mum would always be with her in her heart. That I understood it wasn't the same, not even close, to having her here to see how beautiful her daughter looked, how proud she would have been to see this bright, funny, wonderful woman preparing to make a commitment to a man who supported her and believed in her as much as she had. And that, whether she chose to believe it or not, I believed that her mum was with her today. We'd both mopped up our tears, called in the make-up artist for emergency repairs and I'd watched as the woman walked up that aisle, still missing her mum, but with a sense of reassurance she hadn't had before and that, if I'd stuck to the rule book, she still wouldn't have. Sometimes rules had to be broken.

I'd handed in my resignation a week later, and set about building up my own company where I made my own decisions and my own rules. Every bride, every groom was different and therefore I tailored my approach individually, and my skills in the way I felt was best for each couple.

But Lorcan O'Malley wasn't like anyone I'd come across before. He was sometimes spiky but incredibly kind, occasionally overbearing but thoughtful, closed-off but looked out for everyone. It was a confusing mix and I was still trying, not only to work him out, but also to work out the best way to deal with him that would result in the lowest amount of stress for both of us. At times I felt as if the most successful approach was going to be the one that involved keeping the greatest distance between us, but just as I thought that was the best idea he'd go and throw a spanner in the works and there would be times when the man hiding beneath all those complicated layers showed himself. There was something intriguing about that man. Something that made me—

'Maddie?'

'Oh! Yes, sorry. Miles away.'

Kind of...

'You OK?'

'Yes. I was just thinking how beautiful this is. It's like a secret garden.'

'I believe that was the idea behind it.'

'Then the designer completely nailed it.'

'There's been weddings held here, in the summer obviously.'

'Yes. I imagine the weather can definitely get pretty wild here,' I said, pushing myself up.

'You could say that,' he said, standing too and offering his arm once again. 'Humour me,' he said as he watched me hesitating.

'Thank you.' I took a step and then stopped, lifting my head to meet his eyes. 'I'm sorry. I don't mean to have come across as rude. I'm just used to doing things for myself, and have been for a long time.'

'I can see that. And I'm used to being the eldest brother with three sisters and a brother who often needed scooping up and taking care of and I guess that's also a habit that's hard to break.' He gave a shrug that wasn't exactly apologetic, more that it was just the way he was wired, which I could understand.

'That explains a lot.'

'It certainly does.'

I took his arm and we walked towards the edge of the garden. Beyond a small willow fence, itself host to plants scrambling up and over it, including a jasmine that was releasing the most divine scent, the sea stretched out into the distance. White caps danced on deep blue mixed with slate grey as the weakening sunlight glittered over the surface. Below, the waves rushed on into the solid cliffs, breaking with a crash, booming against the rock before being drawn back into the sea to be swept up and sent forth again.

'This is amazing. I could stand here all day,' I said, hearing the unusually wistful tone in my voice.

Lorcan said nothing but for a moment the muscles in his arm tensed against mine and I knew he understood.

'Do you want to see the other views?' he asked eventually. 'This is the most spectacular one but the others are still stunning and you can see them from the buggy.'

'Do you have time?'

'All the time in the world.' His smile was as fleeting as one of those dancing horses out on the wild ocean.

'That would be great, then, thank you.'

With his assistance, we headed back to the buggy. My leg was actually pretty painful again now and I was glad of being able to see the rest without having to walk too far.

'This really is the most incredible place,' I said, taking in the view of the grand stone edifice from across the lawns, the lush landscape stretching out far beyond behind it. 'Has it always been kept like this?'

'Ah, no, unfortunately. It was well on the road to rack and ruin, left to crumble. Once places like this get past a certain point, it gets harder and harder to restore them. It was sad to watch that happening here.'

'I can imagine. But something stopped it?'

'An investor. Someone who didn't want that to happen. Money and a lot of hard work got poured in and thankfully the castle turned a profit by becoming a destination and event venue. Luckily there was enough in the coffers to enable it to weather the most recent storm of the pandemic and bookings are steady again now.'

'That's great. I'm so pleased. We've lost so many beautiful

houses over the decades, certainly in England. It's such a shame. It would have been so sad if the castle had been left to rot. It's magnificent in itself, but in these grounds, and this location, it's just... wow.' I laughed. 'I'm out of adjectives.'

Lorcan flicked a glance at me. 'I know what you mean. It's a pretty special place. Means a lot to the village too.'

'They must have been pleased that it was bought by someone sympathetic to creating a purpose for the original building rather than demolishing it and building on the land.'

He gave me the briefest of grins. 'There are benefits to being in the middle of nowhere. It's less likely to be developed.'

'Then, I, for one, am very glad it's in the middle of nowhere.'

'Apart from the fact you're stuck here with me.'

'Well, yes, but, as you said earlier, nothing's perfect.'

'Touché,' he said, a low rumble of laughter sending ripples of warmth through my body. I gave myself a mental kick and concentrated on what he was saying.

'It's worked out so far. It's brought trade in but without making the village a tourist trap where locals can't afford to live any more.'

'Sounds like the ideal compromise – saving a beautiful building and restoring it sympathetically for events, which brings in trade and employment for the local community but without destroying the essence of the village.'

'Couldn't have put it better myself.'

'Can I ask something?'

'Sure.'

'How come it was available for Patrick and Peyton at such late notice? I know myself that a lot of the best places are booked up years ahead, let alone with just weeks to go.'

'Patrick's a local boy. Strings sometimes have to be pulled

when it's important.'

'So is there a bride and groom out there who got bumped?'

He shook his head. 'No.' His laugh was deep and warm and once again wrapped itself around me, taking the chill off the air that now had a hint of bite in it from a building northerly wind. 'Stop worrying.'

'OK.'

'Is it playing on your mind?'

'No.'

'Liar.'

Was there something in the air here that gave its inhabitants special mind-reading powers? I'd noticed the same talent a couple of times with Brighid.

I remained silent but evidently my face was having a whole conversation with Lorcan of its own volition. He slowed the buggy down and pulled it to a stop, his eyes still focused out on the vista in front of us.

'Can you keep a secret?'

'Yes,' I answered without hesitation.

'When Peyton started talking about getting married in Ireland and set the date, I had a chat with Calum and they put a reserve on the castle. Just in case they decided they wanted to marry in the village after all.'

'But I thought the wedding was all set for Dublin initially?'

'It was. But I think that was more to do with feeling Dublin would be easier for other people, especially Peyton's side. Travel arrangements and so on. They might be loaded but, even with first-class flights to Ireland, there's still a certain amount of faff involved in getting here, finding accommodation, that kind of thing. Paddy and I both felt she was compromising as she'd seen the castle on visits to his family and always raved about it. Of course, she denied that she was.'

'She's very sweet and I suppose thinking of others' travel plans is sensible.' Personally, I didn't think that was a good enough reason not to have the wedding you wanted but I kept that thought to myself.

'True,' he agreed. 'And sensible is all well and good but not when it comes to a wedding. With that, you have to go with what your heart wants.'

I looked round at him as he once again appeared to read my mind.

'Within budget,' I added as a way to distract myself from the discomforting thought that Lorcan O'Malley might be able to read any of my thoughts at all.

He tipped his head back and the laugh burst from him, transforming the sharply chiselled, hard-edged features. 'And you accuse me of not being romantic.' When he turned, the smiling eyes seemed to look deep into my soul.

'I'm romantic!' I protested.

'Within budget,' he replied, laughter still resonating in his voice.

I shrugged, feeling the blush tinge my cheeks, hoping that he would mistake that for the chill and the breeze rather than a reaction to the teasing in his voice that, when he spoke softly like that, was like warm, melting chocolate.

'Fair enough. Within budget,' he continued. 'But there was something about that original plan that seemed... not right. Patrick's happy to go along with whatever Peyton wants. All he wants is for her to be happy.'

'Yes, I can see that. It's lovely.'

'She's got a good man there.'

'She's very sweet too.'

He turned back to face me. 'She is. She's very lovely. Too much of a princess for me but her and Patrick are made for each other. She's like another sister, really. Not that I need any more!'

'You did give her a bit of a hard time about the whole Irish ancestry thing.'

He dragged his hand across his jaw. 'I know. I guess... Roísín had just finished the genealogy search and turned up nothing. I was disappointed for Peyton, and I didn't want her to get this idea in her head that she had all these roots here when, in truth, she doesn't.'

'But being sarcastic about it probably isn't the best way to go about it, or put her off.'

'No, you're right. It hadn't been the best day. I know that's not an excuse. She's great but occasionally things rub me up the wrong way. It's a culture thing, I guess, and, Jesus, she's just so full of bloody energy, it feels a bit overwhelming at times. She's like a Duracell bunny on steroids. I couldn't cope with that all the time. But she makes Paddy happy and that's all that matters.'

'But you arranged this place, just in case?'

'She's insisted on me being involved from the beginning. Paddy and I are like brothers and I think she hoped it would be a chance for her and I to get to know each other better. Although, as it turns out, I'm spending more time with you than either of them.'

'And you said there was no upside.'

He laughed that laugh again, looking up through envy-inducing thick lashes, and gave me a smile that did funny things to my tummy – and a couple of other places. I put it down to after-effects of the painkillers. Something that strong was bound to have some brain-addling hangover effect. That was the only explanation. Well, the only one I was prepared to entertain anyway.

20

'So are you just anti-weddings or anti-marriage too?'

'You can live with a partner just as easily and with a lot less expense. Weddings can cost a phenomenal amount just for one day. All that hype and stress for a party celebrating something that might not last very long anyway.'

'And you say I'm not romantic whereas clearly your soul is just bursting with romance.'

'Romance isn't all it's cracked up to be.'

'He says to the wedding planner.'

Lorcan at least had the decency to look momentarily chastened. 'Sorry. Just stating the facts.'

'As you see them.'

'As I see them.'

'Can I ask a question?'

'Why do people always say that? Why don't they just ask the question? Does anyone ever say no, you can't?'

I gave him a patient look and he spread his hands. 'Ask away.'

'Did something happen to make you this cynical about marriage?'

He looked away from me, out towards the deep green of the fields stretching away from us, dotted with white balls of sheep. 'Nope. Just all seems a lot of fuss when you can live with someone if you're that bothered.'

'That bothered?' I couldn't help the laugh that escaped me. 'Perhaps you were right earlier when you said you're not the romantic-hero type.'

'Finally, we've found something we can agree on.' He turned, giving me a smile before looking back towards the castle. 'You done here, or do you need to go over any more details with Calum?'

'I'd like to go over the provision of seating, cutlery, glassware, et cetera, so that I can get on to that if I need to.'

Lorcan nodded, and released the brake of the cart. 'I know that's all part of the package here, but I'm happy to take you back.'

'Thank you. You're not going to try and carry me, are you?'

'No. My back's aching now.'

'Oh, ha ha, very funny,' I replied, flicking him on the arm and seeing a grin spread over the handsome face. 'You seem to know a lot about the arrangements of weddings here for someone who isn't interested.'

'Calum and I talked when we decided to have the castle as a backup.'

'How very organised of you.'

'I can't work out whether that's a compliment or a dig.'

'I'll let you choose.'

'Then I'll choose compliment.'

As we pulled into the front of the castle, Calum hauled

open one of the huge wooden doors and came down the wide stone steps to greet us. 'How was the tour?'

'Great, thanks. This is such a fantastic location. I'm definitely putting it on my list in case I have any more couples that want to get married in Ireland.'

'That'd be grand. I know we're going to have such fun working together,' he said, grabbing my hand and squeezing it between his own, enthusiasm rolling off him in waves.

'Madeleine has a few more questions,' Lorcan said, coming around and taking my arm as I hobbled up the steps. Calum quickly took the other and we made our way back inside.

'I've lit a fire in the snug. Let's go in there to chat. Are you ready for another cup of tea?'

'Always,' I returned, laughing and letting go of Lorcan's arm as we got to the top of the stone steps.

'How about you, Lorcan?' Calum asked, still firmly holding my arm.

'Not for me, thanks, Cal. I'm going to leave you two in peace. I've got a couple of errands to run and there's only so much wedding talk I can take in one day.'

Calum squeezed my arm and rolled his eyes at me. 'One day you'll change your mind, you'll see.'

Lorcan gave him a look that, if I didn't know better, contained a warning. 'Not going to happen,' he replied in a tone of finality before turning to me. 'Let me know when you're ready and I'll come pick you up.'

'Thank you. I'm sure I can get a taxi, if the chap's awake.'

'Yeah... he doesn't really do Sundays,' Calum said.

'It's no bother, honestly. And keep her off that leg,' Lorcan said, looking at Calum. 'If she'll let you.'

I shooed him with my hand. 'Stop fussing. I'm not going to

tell the doctor or your mother or anyone else on you. I promise.'

The smile was back before he turned and walked away, the echo of the heavy door closing behind him punctuating his departure as the two of us headed towards the snug.

'Oh, that boy. I don't know what we're going to do with him,' Calum said, fluffing cushions around me and behind my back before sliding a deep burgundy embroidered footstool with stubby, turned mahogany wooden legs in front of me and gently guiding my foot to it. 'There. Comfy?'

'Extremely. I may never leave!'

Calum laughed and poured us the tea that had been delivered by a young girl who smiled shyly before disappearing again.

'Lara,' he said. 'She helps out on the weekends and holidays,' he explained as she closed the door behind her. 'Such a great girl. She's interested in getting into event planning so came to us to try and gain some experience.'

'That's great.'

'I know she's probably got a whole host of questions for you.'

'I'd be happy to help any way I can.' I rummaged quickly in my bag. 'Look, here's my card. Tell her to email me and we can set up a video call to have a chat and obviously I'll be back here before too long anyway.'

'Now, that's something to look forward to.' He grinned, brown eyes twinkling in good humour.

'Oh, you've got all the Irish charm, haven't you?' I replied, laughing.

'I do. Absolute bucketloads of it! Not that it does me much good around here. Still, we live in hope.'

'Have you never thought about moving somewhere else?'

'Oh, God. All the time! But then I think about leaving and, when it comes down to it, I don't want to. Sure, growing up was tough at times. People can be set in their ways, but I have great friends here and my family and that makes up for the rest. If something else is supposed to happen, it will.'

'I can understand you not wanting to leave. It's a gorgeous place and the feeling of community in the village is wonderful. Growing up in an area where your family has so much history and everyone is so close seems wonderful. It's been lost now in so many places. It's great to discover that it does actually still exist.'

'It is.' He chinked his china cup delicately against mine. 'To friendships old and new.'

I smiled, nodded my head in acceptance of the toast and took a sip of the light Darjeeling tea.

'So, Lorcan tells me you have all the glassware, cutlery and crockery available? Is that right? I don't need to arrange extra?'

'No. We cover all that. Found it was easier after a few events just to have our own. That way we know it's always available when we need it, even at short notice.'

'Sounds good.' I took another sip of my tea. 'Lorcan certainly did his homework when he reserved this place for Patrick just in case, didn't he?'

Calum looked at me. 'What do you mean?'

'Well, he knew all this about the arrangements. I assume he must have gone through that with you? I was just double-checking really for my own peace of mind.'

Calum was frowning at me.

'What did I say?'

'Nothing wrong,' he said, laying his hand on my arm for a moment. 'Not at all. I'm just a bit confused.'

'About what?'

'What you said about Lorcan.'

'Yes. He acts all anti weddings, but he's obviously taken the time to ensure everything here is going to be perfect for his friends. It's lovely. There's clearly more to him than he likes to show.'

'He has his reasons.'

'Oh! I'm sure. It wasn't a criticism. It's great, actually. Peyton and Patrick have left a lot of the boots-on-the-ground preparation to me and Lorcan so the more I know he's actually invested in this, despite what he says, the easier that makes my job.'

'Oh, he's invested. Don't worry.'

'Yes, I can see that now.'

Calum was studying me.

'What?' I asked, taking a bite of a feather-light biscuit.

'I mean, he's totally invested in all senses of the word. You know Lorcan owns this place, right?'

21

The biscuit, apparently as much in shock as I was, decided to take a wrong turn at this point and tried to enter my lungs. I coughed, snorted, gasped for breath and finally found some air after Calum, despite being small and lean, gave me a surprisingly hefty 'pat' on the back, which helped reroute things.

'From your reaction, I take it you didn't know that.'

'He owns the castle?'

'Yep. I know he doesn't say too much about it generally, but I thought, as it was all business between you two, he might have mentioned it.'

'No. He didn't. Earlier he said that it was going to rack and ruin and that investors helped restore it and make it what it is now.'

'He's right. There were investors but he's gradually bought them out over the last ten years or so. Some of them had ideas as to how the castle should be run.' He pulled a face.

'Ideas that you didn't agree with?'

'Well, if you want a totally tasteless version of Ireland, complete with the serving staff dressing as leprechauns...'

'Oh, God! That sounds awful!'

'I know. Direct flight to Tacky Central!'

'Dreadful.'

'So, Lorcan was the main shareholder, thankfully, and managed to charm them into waiting a while before we changed the way we were running things. Bearing in mind we were fully booked for months ahead and had rave reviews, things were clearly going well. It bought him time to find the money to buy them out.'

'I'm glad it worked out. What you're doing here is great. I wonder why he didn't mention that it was *his* castle.'

'I don't know. He can be pretty private outside the village – you don't really have that choice as part of it. Everyone knows your business whether you want them to or not. But we've definitely had extra attention in him from a few visitors when they find out he owns the place.'

'Oh-h-h, I see. Well, you and he can both rest assured I'm definitely not interested in him because he owns a castle.'

Calum raised a brow, delight washing across his face.

'That is, I'm definitely not interested in him at all! The fact that he owns a castle is neither here nor there.'

'No, I can see that,' he replied, looking genuinely disappointed. 'Shame. You look good together.'

'Oh, we do not,' I said, laughing now, feeling my initial blush dissipating. 'Anyway, that does explain his inside knowledge. I'll continue dealing directly with you, though, if that's all right?'

'Absolutely. I think we've got most of it covered but we'll definitely keep in touch and make sure everything is going exactly as planned. If you want to send me over the details of who is to be accommodated in the rooms here, I can get that all confirmed.'

'Do you have a list of other recommended places people can stay? Obviously, there's not a lot in the village, other than the pub. And perhaps a more regular taxi service that could be booked?'

'Sure I can. The next biggest town is about half an hour's drive and has a couple of hotels and a taxi firm. I'll send you all the details this evening.'

'Tomorrow is fine. I've put you out enough today. Thanks for seeing me on a Sunday.'

'Honestly, it was my pleasure. Lorcan said he'd do it if I had plans, but I really do love my job and I'm so glad I came in to meet you. Not least to see my boss sweeping you up into his arms.' He laid a hand on his chest and fluttered his eyelashes.

'Oh, shush. This stupid leg is already getting on my nerves. I'm hoping I'll be back to normal in a few days. I have things to do.'

'Don't overdo it. Work can wait. Your health is the most important thing.'

'I have brides who would disagree with that, but yes, I know. I will try.'

'Well, Lorcan will be back over in England so he'll be keeping an eye on you, I'm sure.' He gave another teasing waggle of his brows.

'Stop it!' I said, laughing. 'Patrick and Peyton may have left most of the arrangements to be done on their behalf, but I assure you I will be doing as much as possible myself. I'm used to working alone and that's probably preferable to both of us anyway.'

'Hmm, I'm not so sure. And I know he enjoyed the cake-tasting and narrowing down the catering choices.'

'Yes, well, that's food. That's different.'

'True. We've all been hoping he'd come around to the idea of marriage again eventually, but he seems pretty set in his decision.'

'Again?'

Calum put his hand up to his mouth. 'Mam's always saying I talk too much. Forget I said that. And for God's sake, don't tell Lorcan I said anything.'

I laid a reassuring hand on his arm. 'I promise. Don't worry.' Although just because I wasn't about to try and prise the information out of Calum, which, had I been determined, I guessed would have been fairly easy, didn't mean that his comment hadn't sparked my curiosity. Clearly Lorcan's dislike of marriage hadn't been a lifelong thing, which meant something must have happened to make him the way he was.

But still, that was none of my business and I had plenty more important things to occupy my time. In the meantime, I needed to get back to the pub and answer some enquiries that had come in during the day. I picked up my phone from the table and found Lorcan's contact details.

Ready when you are. Thanks.

Almost before I'd put the phone back down, it sent out a small polite ping and I read Lorcan's message.

Be there in 5.

'Waiting on your message, it seems.'

'You,' I said, dropping the phone into my bag before pointing at Calum, 'are trouble.'

'As often as I can be!' he replied with a wicked grin. 'I'll go and get your coat and we'll get you to the door. If you're sure you don't need a big, strong hunk of love like Lorcan to help.'

'I most certainly don't. And if you don't knock it off, I'm going to persuade my clients to go elsewhere.'

Calum drew in a mock gasp. 'You wouldn't.'

I narrowed my eyes. 'Watch me.'

He gave me a squeeze. 'Back in a sec.'

A short time later we were pulling open the great front door to see Lorcan reaching out for the handle.

'Hi.'

'Hello. Perfect timing.'

'I do my best.'

Calum gave me a subtle elbow in the ribs and I gave him a not so subtle one back, which caused him to giggle.

'Did I miss something?' Lorcan asked, looking from me to Calum and back again.

'Not at all,' I replied, smiling before turning to Calum. 'It was so lovely to meet you, and I'm really looking forward to working with you.' I held out my hand, which he ignored, instead sweeping me into a huge hug.

'Me too,' he said. 'What?' he asked when he noticed Lorcan looking at him. 'We're beyond professional now, aren't we, darlin'?'

'I guess we are,' I replied, unable to keep the laughter from my voice. I loved the warmth that Calum, and somehow even the venue itself, exuded and I really was looking forward to working with him, not just because it meant I'd be back here in this incredible setting and staying in the village that I already felt at home in. My gaze drifted back to Lorcan. Perhaps in other circumstances there might be another interest, but I had too much riding on this wedding to risk distractions.

'M'lady?' Lorcan held out his arm.

I looked up at him, almost silhouetted against the sun that was now lowering behind the soft green mounds of the hills behind him. There was that hint of smile again. Was he always like that, or had whatever Calum had alluded to diluted the wider smile I'd seen him give on occasion? What exactly was the story with Lorcan O'Malley? Although perhaps the bigger question was: why did I care?

I gave myself a mental shake and took the proffered arm.

'Thank you, kind sir.'

Beside me, Calum was vibrating with holding in whatever it was he wanted to say but a glance from me kept him silent. I gave him a wave and turned back to focus on the steps in front of me.

'Look after yourself and we'll talk soon,' Lorcan said, glancing over his shoulder before concentrating on taking as much weight as he could from me as we headed to the car he'd parked at the bottom of the steps.

* * *

'So, I have a couple of projects to check on in Dublin and a short meeting. You're welcome to come with me but I'm sure you have plenty of your own work to do, plus we still need to be careful about that leg. I know a great dog-friendly café that we can ensconce you in, if you don't mind dog-sitting? Would that be OK? I'll take him with me if not. It's not a problem.'

'No, that sounds good. I'm happy to keep Bod with me.'

'Great, thanks.'

I was realistic enough not to read anything into the fact that Lorcan had taken to using 'we' sometimes now, but inside there was a tiny part of my heart that fluttered with warmth when he did. It had been a long time since I'd felt part of a 'we'. On occasions in the past when it had been employed I'd felt uncomfortable about it, my independence being so ingrained in me over the years, but somehow here, with Lorcan, it felt OK. More than OK, in fact. I couldn't help liking the sound of it.

Having said an unexpectedly heartfelt goodbye to Gerry and Brighid, Lorcan, Bod and I were preparing to leave and set off across the country for his meetings and our flight back to London later this evening.

'Can you take Bod if I take your case?' Lorcan asked, already handing me the pooch, clearly knowing I couldn't refuse the fluffy little face looking up at me.

I waved again to my new friends and added in a little paw wave from Bod, a whimsical move that took me by surprise. I didn't do whimsy. I was down-to-earth, sensible Madeleine, fully grounded in reality. But their smiles at my action made me wonder if I'd been missing out on something by being so set in those ways. Oh, Maddie, come on. Of course not. The sooner I got back to my cottage, the better. There was something about Ireland that was determined to try and work some sort of magic on me and I just didn't have room, or time, in my life for magic.

'Ready?' Lorcan asked.

I nodded and his smile stayed in place as he moved towards the door, motioning for me to go first as he opened it.

'Oh!' The woman on the other side jumped, placing a hand on her chest. 'Lord, you gave me a fright.'

'Sorry.' I laughed, turning to Lorcan. My laughter died in my throat as I saw his face drain of colour and the smile he'd worn just seconds ago disappear, his features hardening like stone. The woman followed my gaze.

'Lorcan.' Her eyes shifted between me and him. 'I... didn't know you were back.'

'Just for the weekend.' The words were clipped and his eyes

shifted to me. 'We should get going if we're not going to miss the plane,' he stated, taking hold of the suitcase handles again.

We had hours, not to mention his meetings, before the flight, but he clearly wanted to be out of there.

'I love your dog,' the woman said, shifting her attention back to me. Bod looked up as if realising he was being admired, making sure his best side was on show. Not that he had a best side, of course. He was plain adorable all round.

'Oh. He's... umm... not mine,' I said, returning her smile and feeling inexplicably as if I were betraying Lorcan in doing so.

'A fan of dogs now, are you?' Lorcan flicked a glance at her that would cause a penguin to shiver.

'People can change, Lorcan.'

'Is that right?'

She shook her head. 'Can't we just put this behind us? It's been ten years.'

Lorcan dropped his head and, for a moment, it seemed that he might be considering that whatever the problem was between them had perhaps indeed run its course.

'Mammy?'

Lorcan's head snapped up as a young boy walked up towards the woman. He watched as she wrapped her arm around him. 'Sorry, sweetheart. I won't be a moment and then we'll get you home. I just need to pick up some eggs from Brighid so I can make your favourite sandwiches.' A wan smile lifted the corner of his mouth but his face was pale.

'What's wrong with him?' Lorcan asked, nodding at the boy.

'Tummy bug, the doc says. I've just picked up some medicine for him and I'm taking him home.'

'You'd better get your eggs, then. He looks fit to drop.'

The young boy looked up at Lorcan, then back at his

mother and snuggled closer to her. 'I'm quite capable of knowing how to look after my own son.'

Lorcan took a step back as though she'd physically slapped him and the flash of pain that crossed his face was clear for everyone to see.

'I'm sorry,' she said, her face flushing. 'I didn't mean—'

'Siobhan,' Brighid said, bustling towards us. The glance she sent Lorcan told me that she'd not only heard the exchange but also seen the distress it had caused him before he'd hidden it beneath the blank expression he now wore. And she, unlike me, also clearly understood the reasons behind it.

'I thought you two had left,' she said, wrapping one arm around his waist and the other around mine. 'Have you decided to stay after all?' She laughed, squeezing me a little closer.

'And what can I do for you, Siobhan?' Her tone was still friendly but, with her actions, it felt as if she was providing a support, a show of solidarity with Lorcan – and, by extension, me – against this new arrival.

'I was just seeing if you had any eggs? Tommy's not well and I thought that'd be easy on his stomach.'

'Ah, now. That's not so good, is it, young Tommy? I'll sort you some out. Now, off you go, you two,' she said, turning to us. 'Travel safe.'

Lorcan bent and kissed Brighid's cheek. 'We will, thanks,' he said, releasing the case handles to give her a hug. As he pulled back, there was another exchange between them, this time unsaid but just as clear. Lorcan gave the tiniest of nods and turned to the cases as Brighid hugged me and Bod. 'Look after that boy,' she whispered. 'He's nowhere near as tough as he likes to make out.'

With Siobhan and her son looking on, this didn't exactly seem the right moment to point out that I would likely hardly see Lorcan between now and Christmas when we'd be back here for the wedding, but Brighid's sharp, knowing eyes brooked no argument. Siobhan stood aside so that we could get out of the door and Lorcan indicated for me to go first as Brighid took Siobhan and her son off further in the pub, pulling the heavy door closed behind him.

22

Lorcan was silent as he loaded the cases, then me, then Bod into the car. He folded himself behind the wheel, checking I was OK with the dog on my lap. I sat, waiting to see if he planned to say anything about the situation we'd just left, but instead he turned the key to start the engine. The elephant in the room from the pub had clearly followed us out and was now sprawled across the back seat, making itself comfortable.

'It really is the most beautiful countryside around here,' I said after a while, as Lorcan hugged the car to the bendy road, the ancient cliffs falling away to the sea on one side. The weather today was overcast and as a result the water below was like pewter, looking more ominous than it had yesterday when we'd watched it crash and sparkle from the secret garden within the castle grounds. As I stole a look at Lorcan it felt as if the ocean below us wasn't the only thing mercurial. His eyes concentrated on the road, but his fingers gripped the wheel tighter than they had previously.

'Is everything all right?' I said eventually. Clearly it wasn't but the atmosphere was so thick the elephant in the back seat could have cut it with his trunk.

'Grand.'

Right. Well, that answered that question, then. Silence resumed. I thought about turning on the radio but that seemed a bit presumptuous and had he wanted to listen to something, I guessed he'd probably have turned it on himself. I could understand that. Sometimes when my mind was churning I needed to distract it with an audio book, or podcast. For me, words that I was interested in were a better escape than music in those circumstances. But there were also days when I wanted, even needed, silence. Perhaps that was how Lorcan dealt with things and, if so, then it was only fair to leave him to his musings.

'Sorry you were in the middle of that.'

I turned and smiled at him, a genuinely wide one. 'I'm a wedding planner. Believe me, I've been in the middle of far worse than that. If no one walks away bleeding or with clumps of hair gripped between their fingers, I call it a win.'

Lorcan glanced at me and I was relieved and oddly pleased to see a smile, albeit a shadow of the one I'd found myself admiring over the weekend – purely from the point of view that he would look good in the wedding photos, obviously. Still, it was a smile and that was something.

'Sounds brutal.'

'It can be.'

'But let me guess, you wouldn't change it for the world.'

'No, you're right,' I said, running my hand over Bod's teddy-bear-like fur. 'I love what I do.'

'I imagine everyone thinks you have quite the glamorous life?'

'Yes, I have had that comment on more than one occasion, especially if the event is being held somewhere swanky.'

'Obviously not the same people you're pulling apart when they get in a barney.'

'Ha! No, definitely not. I sometimes think I'm like a swan, or at least try to be. All serene and elegant on the surface and paddling madly underneath where no one sees all the mechanics at work.'

'And from what I've seen so far, you definitely succeed.'

'Thank you,' I replied. 'I hope you still think that once this is all over.'

'This?' He turned his head for the briefest moment.

'The wedding.'

'Oh. Yeah. Right. Sorry. I'm sure I will. And Calum can't stop raving about you. I've already had four messages from him singing your praises.'

'Aah, that's very kind of him. He's lovely.' I paused for a moment, considering what I was about to say and decided just to say it. 'I can see why you hired him.'

We rolled to a stop at a red light in a small town as two nuns crossed the road in front of us. There was something slightly surreal about the scene, and for a moment I forgot the conversation I'd begun.

'What do you mean?' Lorcan was studying me. 'Hired him?'

'Yes. As the castle's manager.'

Lorcan was still looking at me and a car behind us beeped him, alerting us to the fact the light was now green.

'Shit,' he mumbled, thrust the car into first and pulled away, lifting his hand to the rear-view mirror in a signal of apology.

'How long have you known?' he asked.

'Only since yesterday afternoon when you disappeared off.'

I saw him give a small headshake. 'Calum talks way too much.'

'He did mention that his mother says the same thing.'

This, at least, extracted a huff of laughter from him. 'That's a woman with a good head on her shoulders. Talks a lot of sense even though I think she despairs at times of her son having any.'

'I think he has plenty, and clearly so do you otherwise you'd never have put him in that position. The manager of any establishment can make or break it, which you're obviously well aware of.'

'He's very good at his job.'

'So I could see. So why all the cloak and dagger stuff?' My mind drifted back to the meal we'd had with Patrick and Peyton. 'You even went out of your way to make sure Peyton didn't let on. When I asked if you knew the venue well she'd been about to say that of course you did, as it was yours. You interrupted her and, lovely girl that she is, she went along with it.'

'It just saves hassle.'

'And what hassle, exactly, would that be?'

He looked awkward, clearly searching for a tactful reply.

'Would it, by chance, be the hassle that poor little me with my leaking roof and business hanging on by a thread may try and seduce you, thinking you're some sort of rich aristocrat?'

A deep bubble of laughter bounced around the interior of the car. 'One, I'm definitely no rich aristocrat, so whoever thinks that would be in for a big disappointment.'

'And two?'

'And two... don't take this the wrong way.'

'Whenever someone says don't take this the wrong way it usually means that said person is about to insult the other in some way.'

'Not at all.'

I set my features to haughty and waited.

'OK. It's just that, well, you're not really the seductress type, are you, to be fair?' He waited a beat. 'On a scale of one to five, how pissed off at me are you now?'

'Honestly, I don't really care whether you think I could seduce you or anyone else. I'm more than capable of making my own money and don't need to get it from a man. In any case there have been plenty of opportunities to meet other far richer, far more handsome and far more charming venue owners than you.'

'Is that so now?'

'Yes.' Well, it was – sort of. Frankly I had no idea how much money Lorcan had in the bank. He drove a swanky car back in England but, let's face it, there have been plenty of bankrupt people driving around in their posh cars up until the minute the vehicle was put on to the back of a low loader. As for other owners, well, there I might have been telling a tiny fib. Lorcan O'Malley was definitely the best-looking venue owner I'd ever met. But there was no way on God's green earth I was telling him that.

'It's just become a bit of a habit really.'

'What has?'

'Distancing myself from the ownership. It makes life easier.'

'Do the events of this morning tie into that?'

He gave me a momentary glance. 'It's complicated.'

'These things usually are,' I replied, in a tone that let him know that I didn't expect a reply.

'Yep, that they are,' he said anyway before turning in on his thoughts once again as the scenery of Ireland passed us by.

* * *

'You sure you don't mind looking after him?' Lorcan asked for the third time as he pushed his empty coffee mug to the side. Much of the rest of the journey had passed in silence, which had given me the time to enjoy the views and make mental, and sometimes actual, notes about Patrick and Peyton's wedding. I'd noticed my inbox was also looking a little healthier with enquiries too, and answering them was one of the things I planned to get done while Bod and I sat in the delightful dog-friendly café Lorcan had brought us to in Dublin. We'd enjoyed a delicious, home-cooked lunch followed with a slice of home-made cake, which I really shouldn't have had but which tasted divine. What with all the full Irish breakfasts, various cake-tastings, along with the rest of the meals and now this today, the trip had certainly played havoc with my ordinarily regimented dietary routine. I'd seen Lorcan's expression as he watched my hesitation over the choice of cake, clearly expecting me not to have any. Childishly I had some just so that he couldn't be right. It was worth the calories just to see the look of surprise on his face, which he didn't even bother to try and cover. Normally I'd have just added another mile to my run, but my sore leg wasn't quite up to that yet. I'd managed to book an appointment on Friday with my local GP to hopefully have the stiches out and, with luck, things would improve from there. My weight hadn't varied more than a pound or two in years and I liked to keep it that way. I knew where I was then.

'Do you write down every single thing you eat and drink?' Lorcan asked as I closed the app on my phone.

'Yes.'

'Why?'

'It helps me keep track.'

'Of what?'

'What I'm eating,' I said, giving him a look that suggested I had a special pointy hat in the car for him.

'Well, yes. Obviously. But why?'

As I opened my mouth to repeat my previous answer, he waved his hand. 'Exactly why do you need to keep track, I mean?'

'Because I like to. I have a set number of calories I can consume and a set number of calories I need to burn to keep me at the weight I'm comfortable with.'

'You're petite.'

'I'm a size eight and that's where I feel comfortable. I'm not depriving myself and I'm not judging anyone else, just as I don't appreciate people judging me. My mum was slim too.'

He was looking at me with a quizzical expression.

'What?'

'Doesn't that take all the joy out of eating?'

'Not at all.'

His face told me he didn't believe me. 'It doesn't. I'm lucky to have inherited a pretty fast metabolism so that helps and I'm not a fan of junk food anyway, which, again, helps. I just like to keep track of things, that's all.'

'Of everything, it seems.'

I gave a small shrug. 'As I said, I like my life organised.'

'Fair enough,' Lorcan said, stretching his back, raising his arms above his head.. I looked away, as casually as I could and gave Bod, currently curled on my lap, a fuss. Lorcan's indisputably attractive body was the one thing I definitely didn't need to make a note of. 'Just seems like planning every single aspect of your life like you do might suck the joy out of it. Don't you crave spontaneity? Surprise? Living for the moment?'

'No. I don't. I don't like surprises.'

Lorcan had now crouched down in front of me and looked

up from where he was giving Bod a treat for having been such a good boy through lunch. 'What do you mean you don't like surprises? Everyone likes surprises.'

'Clearly not.'

'What sort of person doesn't?'

I let out a sigh and reached down into my bag to pull out my laptop that I'd plugged in last night so that it would be fully charged for today.

'How long do you think you'll be?' I asked, checking my watch and signalling the previous conversation was well and truly closed. I certainly wasn't about to tell Lorcan that once upon a time I'd been far more free-spirited and had loved surprises. Our whole family had been the type to wake up on a Sunday, randomly pick a place on the map, grab a picnic and go. One time we'd even just driven to the airport and asked what flights they had. Mum had packed some cold-weather clothes and some warmer-weather ones, hedging her bets, and we'd ended up with ten days in Montana, somewhere we probably would never have gone if we'd sat down and thought about it. But that was then. Things happen. Things change. Now planning was not only my career – it was my coping mechanism for life.

23

'You going to jot that down in one of your notebooks too?' Lorcan asked.

'No. Just in my phone so I know when to be ready to leave.'

He shrugged his shoulders. 'A couple of hours. I don't know exactly.'

'Oh. I see. Well, that gives me some idea.'

'It doesn't matter. The café stays open late and I've set up a tab so you can get as many drinks or anything else as you'd like.'

'You really don't need to do that. I'm quite capable of paying my own way.' I kept my head up and tried to ignore the fact that Lorcan had already been witness to the state of my roof. It hadn't been spoken out loud but I got the clear feeling he knew I couldn't be wasting any money on indulgent cups of ginger-bread steamers or slices of cake, despite how delicious the last ones had been.

'I know,' he said, 'but it's my fault you're stuck here instead of us being able to get an earlier flight so I'd prefer it if you used it.'

'We'll see,' I replied. 'But thank you for the thought. That's very kind.'

'Right.' He glanced at his phone. 'I'd better head off. If you need me, just call, OK?'

'I thought you had meetings.'

'I do. But if you need something, just call. It doesn't matter.'

I tilted my head at him. 'If you're worried about Bod, I won't be offended if you prefer to take him with you. My only real experience of dogs has been this weekend, so I quite understand if you don't feel comfortable about it.'

Lorcan let a smile slide onto his face. 'Yeah, he looks really stressed. Perhaps I'd better take him after all.' We both looked down to where Bod was now asleep on my lap, pressed up against me with all four feet in the air. I returned the smile. 'And I was talking about you needing anything, not the dog.' I opened my mouth and he held up a hand. 'Not that I'm saying you're not independent or capable of doing anything and everything yourself, I'm just saying if you need anything, ring me. Even if it's just to pick up another notebook for you.' He glanced down at the pile I'd now neatly stacked on the worn mahogany of the coffee-shop table.

'You can never have enough notebooks.'

'I'd beg to differ but somehow I think I'd lose.'

'You would. Obviously.'

'Obviously.' He remained where he was.

'Not that I'm hurrying you out the door or anything, but didn't you say your meeting was at two? It's five to now.'

He jolted out of whatever thought he was contemplating. 'Oh, shit. Right, yeah. OK. I'll be back as soon as I can.'

'Don't worry,' I replied, half laughing. 'I'm fine. I can't go anywhere anyway. You have the tickets.'

'This is true.' He dashed towards the door, drawing a few

admiring glances as he did so. With his size, he was hard to miss. Add unreasonably good looks to that and it was almost impossible. Turning at the door to pull it closed behind him, he noticed me still watching – something I hadn't planned on. He raised a hand in a brief wave and gave me one of those winks that I had already told myself was not at all sexy. Nope. Not in the slightest. Despite the fact on the odd occasion he did it, an uninvited tingle never failed to trickle itself down my spine and detour to areas it really had no place being!

I looked down at Bod, who chose that moment to let out a very polite and dignified fart, which did an excellent job of breaking the spell. I could have done without the accompanying pong, but it was still a job well done. Much to his tired disgust, I moved him onto a little blanket on the floor by my feet, where he curled back up, resting his head on my feet. Lifting my first notebook onto my lap, I checked a few colour-coordinated, bulleted points then picked up my phone and scrolled through my contacts until I found the one I was looking for.

'Isobel Designs. How may I help you?'

'Hi. This is Madeleine Hart. Is Izzy around?'

'I'll just check for you. Could you hold the line, please?'

Izzy had been one of my first contacts when I started my business and I still always recommended clients to her if possible. She made the most incredible bridal gowns and her designs were always perfect. She had an innate sense of what people wanted and could transfer those wishes into reality with the most beautiful fabrics. Isobel Designs had gone from strength to strength in the time I'd known her, with a huge waiting list. But I also loved working with her as Izzy was one of the nicest, most supportive people I'd ever met.

'Maddie!' Izzy's voice sang down the phone. 'How are you? How's things?'

'I'm OK. Things have been a bit not so great but I'm hopeful they're starting to pick up again now.'

'I'm sure they will. I couldn't wait to get back to the studio. Obviously I love Rob to bits but when we were both working full-time from home, it could get a bit tense from time to time. Like most people, I suspect.'

'Oh, yes, this last few years certainly seems to have tested relationships, that's for sure.'

'I mean, how can one man type so loud? I swear he ordered an extra-loud keyboard just to wind me up,' she said, laughing, not actually putting it past her husband to do just that as a tease. Izzy had gone through her own tough time and I was glad she'd found someone who appreciated her for the incredible woman she was. 'Anyway, I'm rabbiting on as usual. What can I do for you?'

'I just wondered if I could pop in and check on Peyton Leigh-Steele's dress? I haven't actually seen it in the flesh yet as she'd ordered it before I took over the wedding planning. I understand you've got the bridesmaids' ones too?'

'Oh God, I heard that the original planner let them down big time, the poor things. That was awful. I didn't realise you'd got the job of picking up the pieces. How's it going? Peyton said something about them not getting married in Dublin now, is that right?'

'Yeah. They've moved the wedding to Patrick's home town. Well, village actually, and I have to say, although it's obviously been a nightmare for them, the new venue is absolutely stunning and the suppliers we've got on board so far are amazing and all so nice.'

'Was it hard to find people there or are they coming in from elsewhere? I seem to remember Patrick mention in passing he comes from a tiny place.'

'The village is small, yes, but luckily I had someone with inside knowledge with me on the trip to recce the place, which has been a huge help.'

'Always good to have someone on the inside,' she said, laughing. 'So when do you want to come in?'

'I'm flying back from Ireland later today and I need to just get organised again.'

'I've never known a time you weren't organised!' Izzy replied, a smile in her voice.

'Goes with the territory,' I said, trying to push away Lorcan's comment about my approach to doing things taking all the spontaneity out of life.

'It absolutely does. I'm so glad Peyton and Patrick have hired you. They're definitely in the best hands now.' Izzy had a way of always saying the right thing. Perhaps that came with her territory, but I think it also came down to her being a lovely woman with a generous, kind heart. 'So when would suit you? I'm in the studio Wednesday and Thursday this week if either of those are any good. Wednesday would probably have to be a later one though as I have a fitting at four. I should be done by half five at the latest so if you want to pop in around six? Is that too late?'

'No, not at all. It will be good to get something else ticked off the list and I'll have the silhouette and fabric more in my head then if I've seen it in person. Peyton's shown me some photos you took, of course, but—'

'It's not the same as seeing it with your own eyes, I know.' Izzy understood completely. 'I can give you some swatches of each of the fabrics her dress and veil have been made up with, as well as some for the bridesmaid dresses too.'

'Perfect. Exactly what I need. See, this is why I love working with you. You know just what I need before I even say it.'

'Works both ways, hon. Do you want to grab a bite to eat with me and Rob afterwards? It'd be lovely to catch up if you have time?'

I quickly scanned my calendar and saw that I had an online Clubbercise session booked for seven. Well, that won't be happening, I thought, glancing down at my leg.

'That sounds great, Izzy.'

'Fab! Any preference?'

'Not at all. I'm happy to leave it to you.'

See, Lorcan, I don't always have to plan everything. I can be just as spontaneous as the next person!

'You sure?' Izzy's tone suggested she wasn't convinced.

I paused. 'Well, I do hear that new Greek restaurant near your place has been getting great reviews.'

Spontaneity is so overrated anyway.

'Demeter?'

'Yes, that's the one.'

'I heard the same. I'll message Rob and get him to book us a table. Are you bringing anyone?' Her words were innocent enough but I knew she was fishing.

'Nope, it'll just be the three of us,' I replied, laughing. 'Do you reckon he'll be able to get us in at short notice?'

'No problem. He's actually done some work for them and they think he's marvellous so I'm sure it won't be a problem.'

'That's handy.'

'Yes, he has his uses.' She giggled. 'It'll be so lovely to see you. Safe flight and see you at six on Wednesday.'

* * *

'Hey.' Lorcan's deep tones made me jump and I looked up, startled, having been absorbed in some provisional ideas for another wedding I'd just been booked for.

'Oh, hi!' I said, returning the smile he gave me. He really did have a great smile. It was a shame he didn't let it show more often. 'How did your meetings go?'

'Really well, thanks for asking.' The smile remained, his gaze hooking on mine for a moment before it dropped to where Bod was back snoozing on my lap. 'It's nice that one of you has noticed my return.' A quick scan of the café told me quite a few people had noticed him, but that didn't appear to have registered. I'd once dated a man who liked to see exactly who was checking him out every time we went anywhere, and wasn't averse to throwing back a smile to those whom he approved of. Needless to say, that particular relationship hadn't lasted very long. Lorcan might be a bit of a player when he wanted to be, from what I'd heard about the trail of broken hearts behind him, but I had to give him the fact he certainly wasn't vain.

'Has he been asleep the whole time?' he asked, scratching the top of the dog's head, who had now finally deigned to open one eye to see what was going on. Of course, once he saw his master, there was a sudden flurry of paws, fluff, ears and tail as he scrabbled to leap from my lap into Lorcan's arms, whereupon his owner's smile became a laugh, his whole body relaxing into the moment, the hard planes and frown of his face softening at the dog's antics. I watched, enjoying the loving warmth reflected from the scene. I liked this side of Lorcan. I'd seen glimpses of it over the weekend, especially when he gave up his Saturday evening to keep me company. I still blushed a little at the memory. I hadn't asked anyone to stay and keep me company since I was a child. Typical that the first time I did so, it would be Lorcan O'Malley that I made the exception for, even if it was through a drug-induced haze.

I couldn't help wonder if the mysterious Siobhan we'd run into this morning had something to do with him developing that tough shell he protected his softer side with. Either way, I was glad to see this crack in it, glad to see the light getting in and showing the world the true nature of this man who, in the short time I'd known him, made me think that he was the most infuriating man I'd ever met – but also the kindest. Lorcan O'Malley was someone whom it would be very easy to fall for if one was so inclined. Thankfully, I was definitely not inclined so that was good. Right. That was that cleared up, then.

24

'You look as if you're very deep in thought.' The melodic tones drifted around me as I watched Bod greeting him as though he'd been away for months, not a few hours.

'Oh! Do I? No, not really,' I replied too quickly, feeling the flush creeping up my chest. Being a redhead with pale skin had never done me any favours when it came to telling fibs.

Lorcan didn't say anything but his eyes locked onto mine and told me he knew better. I gave what I hoped was an innocent shrug, which, judging by the way his mouth tipped up far too sexily at the corners, just made it worse.

'I hope Bod didn't disturb your work too much,' he said, thankfully letting the previous subject drop.

'Not at all. The staff were kind enough to look after my stuff and our seat while I took him out for a walk. It was a good excuse to take a break. They gave me some directions to a place he could have a little run around so we did that and then came back and he had a nap. I was sorely tempted to have one myself. He looked so comfy and content.'

'You should have done.'

'I couldn't,' I said, laughing, 'as nice as that would have been.'

'Not in your schedule?'

The laughter died away and I glanced out of the window at the people passing by the large plate-glass windows, some hurrying, others taking in the scenery, stopping regularly to snap photos or take selfies.

'No,' I said simply, flashing up a smile that I knew didn't reach my eyes. Lorcan O'Malley wouldn't notice that detail anyway. This was why I had my own guards up. Because just when you started to relax with people, they did, or said, something that made you feel foolish. Yes, I was a bit uptight. Perhaps a little too organised but that was how it was. How it would always be because that was what I could deal with and I could do without Lorcan taking the piss. I understood that he didn't have all the relevant information, but it irked me that he couldn't just accept this was the way I worked. Accept the way I was.

Silence hovered between us, thick and heavy, replacing the light and pleasant atmosphere of moments before. Bod pricked his ears and looked between us both as if sensing the change. I'd noticed this action before. The dog was a sensitive little thing – certainly a lot more sensitive than his master anyway, that was for sure.

'You looked busy when I came in,' Lorcan said.

I waited for the follow-up, some further dig about something or other. 'Is business picking up?'

I looked up at him.

'Paddy insisted I follow Peyton on social media and like all her posts. There's an awful lot of wedding ones and I saw she'd tagged you in them.' He gave a shrug. 'She has quite a lot of followers and knows a lot of people. I just wondered if you were getting anything from that. I hoped you might be, anyway.'

I tilted my head. 'What are you up to?'

'Up to?' He looked genuinely confused.

'Yes. You're being nice, and thoughtful. It throws me when you do that. You're easier to deal with when you're being your normal self.'

'My normal self.'

'Yes.'

'Who's to say this isn't my normal self?' he asked, echoing the very thought I had earlier. His propensity to keep doing that was another thing that threw me.

'The fact you keep digging about my way of working and living my life. Anyway,' I said, clearing my throat and deciding it would be safer to change the subject. Lorcan's deep blue eyes were currently locked onto mine and a fluttery sensation tickled my stomach, flitting about in a manner that was definitely not in any of my schedules! 'And yes, I've just got a definite booking off the back of someone seeing some of Peyton's posts, and have three more enquiries from them too. She's quite the influencer. I had no idea.'

'She is. I'm glad more people are noticing your business through it. That's good.'

'It is. So much of business is word of mouth, isn't it? Unless you're some massive corporation, obviously.'

'True. You've done a great job picking up the pieces with this wedding. It can't have been easy and Peyton was a wreck when the original plans fell apart. They thought the whole wedding was in place and that woman just legged it with their deposits.'

'I'd never heard of her. How did she talk Peyton into using her?'

'She's a con artist. That's what she does. She targeted their wedding because she knew there was big money involved. Said all the right words, promised all the right things and Peyton was bowled over.'

'And Patrick didn't suspect a thing?'

'Nope. Neither did I. I didn't get on with her. Just couldn't take to her for some reason but we all put that down to me being a grouchy eejit.' He smiled a self-deprecating half-smile.

'Glad it's not just me, then.'

He flashed me a grin. 'Definitely not. But there was just something about her...'

'You had a gut feeling.'

'I suppose that's what it was, yeah. Hindsight is such a punch in the face. I should have known.'

'Why should you? As you said, it sounds like that's what she does, cons people. And she's clearly very good at it. I'm sure Peyton and Patrick weren't the first and, sadly, probably won't be the last.'

'They might be. Peyton's family have a lot of money and they've got several people dedicated solely to finding and bringing that woman to justice.'

'Wow. I really better not mess up! They're lucky to have you supporting them, despite the fact that you don't even believe in any of this.' I waved my hand to encompass the latest editions of a couple of wedding magazines I'd picked up on my stroll with Bod earlier.

'My opinion on it all isn't what matters. Patrick told me that if I wanted to be his best man, which is what he wanted, then I had to get on board, irrespective of my own outlook on weddings. So I did. And then I ignored my gut feeling and let them down. It was supposed to be my job to make sure they got everything they wanted and then that woman happened.

Peyton was distraught.' His attention was now focused on the little dog, who was snuggling into his master's shoulder, sensing he needed comfort. Lorcan's eyes met mine. 'Peyton is a sweet girl. Admittedly, she's a princess and way too full on for me but she's a good woman in her heart and I've never seen Paddy as happy as he's been since he met her. He lost his mum a few years ago now and they were so close. It broke him and nobody could get through. And then he met Peyton and it was as if the clouds parted ever so slightly. The more time he spent with her, the more he let the sun back into his heart. Even though she exhausts me at times with all her mad ideas and Californian fads and craziness, I'll never be able to thank her enough for bringing Patrick back to us and helping him through the grief he was mired in.'

'It wasn't your fault, Lorcan. None of it.'

He gave me a look that said he begged to differ.

I put my planner down and reached out, taking the hand that wasn't holding up his dog, who was now half hanging over his shoulder, surveying the passing public and basking in the admiring looks cast his way. 'I'm serious, Lorcan. None of it was your fault. You didn't know who that woman was. If you had, of course you would have said something. But you didn't. You couldn't know. Just as no one else could. You can't blame yourself.'

'Says who?' he replied, almost to himself, shaking his head.

'Me,' I said, drawing myself up. 'I say so. In fact, it says so right here in my planner.' I let go of his hand, flashed him the planner before closing it again and putting it back on the table. 'And you know how much of a bible that is. What's in there is truth and gospel. So that's that.'

'That's that?' he replied, reaching up to pull Bod back from his position as he noticed a group of teenage Korean girls gathering at the window watching the dog, and thereby us.

'Yes. End of. It's not your job to make sure Peyton and Patrick have the wedding they want. That's my job, so you can relinquish that burden now. You're there to support them, which you are. You've done so much to help me this weekend, and don't forget I know that you didn't just happen to find a space for them at the castle. You made special arrangements to ensure it was free for them to have the date they wanted, should they need it as a back-up. You risked your own income on the off chance that your friends might need the castle as their venue. We all know how much hospitality has suffered over the last few years and not many owners would do that.'

'They would for their friends.'

'No, Lorcan. They wouldn't.'

'Then perhaps they're not real friends.'

'Perhaps they're just not as good a friend as you are. So let go of all that other stuff. You've got them a venue. You also pretty much single-handedly got them a caterer, a florist and a baker. In fact, I'm beginning to think I ought to give you half my fee.'

'Only if you insist.'

'Well, I wouldn't like to insist.'

Another smile.

'Do you want another drink or some food? We have time before we have to leave for the airport.'

'Have you eaten?'

'I'm OK.'

I waited.

'No, Mam. I haven't eaten.'

I gave him a gentle kick and told him to go and order whatever he knew was good, to which he gave a nod of acquiescence, handing the dog back to me as he did so. Bod snuggled in as if he'd known me forever and I felt the smile spread over my face.

'He does that to people.'

'Snuggles?'

'Makes them smile.'

'Oh, I see.'

'He's a cuddly little chap, for sure, but he seems to have taken a special liking to you.'

'Now you're just being nice. Stop it. It unnerves me.'

Lorcan let out that deep, rumbling laugh again and I turned my attention hurriedly back to the dog. Falling for the dog was one thing. Falling for his owner was quite another. Sensing he'd gone, I looked up to watch Lorcan striding across the café. God, he looked good in a suit. I mean, he looked good in everything. He was just one of those annoying people that did. But today, in that dark blue suit that matched his eyes, all set off with a crisp white shirt, he was – objectively – hot. Subjectively, he was off the Scoville scale.

'That, however,' I whispered to Bod as I shuffled him a bit to get him off my bladder, 'is purely between you and me. OK?'

Bod looked at me and I swear to God, he smiled.

25

'So, what's the plan for the rest of the week?' Lorcan asked as we each tucked into a steaming bowl of Irish stew, accompanied by soda bread, which I'd never had before. This was apparently unacceptable and he insisted on me having some.

'I'm meeting with the dress designer on Wednesday night. I've worked with her before so I know everything's going to be fine, but I just want to see the dress in the flesh, as it were. I might then be able to tie in some aspects of it with the décor and so on.'

'Didn't Peyton have a photo of her in it?'

'Yes. She sent me that but it's not the same as seeing it for myself.'

'You're a stickler for the details, aren't you?'

'It's the details that pay the bills in this job.'

'I suppose it is.'

'I'm sure it's the same with event hosting at the castle.'

'I'm sure it is, which is why I leave all that to Calum.'

'Not a details man, then?'

'I have to be in my job. Like you, it's the details that can be the reason a project is a big success or an expensive flop. That's why I make no attempt to micromanage Calum when it comes to Ballalee Castle. He's more than capable and he has a great team backing him up. I'd only mess things up if I went poking my nose in. Not to mention he'd firmly and not that politely tell me where to go if I tried.'

'Really?' I asked, laughing.

'To paraphrase Shakespeare, he may be little, but he is fierce.'

'He clearly has a knack for what he does and gets things done, judging by the photos in that album. Also, by the fact you're happy to leave him to it. You don't strike me as a man who suffers fools gladly.'

'Definitely not if they're going to lose me money, and Calum's certainly no fool. So what time are you booked in to see the dress woman?'

I gave him a flat look at his terminology. 'Izzy is a designer and a specialised, highly talented bridal atelier.'

'That's what I said.' Lorcan gave a shrug and I let out a sigh. His just-full lips were straight and gave nothing away but a hint of mischievousness twinkled in the blue eyes.

'I'm glad you're enjoying yourself,' I said, trying not to show that I was too.

'I don't know what you mean,' he said. I shook my head as I turned back to my delicious dinner, but I knew he'd seen straight through me. 'So what time are you meeting her?'

'Six p.m. at her studio in London.'

'OK. Do you want me to pick you up?'

I snapped my head up. 'What?'

'Wednesday. Do you want me to pick you up?'

'For what?'

'To go to the specialist bridal atelier.' There was the merest hint of twitch in his dark brow. He was such a smart arse.

'You don't need to come to that. It's just for my own sake. Peyton already had the dress designed and Izzy is going to do a final fitting just before the wedding itself.'

'I have strict instructions that I am to make myself available to you for any and all wedding-related activities.'

'Which I appreciate, but I can handle this one. Thank you, though.'

'No one has any doubt that you can handle anything. That's not the point. If Peyton were here, she'd be going with you, I assume. In lieu of that possibility, I am, instead, at your service.'

'Somehow I don't think the dress will fit you.'

'Shame. Although maybe that's a good thing. I'm not sure white is my colour. I find it washes me out.' He put a hand to his cheek and glanced at the window as if checking his reflection. Laughing, I bopped him with one of my notebooks. He turned back, that smile on full wattage, lighting his face.

Why couldn't he be this guy all the time? Although, as that smile hit me, and my face returned it without prior consultation with my brain, it struck me again that it was probably just as well he wasn't. I had enough on my mind scraping my business back together and running repairs to my house (not to mention running water where it wasn't supposed to be) without adding a tall, dark Irishman who had absolutely no idea how sexy he was. As for that quip about white washing him out, as my eyes drifted to the shirt now on show, Lorcan having discarded his suit jacket, I had to disagree. The tailored cut skimmed everywhere it should, and the pure white acted as a perfect foil for tar-black hair and deep blue eyes. He'd folded the sleeves back and tanned forearms with a smattering of dark hair were now on show, the cords of muscle in them rippling every now and then as he moved. I was doing my best to ignore them, but my gaze would occasionally drift down to them as we chatted when my brain was distracted and not keeping my eyes under strict control.

'I'm not sure Patrick and Peyton meant for you to attach yourself to me on every errand. In fact, I'm certain they didn't mean that at all.'

A thought struck me and I turned to Lorcan. 'Or do they? I mean, I could understand them perhaps wanting that, bearing in mind what happened with the last so-called planner, but I'd rather them be upfront about that with me.'

'No!' Lorcan moved his arm across and covered my hand with his own. 'That's not it at all.' He shifted position so he could take both my hands in his. Bod raised his head to see if he was missing anything, decided he wasn't and went back to snoozing beside his master. Lorcan's hands folded gently around mine.

'Jesus, are your hands always this cold?' he said, laughing, enclosing them together within his own warm ones. 'You mustn't think that. Peyton and Patrick trust you implicitly. Just because they got burned before doesn't mean that they won't trust anyone else now. They're good people and they know that you're genuine and will be doing everything you can to make this the wedding they want it to be, if not better. I promise you.'

I lifted my eyes from where I was studying his hands. 'And you?' I said, meeting his gaze.

'Me?'

'Do you trust me?'

'Of course.'

'You said you felt responsible for not being able to spot the previous woman was a fake. Like I said, I can understand the situation, but I'd rather know where I stand. Especially with you.'

His head tilted a little to the side, the gaze still fixed. 'Why especially with me?'

'Because you're the hardest to work out.'

'Am I now?'

'Yes.' I nodded, slipping my hands from his, ostensibly to tuck a stray lock of hair that had escaped from my clip back behind my ear. The truth was sitting here with Lorcan's warm, strong hands wrapped around my own small, cool ones was beginning to feel just that little bit too good. Too comfortable.

'Whereas you're pretty easy to read.'

'I most certainly am not.'

'Oh, darlin'. You really are.'

'I'm not,' I said, feeling my shields go up. 'And, as I said, I don't need you to attend the designer's studio with me. Thank you for the offer.'

He leant back against the cushions lining the sofa we were sitting on. 'What's up with you?'

'Excuse me?'

'You. You suddenly went into self-protection mode.'

I let out a laugh that sounded a little strangulated and tried to gloss over it, although I'd caught a glance of Lorcan's face and he clearly hadn't missed that it had sounded off. Of course he bloody hadn't.

'You don't like people trying to get behind that organised, put-together face you show the world, do you?'

'I don't know what you mean. I like to be organised and I like to feel put together. There's no "face", as you put it. This is who I am.'

'Is it though?' His voice was soft and enquiring but his questioning was making my hackles rise. I wasn't sure what his intention was. Perhaps it was just curiosity. I'd got used to my own company and keeping myself to myself, especially when it came to my private life. Well, as much as you could in a village and with Betty as a neighbour. Thank God the village wasn't like Ballalee though, where you really couldn't have any secrets. Everyone seemed to know everything. And the curious thing to me was that no one seemed to mind. Maybe it was just the nature of the place, the people. And maybe it was simply that nature that prompted Lorcan to ask the question he had. I did my best to keep that in mind.

'It is,' I said, smiling briefly before turning my attention to sweeping up the crumbs on the table in front of us with a napkin before depositing them on the side of the plate.

'I see. I wondered if the real you was the one I saw Saturday night when doc's drugs had you dropping all those barriers.'

'I don't have barriers,' I said, struggling a little more now with keeping my polite smile in place. 'My job requires me to be a people person. I can't afford to have barriers.'

'Rubbish,' Lorcan countered. 'You can be excellent at your job, which you clearly are, and still have personal barriers. In fact, maybe it's a necessity at work, but I get the feeling there's more to it when it comes to you.'

I looked up in order for him to witness my exasperated sigh but instead found myself hooked into that deep blue gaze and for a moment it felt as if he could see straight through me. Right back to that night. Right back to the moment when my life changed forever and I was hit with so much pain that I went out the other side of it into a place where I felt completely numb. A place I'd never thought I'd return from. A place perhaps I hadn't truly come back from, not entirely. But no one had ever called me out on it before. Of course, Lorcan O'Malley was different from anyone I'd met before and that meant Lorcan O'Malley was dangerous.

'What time do we need to leave for the airport?' I asked, gathering up the neat pile of work I'd tucked beside me when the food arrived and putting it in my carry-on suitcase.

'OK, I guess that's the end of that conversation.'

I looked up from my task with what I hoped was an innocent expression. 'Oh, I'm sorry. I thought you'd finished. I just don't want us to be late.'

Lorcan raised a hand and gave a little wave to the woman behind the counter, signalling for the bill as he spoke. 'We won't be late, don't worry. I'll just settle up here and we can head off.' The worn, comfortable leather of the sofa creaked as he stood, unrolling his sleeves and deftly fastening the cuff buttons, before slipping his jacket back on. The fabric momentarily stretched across his broad back before settling into just the right position.

'Let me give you some money for the bill,' I said, reaching into my purse.

'No need. I'm here for business meetings. Had I not been we wouldn't have had to stop off here, ergo you wouldn't have had to eat here and may, in fact, be at home now knocking back some vile green juice thing instead of a hearty Irish stew. So, my meetings delayed us, therefore the onus is on me to pay.'

I let out a sigh. 'Fine.'

Lorcan looked down, as though studying me. 'You know, most people would just say, "Ah, thanks, Lorcan, that's grand. I'll get it the next time."'

'Well, I'm not most people, plus it's unlikely that there will be a next time so it would have just been simpler if we split the bill now, but, as you seem so determined, I won't object.'

A smile spread across his face and that ripple of danger

tickled my spine once more. 'You're quite the woman, Miss Madeleine.'

'Well, that sounded patronising,' I said, straightening my back as much as I could in a desperate effort to try and gain even a grain more height. It wasn't working. Lorcan still towered over me. The smile slid from his face.

'Sorry. It wasn't meant to. It was actually meant to be a compliment. Clearly not well delivered. My apologies.' His frown had deepened again and the eyes were clouded with concern. The relaxed body language he'd had a moment ago had now tensed. All of it told me that he'd meant what he'd said and I was sorry now I'd misunderstood, uncomfortable that the moment of... whatever it was – truce, perhaps – had gone. Between us we really were quite the pair. He turned to head towards the counter and I caught his hand. The surprise on his face as he looked back made me pause.

'I... erm... I...'

Bloody hell, Maddie. Spit it out.

Lorcan turned his body more, so that he was once more back in the position we'd been a moment ago, but this time a little closer. I could smell the woody notes of his aftershave. It suited him. Real. Earthy. Solid. My gaze drifted down from his face and I realised I was still holding his hand.

'Thank you for the compliment.'

The smile returned and for a second he closed his hand around mine. 'You're welcome. Apologies again for the poor delivery. I'm a little out of practice.'

'Perhaps that's something I need to add to my schedule, then.'

He tilted his head in question.

'You're supposed to be very complimentary in your speech

at the wedding about Peyton, the bridesmaids and a host of other people.'

The penny dropped. 'Ah. Yes. Good point. Schedule me in, then. Do you charge extra for private tuition?' The smile was back now and so was the tingling in my spine, except right now it was whizzing around my whole body, completely ignoring all the no-entry signs for specific areas. This wasn't good. But... oh, my goodness, it felt wonderful.

'Uh... no.' I cleared my throat. 'All part of the service,' I added. 'I would obviously want to hear your speech anyway. Make sure it's appropriate.'

The mischievous twinkle was back. 'Ah now, Madeleine, are you saying you don't trust me?'

'No, not at all. Again, just all part of the service.'

He shifted his weight and I could feel his warmth, the strong, solid bulk of him. Perhaps I did trust Lorcan. But right now, I wasn't sure I could say the same of myself.

'I'll go and pay,' he said, giving my hand a final squeeze before dropping it gently and striding across the stripped wooden floor, his Italian leather shoes making a small tap with each long step he took. I let out the breath I didn't know I'd been holding and plopped back onto the sofa, disturbing Bod, who shuffled round and climbed onto my lap. I cuddled him to me.

'Your owner is far too... everything for his own good. More to the point,' I added as Bod listened intently, 'he's far too much of everything for my own good. I need this job to go well and I definitely don't need a broken heart, so you're going to have to help me, OK?'

Bod studied me for a moment, then did a massive yawn that ended with a squeak, flopped back down on my lap and looked out of the window, fuzzy brows twitching occasionally as something interested him.

'Good,' I said, running my hand down his back. 'Glad to see you're on top of things.'

'Everything OK?' Lorcan asked, returning to the table as he tucked the folded receipt into the back of his wallet.

'Yes, thanks. All good. Just impressing Bod with my scintillating conversation.'

'He's a great dog but not always appreciative of the good things in life.' Lorcan gave a wink, lifting his pet with one large hand and grabbing his case with the other. 'Ready to go?'

'Definitely.'

More than you know...

26

Thankfully the flight home was far less eventful than the trip over and, despite me trying to insist on Lorcan taking it, I was once again sitting in the window seat, staring out at the green patchwork of Ireland as we lifted off, leaving the sunset behind us as we headed back home.

'So, what did you think of Ireland?' Lorcan asked as we sipped a whiskey each that he'd advised we must have to toast my first trip to the Emerald Isle. I'd given him a small eye-roll but agreed anyway and was now enjoying the smooth taste as it warmed its way down.

'It's very beautiful. There's definitely a magical feel about it. I think the wedding is going to be gorgeous.'

'I wasn't asking what you thought about it as a backdrop for weddings,' Lorcan said, studying me. 'I want to know what *you* think about the place – not Madeleine the wedding planner.'

'Oh... well, I suppose I think the same.'

'You suppose?'

I took another sip of whiskey and pondered the question. Every place I saw, every view, every village I drove through I saw from a work perspective and how it could feature in a wedding. I hadn't even realised I did it until Lorcan pointed it out.

'You're always looking at things through the eyes of a wedding planner, aren't you?' he prompted as I took another sip, delaying my answer as I realised that my career had, in effect, taken over my life. Everything I did, everywhere I went, everyone I met was unconsciously assessed on how they would fit into a wedding. Even every flower I smelled, I realised now, I processed only in relation to how it would look in a bouquet. It was as if I'd forgotten to appreciate things for being beautiful in and of themselves.

I turned away from the window and met Lorcan's eyes. 'It's hard not to become absorbed when it's your own business. Everything you have goes into it and with the last couple of years...'

'I get that. And you're right. It's hard for me to look at a place now without considering what I would have done, had I been the developer. At least it was. I'm better at it now. You have to take a step back from work sometimes otherwise you find that's all you have.'

'It's not all I have. I do plenty!'

He studied me before replying in that calm, knowing way. 'I was saying that from my perspective. I wasn't suggesting you don't have lots of other things in your life. In fact, you showed me your diary. There's definitely not a shortage of things in your life.'

'It's good to keep busy. Take all the opportunities you can.'

He gave his whiskey a gentle swirl and watched the golden liquid thoughtfully as it circled the glass.

'By the look on your face I can see you don't agree.'

'It's not that I don't agree as such,' he said, lifting his gaze to mine. 'It's just that it's always good to have balance.'

'I'm balanced,' I shot back. 'I'm totally balanced. Even though you seem to take such enjoyment in criticising my organisation, what you're missing is that it enables me to schedule all the balance I need into my life.'

Lorcan's eyes looked deep into mine and I felt my chest expand more than it should. I really needed to have a sit down with myself when we got home and talk about my body doing things of its own accord – especially when it came to Lorcan O'Malley. Thankfully, having a break from him once we were back in England should make that easier. Getting away for the first time in years, being drawn into the romance of this wedding and the magical spell of Ireland were a lot to deal with in one go. Once I was home and in the swing of things I'd drop back into reality. Romance was high on the list in my life – just not for me. As handsome and charming as Lorcan could be, and as much as I loved being with him, I couldn't let him into my life. He liked spontaneity, going with the flow. I needed to know exactly where the flow was, where it was going and what time it would get there. We were too different. And that was probably just as well.

'If you say so, Miss Madeleine.'

I shot him a look and downed the rest of my drink.

* * *

'You've definitely got a fan there,' Lorcan said as he opened my door and took a protesting and very yawny Bod from my hands so that I could exit the vehicle.

'So, what time shall I pick you up Wednesday?' Lorcan asked as he placed my case in the small hallway of the cottage. I'd motioned him in as I'd already seen Betty's curtain next door twitching, although inviting him in had probably made things worse. Oh, well. At least this way I got a proper goodbye snuggle from Bod.

Lorcan and I hadn't spoken much on the rest of the flight or on the drive back from Heathrow and I got the impression that, although Bod might be a fan, his master was far less so, which was why his question surprised me. I'd already said it wasn't necessary for him to come to see the dress and had assumed the matter was settled. But no, of course not. This was Lorcan O'Malley. Why would things be that easy?

'We had this discussion. You don't need to come.'

'Yes, we did, and I never agreed. I just let it go rather than wind you up. There was a vein throbbing in your forehead that was a little scary so I dropped the subject. But now I need a reply. I don't like to be late so I'll ask again. What time shall I pick you up and from where?'

I frowned up at him. This man was utterly impossible. Absolutely bloody gorgeous but impossible.

'You're racking your brains trying to think of a reason for me not to come, aren't you?'

'Of course not!'

Absolutely!

'Liar.'

'Arrrrghhhh!'

Bod looked at me and cocked his head. Lorcan chuckled.

'It's literally a quick visit for me to see the dress, check out the fabric and then I'm done. There's absolutely no need for you to be there.'

'I disagree. It's part of the wedding prep, therefore I should be there.'

'It's bad luck for the best man to see the wedding dress before the actual day and I know you wouldn't want to be responsible for risking any more of that for Patrick and Peyton, especially considering the setback they already had.' I fixed on my most understanding expression as I tilted my head back to meet his eyes.

He took a step closer, transferring the dog from my arms to his, our hands and arms brushing as he did. His voice was low when he spoke.

'Even I know that it's the groom who's not supposed to see the dress, not the best man. Besides,' he added, the voice still low and melodious and dangerously intimate in the soft glow of the small table lamp, 'you know if you don't tell me, I'll just ring the designer and meet you there.' His voice was close to my ear now and I could feel warm breath tickling it. I turned my head, ostensibly to tell him firmly that his assistance was not needed once and for all. But as I did so I found myself perilously close to his lips, and staring directly into the deep pools of blue that could transform from calm sea to thunderous sky in seconds, and for that split second my mind emptied of everything but the thought of how it would feel to have those lips on mine, on me, on my—

'I have to be at the studio at six!' I blurted in an octave higher than usual, stepping back as I did so and tripping over a heavy doorstop in the shape of a hippo. Lorcan's free arm reached out and steadied me, his brows drawing together.

'Everything OK?'

'Yes.'

He paused a beat or two, watching me. 'Message me where to pick you up from once you've checked your schedule. See you Wednesday.'

I gave him a tight smile as he began to head down the path.

'Thanks for looking after Bod today,' he said, turning back. 'I appreciate it.'

'That really was my pleasure,' I replied, this time with a genuine smile.

He gave a short nod. 'And if you ever figure out a way to think about it separate from work, I hope you find you enjoyed Ireland.'

I gave him an exasperated shake of my head and squelched the rebellious smile that was trying to curl my lips.

'Don't think I don't see that smile, either.'

Honest to God, how did he do it? It was practically dark. I swear he had Leprechaun blood flowing in his veins.

'I'm not smiling,' I called out.

'Liar,' he called back lazily as he slid into the driver's seat, a low, disturbingly sexy chuckle drifting after it on the still night before the low growl of the engine swallowed it up. With another wave, he drove off into the darkness. I closed the door before the tail lights disappeared and leant against the thick wood for a moment before heading straight up to the bathroom to take a long, hot bath. Although, as the memory of Lorcan's mouth drifted uninvited back into my thoughts, I considered that perhaps a cold shower might be more appropriate.

* * *

The following morning, after a good sleep in my own bed and my usual green smoothie for breakfast, I was feeling more like my old self and wondering what all the fuss my mind (and body) had made over Lorcan O'Malley was about. As I had suspected, it was clearly just to do with being out of my environment for the first time in ages – the magical surroundings of Ireland, a romantic castle setting and the kind, genuine people I'd met. I'd be more prepared on my next trip and on top of my game, able to deal with anything and – more importantly – anyone, without getting distracted.

'Hello?' Betty's voice called through the letterbox when I ignored my doorbell while trying to get a session of Pilates in – something else that had gone amiss at the weekend. I'd had to modify my practice thanks to my injury but at least I was getting some exercise. Well, I had been but my neighbour could be persistent, especially when she'd clearly spotted me getting out of a car, aided by a good-looking man. To be fair, it had been a long time since she'd had the opportunity to good-naturedly spy on such an occurrence, but still. I was desperately trying to get back to my schedule and Tuesday mornings from eight until nine, clearly marked, in purple, were Pilates.

'Hello-o-o-o-o-o!' she called again.

I flopped back on my mat and let out a sigh.

'Coming, Betty.'

27

I pushed myself up off the mat and went to answer the door. 'Hi,' I said, pulling it open.

'Hello, dear. I'm not disturbing you, am I?' She glanced at my workout top and shorts, then noticed the dressing on my leg. 'Oh! What happened there?'

'Come in, Betty. Nothing much, I fell over at the weekend and cut it.'

'Oh dear. Is it bad?'

'A couple of stitches. I'm having them out in a few days.'

'You poor thing,' she said. Then a faint smile began to form on her kindly features. 'Was it...?' She made a drinking gesture.

'Not at all,' I replied. 'Like I said, it was a business trip. I was working the whole time.'

'Oh. Was that nice Irish man there all the time too?' She arranged her face to look innocent but I could see the interest in her eyes flickering behind her glasses.

'Some of the time. But,' I repeated, 'it was a work trip and the only reason I was with him was because my clients want him kept up to date while they're out of the country. Lorcan offered his assistance with the area as I'm unfamiliar with it. That's all.'

My mind fluttered back to the night I'd fallen, when Lorcan had sat with me on the bed keeping me company – hardly in his remit – and I turned away from my visitor momentarily to shuffle through my post and hope that the blush I felt on my chest didn't betray me by creeping up to my face.

'Oh, that's a shame,' Betty said, sounding genuinely disappointed. 'He seemed such a nice man.'

'Looks can be deceiving, Betty.'

'Is he not, then?' she asked, bustling through to the kitchen and placing a plate of home-baked biscuits on the table as I glanced at my colour-coded schedule for the day tacked to the fridge. The weekend had ended up entirely unscheduled but today at least I hoped I'd be able to get back into my normal pattern.

'He's...' I thought of how many times Lorcan had wound me up over the weekend, but I also remembered his kindness on the plane, his concern when he realised I'd hurt myself, and his devotion to his little dog. I tried not to remember the lingering woody scent of his aftershave when he was close to me, his laugh that wrapped itself around me like a cosy blanket, and the way his warm breath had tickled my ear when he spoke close to it, the deep tones sending waves throughout my body.

'He's what, dear?' Betty asked, studying me with a casual air. From the outside, she looked like a kindly, older lady who baked and always checked up on others in the village, especially if they hadn't been seen for a few days. But Betty was as sharp as a new pin.

'Complicated.'

'I see. Perhaps he has a reason to be complicated.'

'I'm sure he does. But it's not part of my job to find out so...'

I turned up my palms and smiled, hoping that was an end to the discussion.

'Not everything is about work, you know, love.'

'Right now it is, Betty. My business took a massive hit during the pandemic and I need to save it, so the last thing I have time for in my life right now is complicated men. Besides, Lorcan and I are far too different. We do, and would, drive each other round the bend inside a week.'

'Sometimes those are the best ones...' Betty replied, her eyes twinkling.

'No, Betty,' I said, laughing. 'Definitely not now and most definitely not this man.'

'Well now, that's a shame. You looked ever so good together and he's very handsome.'

'Sometimes those are the worst ones,' I said, turning her words back on her and she shook her head, laughing.

'What are we going to do with you?'

'Nothing, but thank you for the offer. Really, I'm perfectly happy as I am.'

My neighbour gave me a look that disagreed. 'I see Tom was here, checking on the place at the weekend.'

'Yes. I have a slight problem with the roof.'

'He told me it was leaking like a sieve.'

Thanks, Tom.

'I'm working on getting it fixed.'

'Tom said he'd told you he'd happily get it done for you, and that you could pay him later.'

I really needed to have words with Tom about how much of my business he discussed with the rest of the village. The fact that he'd told the neighbours this, obviously in all innocence, only backed up what I'd said to Lorcan about gossip. If Tom went around happily telling villagers that he'd done my roof 'on credit', firstly, everyone would know my financial situation and secondly, it would undoubtedly cause at least a few to wonder if he was receiving payment in other ways. Which was why I was sticking to my original sensible plan of praying to any god who would listen – I wasn't fussy – for dry weather until Peyton's big wedding and I could begin to get my finances back on track, and my roof back to being weathertight.

'Yes, I know. It's very kind of him, but I don't like to be beholden to anyone and it's not fair. He's a small business too so it's hardly likely he's got plenty of money sat around in the bank to be doing favours to people.'

'Yes, but we both know you're not just any old people when it comes to Tom, don't we?'

'No, Betty, we don't,' I replied in a definitive tone, which she merely waved away.

'Oh, pssh. He's had a crush on you since the day you moved in. You must have noticed.'

I thought back to what Lorcan had said about Tom having a 'thing' for me. The truth was, I hadn't noticed. I was always too busy to notice.

'You really hadn't, had you?' Betty read my face.

'There's nothing to notice. Anyway, isn't he living with someone? Dark hair, a hairdresser or something?'

'They broke up about a year ago, love.'

'Oh...'

'He was asking what I knew about your Irishman.'

'Well, you can start by telling him he's *not* my Irishman.'

'Yet.'

'Ever!' I turned back to her. 'What did you say?'

'Not much I could say, dear. Just that he'd been here once before when I popped round and seemed very nice. Lovely manners.'

'He said the village looked like something out of *Midsomer Murders* when he first got here, so not that polite actually.'

'Oh, love, you know everyone says that.'

'Yes, but it was the way he said it.' I flapped my hands. 'Anyway, it doesn't matter. None of it is relevant. Thank you for the biscuits, Betty. You really shouldn't.'

'Nonsense. You know I enjoy it. Now, I'll get out of your way. I'm sure you have a ton of things to do as usual.' She smiled as she turned, and I didn't miss the glance she gave to my weekly planner. 'You should take some time off occasionally,' she said, making her way back to the front door.

'Oh, that's not just work. That's personal stuff too. See? I have plenty of time off.'

'It's all very... regimented though, isn't it, love?'

'Best way to get everything you want done is to plan it.'

Betty paused on the doorstep for a moment before reaching out and taking my hand. 'The thing is, love, you can't always plan. Sometimes life just happens.'

I was the last person who needed to be told this although I couldn't tell Betty that, as it would mean unpacking a whole lot of things I wasn't prepared to. Not now and likely not ever. When things happened, you found ways to cope. This was my way of coping, which was certainly a healthier option than my initial choices had been. And as much as I appreciated my neighbour's concern, I needed to get back onto today's schedule. Betty sensed my reluctance to agree so merely smiled, gave my hand a couple of pats and bustled off down the path. I waved as she turned to close the gate, before lifting my eyes to the sky. The early sunshine was gradually being covered by a thin layer of high cloud. Good, that was weather I, and my roof, could deal with.

'Just a bit longer,' I said quietly to the sky. 'Please?' I looked back to find the postman standing in front of me, his eyes going from me to the sky, and back to me again.

'All right?'

I cleared my throat. 'Erm. Yep. Great, thanks. How are you?'

'All right...' He looked back up at the sky. 'Who you talking to?'

'The weather.' In for a penny, in for a pound.

'Right.' He nodded before handing me today's mail and turning round and heading back out of my gate. I watched as he did so. Where once there had been an audible and unmissable squeak as the gate opened and closed, there was now silence, which was how I'd got caught standing out in my front garden talking to the sky. The squeak, although irritating at times, I had left purposely, partly as a pre-warning of visitors but also a security alert. I lived alone and it occurred to me keeping the noise might not be the worst idea. I assumed that Tom, on a check of the house after the downpour we'd apparently had, according to a message he'd sent while I was away, had taken it upon himself to 'fix' it. I turned back into the house and began closing the door.

'Hi, Maddie.'

I jumped for the second time and, turning, found Tom standing there, having also come through the now silent gate.

'Tom. Hi.'

'I, err, I fixed your gate.' He pointed almost shyly to it and I didn't have the heart to say that actually I was kind of cross about it.

'Yes. I noticed. That really wasn't necessary though.'

'No problem. How was your weekend away?'

'Busy,' I said. 'There's a lot of planning to do for this wedding. It's a big event and I need to make sure everything is absolutely perfect.'

'So the guy you were with is the one getting married? I noticed his accent.'

'No. He's the best man.'

'Looks like he got the best job, accompanying you,' Tom said, before flushing the same red as the late rose blooming in the border next to him.

Oh, crikey. Betty – and Lorcan – were right! Tom was sweet but not my type. Not that I really had a type or even the time to decide on a type. But I didn't want to hurt his feelings or pretend I was interested when I wasn't.

'Somehow I don't think he'd agree with you. Anyway, what can I do for you?'

'Nothing. I was just passing and knew you were back today so thought I'd, you know, say hello.'

'Well, that's a coincidence, I was just doing the same thing myself.' Lorcan's deep, sing-song tones drifted in the still air as he came through the gate, ducking under the arch where a rosy pink, late-blooming clematis was just hanging on before the first of the frosts blackened it. 'Tom, isn't it?' He held out his hand and Tom shook it, shooting a glance at me as he did so but all he'd have seen there was total bewilderment. What the hell was Lorcan doing here? 'Nice to see you again.'

Tom nodded, and offered up a smile. 'Well, I'd better be heading off.'

'Oh, OK. Thanks again for keeping an eye on the house, and for fixing the gate, of course.'

He smiled, wider this time. 'Any time,' he said, before nodding once at Lorcan and heading back out of the garden and on into the village.

'Got your own personal handyman now, have you?' Lorcan grinned.

'No. He oiled the gate and frankly,' I said, dropping my voice, 'I'd prefer if he hadn't. I left it squeaky for a reason.'

'Advance alert system?'

'Yes!' I said, turning to Lorcan. 'Exactly.'

'He means well, I'm sure.'

'He does. I know. And I'm aware I sound very ungrateful. I just prefer to do things myself if I can.'

'Yeah. I know. We spent the weekend together, remember?'

'Shooosh!' I said, flapping my hands at him and shooing him into the house before closing the door behind us. 'We did not spend the weekend together.'

'I'm not suggesting anything,' he replied.

'OK, fine but it sounds wrong when you say it like that.'

'Wrong?'

'Yes. Like we "spent" the weekend together,' I explained, dipping my fingers into air quotes.

'And that would be wrong?' He raised one eyebrow and a smile drifted around his lips.

I had a feeling that spending a weekend with Lorcan O'Malley would be the very opposite of wrong. Which was exactly why I stuck to my guns now.

'Yes. Very. Incredibly.'

'I'm wounded.'

'Oh, you are not. I drive you up the wall just as much as you do me.'

He made a head gesture that was a maybe yes, maybe no, as he stepped through to the kitchen and studied the schedule on my fridge. 'How on earth do you function like this?' He tapped the paper.

'Very well. When people don't interrupt.' I gave him a meaningful glance.

'It's lovely to see you, too.'

I raised an eyebrow. 'What are you doing here?'

'Just passing.'

'Really.'

'Yep,' Lorcan said through a mouthful of one of the biscuits he'd helped himself to. 'Are these Betty's? They're amazing.'

'How do you know they aren't mine?' I asked.

Lorcan pointed his second biscuit at the fridge door. 'No baking scheduled.' He moved across to take a closer look. 'What are you supposed to be doing this morning? Let's see. Hmm,' he said, turning his head briefly, 'I see chatting up young Tom wasn't in the schedule. Interesting.'

'You think you're so funny.' I rolled my eyes and moved across the kitchen to stand in front of my planner. Unfortunately, this placed me closer to Lorcan than I'd anticipated and he looked, and smelled, just as good as I remembered.

'You didn't answer my question.'

'Yes, I did. Just passing.'

'Why on earth would you be just passing here?' I asked, disbelief radiating out in waves as I crossed my arms in front of my chest.

Lorcan shifted his weight and tilted his head down a little more, meeting my eyes. 'I hate to pop any balloons, but, unlike Tom, I've no hidden agenda. The only reason I'm here is...' his eyes scanned my face as he took a breath, his broad chest expanding and tightening against the pale blue shirt he wore, the collar open at the neck '... work.' He turned away and I felt the breath I'd been holding escape. He was such an arse. I'd pop his bloody balloons if he wasn't careful.

28

'What possible work reason would you have in the village? It's fine just as it is. We certainly don't need people like you coming in and sticking new houses or blocks of flats on any tiny piece of ground you can get your mitts on!'

'Woah!' Lorcan held up the shovels he called hands. 'Little protective of the village there, are we?'

'Yes, I am. And I'm not ashamed of it. So if that's your plan... oh, no, it's the schoolhouse, isn't it? They've been trying to flatten that and build on the land for years. Is that why you're here?'

'Yes.'

The schoolhouse was the most beautiful Victorian building at the other end of the village, backing out onto sweeping countryside. There was an orchard within its grounds too but that was now really just an overgrown thicket. I'd fallen in love with the place the day I'd taken my first walk around the village. Several people had tried to buy it over the years but it needed a lot of work. It hadn't been touched since it was built so would literally need a new everything to make it a comfortable home.

It was a big job and planning departments were more inclined to grant permission for multiple houses these days, especially with the income local government would then get from taxes and utilities, et cetera.

'A group of us have been trying to get it granted listed status so it can't be flattened but we didn't have any luck. So I presume now we're too late. Well, Betty might think you're a nice man now but once she hears you're tearing that down to build square boxes that won't blend in with the village at all, she'll soon be changing her mind.'

Lorcan smiled. 'Betty thinks I'm a nice man?'

'Yes. She's only met you briefly. Easy mistake to make.'

'Ouch. By the way, remind me at what point I said I'm tearing the schoolhouse down and replacing it with modern housing?'

'I asked if you were here about the schoolhouse and the fact people want to flatten it. You said you were.'

'I am. But I don't agree with those plans. I think the place should be restored. Converted for modern living, but sympathetically. I agree with you that it would be a shame for it to be lost but the longer it's left in its current state, the more likely it is that modern housing will take its place. Which is why I bought it. I'm headed over to the local solicitor shortly to sign the papers. Hence, as much as I would like to admit that I drove all the way out here just to see you, if that would bring a smile to your face, I really am here for work.'

'You're buying it? And saving it?' I grabbed his arm.

'I am.'

'Lorcan! That's amazing!'

'Well, I'd rather you'd smiled like that just to see me for no reason, but as you don't smile nearly enough, I'm going to take this as a close second.' His own smile softened his face as he chuckled.

'I smile plenty, thank you.'

'No, darlin', you don't, which is a great shame as when you do, it's a beautiful one.' I stared at him and he gave a tiny shake of his head, a grin sweeping across his face. 'And as much as I'd like to find out why you don't smile more often, I better get going for this meeting.'

'Go, go!' I said, almost bundling him towards the door. 'Don't you dare lose the deal now.'

Lorcan turned and stopped as he got to the door. My own momentum took a moment to catch up and I slammed into his broad chest and immediately halted.

'Whoops. You all right?' he asked, gently wrapping his hands around my upper arms and standing me back a couple of steps.

'Fine, fine. Sorry. But you mustn't be late.'

'I won't be,' he said, still not moving. 'But I meant what I said about finding out why you hide that beautiful smile.'

'You've got all the blarney, haven't you?' I said, laughing. 'Even Fiadh said you always had the right lines.'

'That she did. But sometimes the right lines are just the right lines. It doesn't mean they're not sincere.'

Bodily, I turned him around and then opened the door. 'If you mess this up, I will never forgive you and I will also persuade Peyton that all the best men this season are wearing bottomless chaps.'

'That's OK. My arse is one of my finest attributes, so I've been told.'

To be fair, he had a point. He did have a great bum. Of course he did.

'Seriously, you'd have an answer for the devil if he popped up in front of you.'

Stepping out onto the doorstep, Lorcan turned around, laughing now. 'My mam said that to me many a time when I was growing up.'

'And probably whenever she sees you now too.'

'Possibly,' he replied, grinning now and looking far too handsome for my own good. 'She'd love you.'

I didn't know what to say as a swirl of emotion engulfed me at his words, so I gave a brief smile and made a point of looking at my smart watch to check a notification. Lorcan had a habit of being able to read me and I didn't want to afford him that chance right now. Or see the tears threatening in my eyes as I thought how much my own mum would have loved him too.

'I'd better go,' Lorcan said, his own face more serious now. 'Message me where to pick you up tomorrow for the designer.'

I nodded – I clearly wasn't going to win on that front. Still it would only be for half an hour at the most as Izzy, Rob and I were going out to dinner afterwards.

Lorcan turned to leave, then quickly faced me again. 'Did I say something wrong?' he asked. 'More than usual, I mean,' he added, with a self-deprecating one-shouldered shrug.

'No,' I said, reaching out and laying my hand on his forearm, feeling the solidity of it, the corded muscles under my fingertips. 'Really.'

His brow remained creased as his gaze dropped to my hand and he placed his own over it. 'I saw your face, Maddie. If I caused that,' he said, 'I'm sorry.'

I squeezed his arm. 'I promise you didn't. Thank you.'

His gaze lifted and met mine. 'It's true though. You're a complete pain in the arse but I think Ma would like that.'

'I'm only a pain in your arse. Everyone else thinks I'm fabu-lous,' I teased.

'Is that so?'

'Of course.'

'Must just be me, then.'

'Must be.'

'I'll see you tomorrow.' He glanced down. 'And look after that leg.'

'I promise. Now go and save our schoolhouse before I go off you again.'

Lorcan gently squeezed a couple of my fingers then turned and headed down the path, through the now silent gate, and strode off towards the centre of the village and the solicitor's office.

* * *

The rest of the day thankfully stuck more on schedule and by the appointed time that night I'd had a twenty-five-minute bath and was in bed, ready for my half-hour of reading before turning out the light. I was just about to put my phone into flight mode when a message notification came in, a little red number one showing on my WhatsApp icon. Opening the app, I saw that it was from Lorcan.

Sorry to disturb you. I know from your schedule you're tucked up in bed now with your book...

There was a winky face after this and then one with its tongue poking out. Smart arse.

Wanted to let you know that the sale has all gone through for the schoolhouse. I'm officially the new owner. (Don't worry, I won't be there too often during the renovation).

Another winky face.

I can tell you more tomorrow when I see you. See you at 5.55 p.m. outside the studio x

Smiling that the beautiful building and its grounds were saved, and also that Lorcan had let me know, I was about to set the phone down – his message hadn't seemed to need a reply – when I saw that he was once again typing. I waited, watching the screen.

Ps, I really am sorry if I said something that upset you earlier. Sleep well x

OK, so here was a dilemma. I didn't feel that I was yet at the 'send a hug' stage with Lorcan, but would saying nothing seem rude? And the words 'I'm fine' could be interpreted in so many ways, that could come across wrong too. Oh, for goodness' sake...

'Hi.' Lorcan answered the video call, surprise showing on his face.

'Hi. Sorry, I hope I'm not interrupting anything.'

'Not at all,' he replied, settling back into his sofa (a warm, rich red velvet number rather than the cold black bachelor leather I'd imagined). 'This is a nice surprise.'

I paused, trying to decide whether he meant it or whether it was another of his wind-ups.

'Wow.' His laugh was deep, rich and relaxed. 'I really have done a number on you, haven't I? I mean it. It is a nice surprise.'

'Oh. Right. Well, thank you.'

He smiled.

'I just wanted to let you know that I'm fine. I mean, earlier. You didn't upset me. And things don't always come out as you mean them on text. So... yep. Fine.'

God. I felt as if I was about thirteen again.

'Thank you for calling.'

He really did have the sexiest voice. The soft accent made the deep, gentle tone so melodic and I knew from experience that, up close, it only got better.

'You OK?' His frown deepened.

'Me? Yep. Fine. Good. Thanks.'

Oh, Christ. Calling had been a bad idea. Note to self, stick to text next time and deal with any consequences later.

'So, anyway, that was it really.'

Lorcan glanced at his watch. 'Still got twenty-five minutes reading time left.'

'Interesting that you were able to absorb so much of my schedule in a short time.'

'Not as green as I'm cabbage looking,' he replied, giving me one of those winks. 'I'd better let you go anyway so you can get your reading in.'

'Oh... yes. Right.'

Lorcan gave a brief smile, lifted his hand in goodbye and hung up. I switched the phone onto flight mode, and picked up my book. As I opened it to the correct page, a flicker of thought passed through my mind that it might have been nice not to have had my life scheduled so rigorously this evening, that talking a little longer with Lorcan, relaxed and calm, might have been more enjoyable. I let out an irritated sigh and wriggled in the bed to get comfy. Of course that wasn't the case! I was exactly where I should be, at exactly the right time doing exactly what I should be doing. So if that was the case, why did I wish Lorcan hadn't been as respectful – for once – of my planning and carried on chatting?

After ten minutes of reading my book and not taking in one word, I closed it a little more forcefully than required, switched off the light and buried down under the duvet. I desperately needed this wedding job, but both the location and the best man were having some very strange and unexpected effects on me. The sooner this was all done, the better it would be. Then I could not only get my roof fixed but I could go back to my normal routine and know for certain, as I had for years, that this was the best way to live my life. Closing my eyes, I began counting sheep, but that only brought with it images of rolling, lush green fields and tall, dark, handsome Irishmen.

Slamming back the cover, I grabbed my phone, found a true crime podcast, switched it on and eventually drifted off to sleep.

29

'He's yummy!' Izzy whispered, taking advantage of the fact that Rob had just started chatting to Lorcan about rugby and found a willing listener. 'Is he single? And if so, why aren't you seeing him?' Her eyes sparkled with mischief and delight as we pretended to be looking through some new stock.

'Yes, he is. And because he's a member of the wedding party. Also, a lot of the time we drive each other bananas.'

Izzy waved her hand. 'That's nothing. Remember how Rob and I got together and we're still happy as anything.'

'Yes, but it's not the same.'

'Why not?'

'It... just isn't.'

'Oh. So long as you have a good, solid reason,' she replied, grinning, and I shook my head, unable to stop myself being swept up in her giggles.

'Have you seen everything you need to here?' Izzy asked.

'Yes, that's all great, thanks for staying on a bit later. Peyton's dress is absolutely beautiful. I mean, you made it so it would be, but seeing it in real life is just so much better. She's going to look amazing. You're so talented.'

'Thanks, hon. Peyton had some great ideas, which was helpful.'

'She's on this mad diet from her nutritionist at the moment. Did she mention it?'

'Yeah,' Izzy said, rolling her eyes a little. 'I told her she already looks perfect and I can make alterations if needs be.'

'She wouldn't even risk trying any cake. Fair enough, the baker turned out to be in Ireland but still. Lorcan and I ended up having to suffer the calories.'

Izzy looked at me. 'You and Lorcan went to Ireland... together.'

'Not like that,' I whispered, hastily, widening my eyes in warning.

She shot him a look. 'Shame.'

'You ready, Iz?' Rob called from across the studio.

'Yep, just let me get my bag,' she said, tapping across the wooden floor in her adored Louboutins. Izzy and I shared an appreciation for beautiful shoes, which had also helped our friendship, although not necessarily our bank balances.

'Got it,' she said, hefting a massive tote onto her shoulder, which Rob immediately took from her and slung up onto his own. 'Bloody hell, have you got a sewing machine in here?'

'Stop whingeing,' she said, reaching up on tiptoe to kiss him. 'And thank you.'

'You're welcome,' he returned, looking at her just as adoringly as when they had married, as though she were the only person in the room. 'I managed to get the restaurant to do a table for four rather than three, now that Lorcan's coming.'

'Oh, fab!' Izzy grinned at him before swinging her gaze to me.

Lorcan's coming?

* * *

'I did try to say no,' he explained as we drove back towards my cottage later. 'I knew you'd be less than thrilled if I came.'

'It wasn't that. I mean, that's not why I didn't invite you.' My words were tumbling out faster than my brain could organise them. 'Izzy suggested dinner before I knew you were coming and then I thought if I asked if you wanted to come to dinner, you might think it was unprofessional of me, or that I was coming on to you, either of which would be awkward. And frankly, I thought the last place you'd want to be sat this evening was at dinner with me again, after having had to chauffeur me around the entire weekend, so I didn't want to make you feel awkward by having to find a polite way to say no thanks.'

'Truth?'

I nibbled my nail. 'OK?'

'It *was* kind of awkward when Rob mentioned it was a shame I wasn't coming to dinner. He was already off dialling the restaurant before I could say anything.'

'I'm sorry.'

'It's fine. I guess I just felt uncomfortable that, as you said, my company was forced on you once again and this time with your friends. They're really good people, by the way. I like them.'

'They are. Really lovely. He adores her so much. Well, obviously she does him but when he looks at her...'

'Yep. He'd do anything for her. That's pretty obvious.'

'Yes. And I'm sorry I didn't mention it earlier. I suppose part of me didn't want Izzy and Rob thinking anything was going on.'

'Wow, I'm that bad.' It was a statement rather than a question, which he spoke with a chuckle.

'No, it's not that. It's just…'

Lorcan turned his head as we waited at a red light.

'Just?'

A beep from behind us caused Lorcan to glance in the rearview mirror, saving me momentarily from answering. Silence drifted down like a blanket over the interior of the car.

'I'm waiting for the "it's not you, it's me",' he said, glancing briefly across. In the low-lit intimacy of the car's luxurious interior I could hear the smile in his voice.

'Oh, no. It's definitely you.'

His laughter wrapped itself around me and I felt myself relax into the soft leather of the car seat as we continued in the darkness.

* * *

The leaves on the village green's trees burned orange and gold before falling, leaving the bare branches to fare against the winter chill. I'd finally seen the sense in Tom's suggestion of fixing my roof before the winter set in and scraped together a deposit for him to satisfy my reservations. I'd been pleased to see him out a couple of times walking with a petite blonde woman, his arm wrapped around her waist, both of them bundled up against the weather.

'Looks like you hesitated too long with old Tom,' Lorcan had teased as he'd entered my cottage one frosty morning, both of us waving to the couple as he came in.

'They look sweet together,' I'd replied, pleased to see that

Tom had found someone. He was a good man and deserved his affections returned.

'They do that,' Lorcan had replied, before heading through to my kitchen to see if Betty had delivered any more goodies recently. Between Lorcan's unexpectedly regular company, and a rapidly filling work diary, the weeks passed quickly until the big day was almost upon us.

* * *

'Oh my God! I can't believe it's nearly here!' Peyton squealed in a tone so high I was sure several local dogs were currently looking around with confused expressions.

'Want to take it down a notch, there, Pey?' Lorcan asked as Bod looked up, slightly stunned.

'Oh! Oh, yes, sorry, Bod, sweetie,' she said, petting the little dog and making baby noises at him, telling him how cute he was, which Bod was making the most of.

'She's allowed to be excited about her wedding day, Lorcan,' I pointed out as we sat in my garden studio and ran through the list for the final time, double and triple-checking.

'I agree. But she's not allowed to deafen my dog.'

'He wouldn't be deafened if you hadn't brought him,' Patrick pointed out.

'He's officially part of the wedding planning team. See?' Lorcan held the little dog up to show that he was currently sporting a deep-wine-coloured tee shirt that said 'wedding crew' to coordinate with the wedding colours. Over dinner, Izzy had found out about Bod and within days had whizzed up a little tee shirt for him and sent it over. To be honest, when I'd presented it to Lorcan, I'd expected a sniff of derision, but his reaction had been entirely the opposite and he'd immediately sent Izzy flowers – from Bod – as a thank you and sent Rob a photo of the dog modelling his wife's latest creation, knowing he'd show Izzy. The two men had bonded over rugby during our dinner out and were now firm friends.

Having known him for a while now, I'd thought I'd have had Lorcan O'Malley all figured out, but he continued to surprise me. Although there was still one subject we butted heads on and that was the whole wedding/marriage thing. There seemed no changing his mind on that and as much as I found him attractive – even if it hadn't been for the whole 'no mixing business with pleasure' thing – that was a deal breaker. Stealing a glance at his profile, the hard biceps peeking from the tee shirt he wore, perhaps that was just as well. I already knew from his friends Lorcan was a heartbreaker. But I hadn't forgotten about the strange exchange with the woman who'd entered the pub just as we were leaving. There was definitely history there. He'd not spoken about it, despite the fact we'd been spending more and more time together. He'd been nothing but helpful and determined to help his friends have the wedding of their dreams and, despite our initial ability to rub each other up the wrong way, we seemed to have adjusted. Not that he didn't still give me a hard time about the fact I planned everything, but I was better at ignoring his digs now or providing pithy comebacks if I was feeling in the mood.

'So, your flights are all booked?' Peyton asked me for the fourth time.

'Babe, she's already confirmed that,' Patrick said, taking her hand and coaxing her to sit down. 'Stop worrying.'

'I'm not worried,' she said. 'I know Maddie has everything totally under control.'

'The only person I haven't met yet is the photographer,' I pointed out. 'Ordinarily I'd have liked to have gone over things with them by now. I've made a few attempts at getting in touch with him, but he's not called me back. Would you mind speaking to him and asking him to ring me so that we can set up a meeting? I'd really like a chat with him and to do a walk-through at the venue before the day itself so that I know exactly what the plan is.'

To be honest, the lack of communication and cooperation from the photographer was the one thing about this wedding that had me nervous. I didn't really do nerves. I couldn't afford to in my job. I was there to smooth things over for everyone else, which I was able to do because I knew exactly what and when everything was happening. Usually. But I'd never worked with this photographer. I wasn't sure he was even a professional photographer, which was fine. I'd seen amazing moments captured in beautiful shots by amateurs over the years, but I did need communication from him. Ordinarily I'd have spoken to Peyton about considering having a back-up – although finding one at this late notice would be a challenge, but I would manage. The situation, however, was proving more tricky as Peyton was adamant about using this guy. Apparently she'd known him since college and thought it would be lovely to have a photographer she knew and trusted and felt she'd be more relaxed for the photos that way. All that was great – but I had my reservations.

'You're worried about the photographer, aren't you?' Lorcan said as I turned back from waving the bride and groom-to-be off.

'Stop reading my mind. You know it unnerves me.'

He shrugged. 'I'd say sorry but then I'd be lying. It amuses me.'

'Such a child,' I said, moving him out of the way to get to my filing cabinet. 'But yes, I am. I've normally got all this locked down by now but I haven't even been able to speak to the man yet.'

'I'm sure Peyton will get onto it now.'

'I've mentioned it to her a few times already and he's still not made contact. It's odd, not to mention unprofessional.'

'Maybe he's a bit of a prima donna and thinks – don't take this the wrong way – that he doesn't need a wedding planner poking her nose into his "art".' He did the actions. 'Remember this is just a theory and not what I think,' he said, eyeing the letter opener glinting under the lamplight on my desk. 'Just to be clear.'

'Don't worry, I'm not going to stab you,' I said, following his eye line. 'I don't have time to clear up the blood.'

'Right. I'll just keep an eye on any of my drinks tasting a little funny, then.'

'Oh, sweet boy. You don't really think I'd use anything you could actually taste, do you? Bless you. So naïve,' I said, giving a shake of my head. Lorcan's deep chuckle made me smile as I tidied up my desk, making sure everything was in place to start again tomorrow morning. Peyton's wedding was going to take all my time once I was in Ireland – ordinarily I'd only go for a day, perhaps two for big weddings, but Peyton had a week-long hen night booked in New York, meaning she wouldn't be getting to Ireland until shortly before the wedding. That meant it was up to me to make sure everything was perfect. Now that Calum had found out there were some well-known faces going to be at the wedding, he'd had a flutter of nerves, which Lorcan had calmed by saying I'd be there several days prior to go through everything with him.

'Hungry?' the deep lilting voice broke into my thoughts.

I glanced up at the dove-grey wall clock, highlighted against the white walls of the studio.

'Crikey, is that the time?' Lorcan had fed Bod some time ago but I'd been on a call and hadn't really taken note of the hour. The dog was happily snuggled up in his bed now between the sofa and the desk, snoozing away, one ear flopped over the edge of the fabric. 'You must be starving. Why didn't you say something ages ago? You don't have to stay anyway, you know. Half of this stuff is for other clients and if anything comes up with our wedding, I can always call you.'

Lorcan's eyes were fixed on mine and I frowned for a second before my brain hit 'replay'.

30

'Not *our* wedding, obviously! I didn't mean...' I flapped a hand that roughly encompassed the two of us. 'I just meant... you know, the one we're... Patrick's wedding.'

Lorcan was still looking at me.

'What?'

'I think that's the first time I've ever seen you get flustered.'

'I wasn't flustered. I'm not flustered. Why on earth would I be?' I said, a trickle of laughter following the words that, even to my ears, sounded totally awkward and fake.

'You know you're not making it better, right?'

'I have no idea what you're talking about,' I replied, hoping to God that my foundation was strong enough to cover the blush I knew was lighting up my cheeks right now. 'So, anyway. I'm sure you're hungry so you should probably leave and get yourself some dinner.'

'And what are you going to do?'

'I have a bit more to do here and then I have something in the fridge.'

'Don't tell me, you have a Monday to Sunday pile of tubs

that you prepared in advance.' The deep, annoyingly sensuous laugh filled the small, low-lit studio.

I remained silent and Lorcan's laugh suddenly died away. 'Oh, God, you do, don't you?'

'As I said,' concentrating on a task in front of me without really taking it in, 'you ought to go and get yourself some food before it gets too much later and you go past it.'

'I rarely go past it.'

'Even so.'

I turned in my chair to file something in the low cabinet behind me and when I turned back, Lorcan was standing in front of the desk. My backside practically left the chair. 'Jesus!' I said, my hand flying to my chest. 'Your dog makes more noise moving than you. You scared the life out of me.'

'Sorry.' He screwed up his face in a grimace.

'It's fine. We just need to fit you with a bell or something. Are you off, then?'

'Sorry,' he repeated.

'I said—'

'No, I mean I'm sorry about what I said about the meal-organisation thing. There's nothing wrong with that. It's actually a good idea, especially when you're working long days.'

I tilted my head back to meet his eyes, tucking an errant curl behind my ear as I did so. 'Lorcan, it's fine. I know you and I work and think completely differently and that's OK. You feel I over-plan and schedule my life too much and that's your prerogative. I do what works for me and you do what works for you. It doesn't really bother me what other people think.'

'Is that so?'

'Yep.'

'So if you're so unaffected by other people's opinions, why did you go the same shade as those roses?' he asked, pointing to the scarlet arrangement I'd set in a crystal vase on my desk. 'Secret admirer?'

Clearly, I needed to add 'find a better foundation' to my to-do list for tomorrow.

'I did not. It's just the light in here and your propensity to try and wind me up, which I'm afraid to say you've failed to do. And no, they're not. Fiadh sent them as a thank you for using them for the wedding.'

Lorcan did that sexy half-smile, clearly remaining unconvinced. 'If you say so.'

'Think whatever you like,' I said, shrugging my shoulders and putting a hand up to rub my neck as the action alerted me to a tightness in my left shoulder.

'Come on,' Lorcan said. 'Give it a rest now. You're tired and hungry and you've been up since five-thirty this morning.'

'How do you know what time I got up?'

He pointed to the calendar on my wall, a copy of the one on my fridge.

'You're far too nosy for your own good, you know that, don't you?'

'I've had worse said about me. So? Dinner?'

'Yes. Go, go,' I said, shooing him out as I returned to my task.

'I meant together,' he said, moving around behind me, his hand creeping towards the power button on my computer.

'Touch that before I've saved my document and that letter opener is coming your way, sod the blood.'

Lorcan's hand shot back into his pocket but soft laughter filled my ears and the faint scent of aftershave wrapped itself around my senses. There was never enough to overpower, but just enough to make you want to get closer and—

'You know what? You're absolutely right. I definitely need

food,' I said, hitting save and then shutting down my screen. 'I think I'm feeling a bit light-headed.'

'Are you?' he asked, moving my office chair round gently so that I was facing him. Oh, great. Well, that rather backfired. Now sight has joined its mates, scent and hearing, in the game of 'let's see how attractive we can make this entirely inappropriate man appear to Maddie today'.

'Look at me.' His words were gentle and held a note of solicitude, the coal-black brows knitting together as he studied me. What was it about that accent? I'd never really thought I'd been one to be affected by accents before. Of course, I would find out to the contrary at the most inconvenient time possible.

'Lorcan, I'm fine, really,' I said. 'I'm sure, as you say, I just need some food.'

His hand caught mine, the long, strong fingers gently wrapping around my wrist.

'Your hands are clammy.'

'Maybe don't lead with that on your next date.'

He flicked a glance to me, amusement in the blue eyes as they focused on mine. I was steaming ahead with four of the senses and the only one left now was taste... Oh, hell.

'Your pulse is racing.'

You don't say...

'We need to get some food in you. What's in that dinner box for tonight?'

I glanced at the calendar. The last few weeks had been a whirlwind and half the time I didn't know what day it was.

'It's Friday,' Lorcan said, having worked out why I'd paused.

'Yes. Right. So that would be chicken salad.'

He looked up from where he'd been gathering my things for me.

'For your information, it's curry tomorrow, and shepherd's

pie the day after that.' I drew myself up as I stood, glad that my leg had now healed, albeit having left a bit of a scar, but at least I was once again able to wear my beloved heels and thereby gain a bit of height when I needed it. 'Go on. Have a good laugh.'

'I'm not laughing.'

And, despite my expectations, he wasn't.

'Why not?' I asked, suspicious now.

He shrugged. 'It's what works for you. I don't necessarily think it's a great idea, having everything planned out to that extent, but frankly you're in no state to get into an argument with me about it right now.'

He did have a point and, from the twinkle in his eyes, he knew I knew.

'I'd still win though, if I could be bothered.'

'Of course,' he conceded, without meaning a word of it. 'Bod, come on. We're heading inside.' Bod, having moments before been in a deep sleep, was up, stretched and waiting by the door within seconds.

* * *

About forty minutes later, the last vestiges of the pizza that Lorcan had ordered were sitting in the box with the main bulk of it, plus the cheesy garlic bread that we apparently had to have as it was on offer, now resident in our full stomachs.

'Don't you feel better now?'

'I definitely feel fuller now, that's for sure. Not to mention fatter.' I prodded my tummy and Lorcan rolled his eyes.

'It's because you're sitting down. You're fine, woman.'

'I think we can agree that pizza has more calories than the chicken salad I had planned. Honestly, every time I'm with you,

you mess up all my careful organisation. The sooner this wedding is done, the better, I think.'

Lorcan slid a glance across to me. 'You know, a lesser man could take great offence at such a comment.'

'And yet I know your ego can take that and more.'

'Ah, you do now, do you?'

'I do,' I said, preparing to push myself up from the sofa where he'd led me to from the garden, and insisted I sit while he made arrangements for food delivery, asking my preferences on toppings, et cetera. It was so long since I'd ordered pizza, my mind had gone a bit blank. I'd fallen into the eat-super-healthy routine some years back and I did, for the most part, enjoy it, but, now that I considered it, perhaps there was a little wiggle room for the odd treat now and then. I hadn't enjoyed a meal as much as that pizza since... well, since Brighid's cooking back at the pub in Ballalee. I wasn't about to abandon all my good intentions but perhaps I could mix things up a bit more. I could still make my lunch and dinners in advance, but perhaps not label them for each day. I rolled that thought around my brain and found that it didn't actually hurtle about in panic, bouncing off my skull as I'd initially feared. Interesting.

'You know you're going to miss me when this is all over.'

'Is that right?'

'Why can't you just admit it?'

'Perhaps because it's not true?'

'See, now I know you're definitely fibbing because you've got that cute little blush going on, just here.' He tapped the top of his unfairly chiselled cheekbones and raised one dark brow.

'Oh, I have not. Isn't it time Bod had a walk?' Just because I could feel the warmth in my cheeks didn't mean that I was going to admit that to Lorcan.

'Yeah. He looks desperate, doesn't he?' Bod was once again

asleep, this time upside down with all four feet in the air, the two front paws hurriedly scooting along in thin air as he charged along in his dream, the odd cute little noise emanating from him as he did so.

I gave Lorcan what was supposed to be a patient look, which clearly didn't have the amount of patience in it that I'd aimed for.

'Fair enough. It's not fair arguing with you when you're this shattered anyway. Gives me the advantage.'

I gave a snort of disbelief.

Lorcan didn't say anything, but the warmth that lit his eyes and turned one corner of his mouth up said plenty. 'You feeling better now?'

'Yes, I am,' I answered honestly. 'Thank you. It's easy to get carried away with work sometimes, isn't it?'

'It is, I agree. That's another bonus of having a dog. They certainly let you know when you've had enough. Or when they have. Plus it forces you to have a break, go for a walk.'

'Yes, I can imagine. Unfortunately, I don't think having one would work with my lifestyle. I'm all over the place – at least I am when business is booming.' I leant over and knocked on the oak end table for luck. 'It wouldn't be fair on an animal.'

'True. They are a commitment but that's not always a bad thing.'

'Says the man who's allergic to commitment. Or does that only apply to two-legged creatures?'

'I've just found the four-legged varieties more reliable.'

'Now that sounds like a story.'

Lorcan released a laugh on a soft huff of air. 'It's really not.'

'So why don't I believe you?'

'I don't know, now. Why don't you?'

'Because you're blushing, just here,' I said, imitating the gesture he'd made earlier to me.

This caused the soft laugh to morph into a full-bodied one. I did my best not to enjoy the sound of it so much and dutifully squashed the flickers of flame low down in my stomach it produced. If I was totally honest, I would miss Lorcan once all this was over even though, had you asked me that several weeks ago, the answer would have been entirely different. He'd grown on me. Where once I would have avoided his company, now I missed him when we parted. He was caring and funny, and more complex than I'd given him credit for. And I liked him. Perhaps a little more than I wished to.

'You look exhausted. We really are going to get out of your way now. Please don't let me find out you went back to work after we left...' he said, studying me from his height advantage as he heaved me up from the sofa with a lot less effort than it would have taken if the position had been reversed.

'No, I'm not. That's another benefit of being able to use my garden office again now someone kindly had a path put in.' I looked up at him through my lashes. 'It's easier to separate work and home again now. When it's all there staring at you on the kitchen table...'

'Yeah. Five minutes more is easy to say but harder to stick to.'

'Exactly. But I am paying you for that path.'

Lorcan held up his hands. 'Seriously, like I told you, you did me a favour. I don't know how I managed to over-order but trying to split and return some of the goods...' He shook his head. 'Just a massive headache.'

'Funny how it was exactly the paving slabs I happened to have chosen when you were apparently innocently chatting about what I'd thought of for the path though, isn't it?'

'I don't know what you mean,' he said, bending down and scooping Bod up with one large hand. 'You, Miss Hart, are a very suspicious woman.'

'You, Mr O'Malley, make me so.'

He did that grin, the one that lit up his whole face and made those incredible eyes sparkle before turning towards the door.

'Thanks for the help today,' I said.

'No problem. It's not like I have far to go at the moment, now the schoolhouse project is under way.'

'Yes, you've made yourself quite the local hero saving that.'

'With everyone except you, it would seem.'

'Oh, rubbish. You know I was thrilled when I found out. It's just that I know you're not as angelic as Betty and the others think you are.'

'Ah, I see. You know the true me, then?'

'Exactly.'

Lorcan's gaze caught onto mine and, for a moment, it felt as if both of us forgot to breathe. At least I did, and from the flicker in his eyes I knew there was something else behind them too. I just couldn't quite pin down what it was. The truth was, as much as he showed me snippets, I still wasn't sure I did know the real Lorcan O'Malley. In fact, I wondered how many people did. And what, exactly, Siobhan back in Ballalee had had to do with that.

31

'Hi, Maddie, how was your flight?' Lorcan answered on the second ring.

'Hi. Yes, good, thanks. Smooth, thankfully.'

'Glad to hear it. Everything OK?'

'Kind of.'

'What's up?'

'Nothing really. I was just trying Calum but his phone is going straight to voicemail.'

'Yeah, he messaged earlier to say he had a meeting with a couple so he'd be offline for a while.'

'That's fine. I was just letting him know I was on my way. I've messaged now. I'll see you later, then. Thanks, Lorcan.'

'OK. Call if you get lost.'

'I have satnav.'

'Like I said,' he repeated, 'call if you get lost.'

'Funny. Bye, Lorcan.'

I could hear the smile in his voice as he said goodbye and disconnected. I turned back to the young man who had led me to my hire car for the trip. Or more accurately, shown me the tank that had been booked by Peyton, who'd had a moment of crisis and felt she hadn't done enough towards her own wedding. In order to dispel her wobble, I'd asked if she could arrange a hire car for the duration of my trip. I'd flown to a more local airport this time as I didn't have any of the special luggage requirements that Lorcan had with Bod, but this car just wasn't going to work.

'Can you find me something smaller, please? I don't need anything this big.'

The young man frowned at me and glanced down at the paperwork then back up at me. 'But this is what you ordered. Top level. She's a lovely machine.'

'It's big enough to start a small haulage firm. I am a five-foot-three female with a single case and will be driving through tiny country lanes. This,' I waved at the car, 'is excess to my requirements.'

'But it's right here.' He tapped his paperwork. 'The lady that booked was most insistent we reserve the most expensive option we had.'

'I'm sure she did,' I said, smiling at Peyton's thoughtfulness, 'but, seriously, I don't need anything remotely this size. Can you please find me something smaller?'

'I can see what we have.'

'Thank you. I'd really appreciate that.'

* * *

Lorcan was sitting on the wall of the pub as I swung in, a beanie hat pulled low over his ears and a green and black striped scarf wrapped around his neck. At his feet, Bod pootled around on a slack lead, exploring a host of interesting sniffs.

'Did they not have anything smaller?' he asked, opening the car door for me, his nose red from the cold.

'Don't start. And actually, this is perfect, I may be in love,' I said, hopping out of the Smart car the hire company had swapped the tank for.

'Is that so?'

'Absolutely. You wouldn't believe what they gave me first.'

He cocked an eyebrow that disappeared up under his hat.

'Let's just say you could probably have got about four of these in it.'

'Is that the one Peyton booked?'

'Yes, bless her. But it just wasn't practical. I'll explain tactfully when I see her,' I said, opening the boot to retrieve my case, pausing first to scoop up Bod into my arms and give him the fuss he was demanding.

'He's missed you.'

'Is that so?' I said, talking to the dog rather than his owner. 'Did you miss me?' Bod was currently doing his best to snuggle down into my coat, pressing his little snout against my neck, his curly fur tickling my ear as he did so, and I felt the tension in my body melting away. When I looked up, Lorcan was resting on the car and had shut the boot.

'I need to get my case out,' I said, putting the dog back on the ground reluctantly.

'I know.'

'OK... so why did you just shut the boot again with aforementioned luggage still inside?'

'Slight change of plan.'

'No,' I said, holding up my finger. 'No, no, no. No change of plan. Everything is set and in place. There are no changes of plan allowed now.'

'It's nothing major. There's just been a tiny hitch with your accommodation.'

I inhaled a long, cold breath attempting to find my centre of calm – or whatever it was I was supposed to find. Right now, I'd likely need a map, compass and Ray Mears.

'Explain tiny hitch.'

'Don't get mad.'

'Not helping.'

'There was a last-minute guest request from one of Peyton's oldest friends. She'd already rsvp'd that she couldn't come but I guess things changed and now she's coming but the rest of the guests have taken over all the accommodation in the local area. Patrick did suggest her friend stay somewhere further out, but it would be a bit of a trek and it seemed important to Peyton this girl was closer as she doesn't get to see her much.'

'No, I understand. I mean, of course. But... what I'm picking up from what you're *not* saying is that the upshot is I don't have anywhere to stay.'

'No.'

I slumped against the car, wishing now I hadn't changed it. At least I could have lived in the tank and I was sure Brighid would have let me use a shower.

Lorcan scooped an arm around me and stood me back up straight, his hypnotic gaze drawing mine.

'I seem to be explaining this badly. Yes, your room at the pub has been signed over to Peyton's friend, but no, you're not homeless for the duration.'

'So where am I staying?'

'With my mam. And, umm, me.'

I blinked.

'Pardon?'

'She's great,' he said, his speech speeding up. 'And seriously, if there'd been any other option, I'd have found it, believe me.'

'Ouch.'

'No! I don't mean like that. I just knew that you weren't going to be thrilled about it. I mean, you like your schedules and plans and things just so and knowing exactly where you're going to be when.'

I let out the breath I'd been holding, watching as it clouded into a white mist in front of me.

'When did this all happen? Why didn't someone contact me? I am supposed to be the planner.'

'I know, but Peyton only found out late last night and she seemed so thrilled. It was late, you'd have gone to bed and, well, I asked her not to say anything to you until I got back to her. I spoke to Brighid this morning and Mam was over the moon. She loves having people to stay.'

'You still should have told me. I was up early enough.'

'And I didn't want you worrying about it on the drive to the airport, or the flight. You have enough on your mind as it is.'

'That wasn't really your decision to make.'

'I had to find the girl somewhere to stay!'

'No, I don't mean that. And yes, you did the right thing. It's what Peyton and Patrick want that's important. I meant that it wasn't your decision what I should and shouldn't be told. I'm a grown woman, Lorcan, and, while I appreciate the sentiment behind the gesture, I don't need to be mollycoddled.'

He chewed the side of his cheek for a moment. 'Fair enough. And I apologise if I overstepped the mark. Like I said, I'm used to looking after my siblings, who to be honest often say the same as you, but I'm their brother. It's my job to look after them.'

'Apology accepted, but, Lorcan, it's not your job to look after me.'

'True. But that doesn't mean I don't still want to. Maybe it's just been so long since you actually let anyone take care of you that you've forgotten how it feels.' His words were soft but the look in his eyes, contrasting with the soft grey beanie, was intense.

The sea crashed fiercely against the nearby cliffs and suddenly it felt as if that was all there was. Lorcan, me and the thundering sea below. Everything else stopped for a split second that felt like forever – and then the memories flooded in.

'You're being ridiculous.'

'Am I?'

'Of course.'

'When was the last time you had a decent relationship?'

My mouth dropped into a perfect 'O'. 'That is absolutely none of your business!'

'Probably not, but I've asked it now.'

'Well, I shan't be answering it. You're hardly an open book yourself.'

'What's that supposed to mean?' he snapped back, his expression hardening.

'We both know what it means but, right now, it doesn't matter. In fact, none of it matters. Once this wedding is done, I can go back to doing what I do and you can go back to doing what you do. In the meantime, I'm bloody freezing and desperate for a wee so do you mind showing me where I'm supposed to be staying? Assuming I'm still invited.'

He rolled his eyes. 'Who's this insured for?' He gave a side nod to the car.

'Both of us, apparently. They already had your details.'

'Good. Easier if I drive, then. Is he all right on your lap?' He looked down at the dog.

'Of course,' I said, lifting Bod up and laughing as he snuggled in for more cuddles, his tail wagging madly. I glanced over at Lorcan, the dog's antics for the moment breaking the tension that had slid between us.

'Told you he'd missed you,' he said as he opened the door for us and I clambered in, busying myself with fussing the little dog as Lorcan strode round to the driver's side and slid the seat back in order to get in. 'It's actually pretty roomy in here. I thought I'd be ducking.'

'I know. Great, huh? So cute.'

He turned the key. 'It is. You should get one next time. It suits you.'

Forcing myself to try and forget our spat, I smiled up at him. 'A few more weddings like this one, and maybe I will. Assuming it goes well, of course. If it doesn't, I think I'll be walking for ever more.'

'Relax. It's going to be just fine.'

32

'I don't like him,' Lorcan said as we drove away from the castle after I'd finally managed to pin down the photographer for a quick meet and greet. Calum had then insisted we stay for a cup of tea, taking advantage of a moment of calm in the planning, before we headed back to Lorcan's mum's house.

'You don't have to like him.'

'You don't like him either.'

'I didn't say that.'

'You didn't have to. I'm good at reading body language,' he stated. Somehow that wasn't too hard to believe.

'Fine,' I agreed. 'I don't like him either. But it doesn't matter. All I have to do is make sure he does a good job with the photographs.'

'He's shifty.'

'Maybe it's nerves. He's not done anything this big before. I think he's hoping it will help his portfolio.'

'It won't help yours if he cocks up.'

'Yes. Thank you for that insightful comment,' I snapped.

'Sorry. I didn't mean...' He ran a hand back through his hair, the soft black waves parting as he did so. 'I just don't want him messing anything up for these two after the first debacle and... I know how hard you've worked on this and what it means to you, in more ways than one.'

I nodded. 'Yes. I know. And I appreciate all of that. I just need to keep an eye on him.'

'We.'

I looked up at him and a small smile curved my lips, a feeling of warmth curling its way through my body at the sincere tone of support issued in that one word.

'We,' I agreed.

* * *

'There you are, now.' Maria O'Malley came hurrying towards me as we returned to Lorcan's family home having seen the photographer and done our best, unsuccessfully, not to judge him. 'I'm so sorry I wasn't here to greet you properly yesterday. The perils of being a grandma. Always on call for emergency babysitting.' I could see now where Lorcan got his eyes and smile from. His mother's smile, however, seemed far more easy when I'd thanked her for opening her home to me at such short notice, especially around the Christmas period.

'It sounds like you have quite a big family, so I'm sure the last thing you need is to be having me under your feet right now.'

'Oh no, no. I love some company, don't I, darlin'?' she said, looking up at her son and picking a bit of fluff from his jumper as she did so. 'Although from what I hear from this one, I doubt I'll be seeing much of you, which is a shame as I've heard so much about you.'

'You have?' I asked, looking round at Lorcan.

'You were a new face in the village. People like to talk.'

'About what?'

Again, he gave a shrug.

'Helpful,' I said, giving him a tight smile.

'Oh, just ignore him.' His mum patted my arm and steered me to a chair near the Aga. 'Have a seat here now and tell me all about yourself. You'll have a tea, won't you?'

I opened my mouth to reply.

'Of course you will,' she said, patting my shoulder as she answered her own question, smiling as Bod put his paws up against my chair and looked up at me with his little black button eyes. Reaching down, I lifted him onto my lap where he quickly made a little nest and hung his front paws over the edge of my leg, basking in the warmth of the large but cosy kitchen. It was easy to see this being the heart of the family home, presided over by the smiling, chatty Maria.

'I see he's got you wrapped around his little finger,' she said, laughter in her gentle sing-song voice as she nodded at the dog. 'Lorcan, reach me the teapot, would you, love? Diarmaid put it away for me the other day, bless him, and it's in the wrong place and I can't reach it up there.'

'Tell him next time. He knows you can't get up there on a chair with your vertigo.' Her son shook his head. 'All he has to do is ask where it goes.'

'Oh, don't be such a grump. He's trying to be helpful,' she replied, sending him the sort of look only a mother could conjure up. 'Diarmaid's my son-in-law,' Maria said, keeping me in the loop.

'I'm helpful!'

'Aye, when you're here and when you want to be.'

Lorcan shook his head. 'At least I put the teapot in the right bloody place,' he mumbled and I bent a little to fuss Bod's fur, hoping the movement would hide the grin spreading across my face at the six-foot-five bulk of Lorcan getting told off by his far smaller mum. I had a feeling there was a lot more to Maria O'Malley than met the eye. It seemed to be a recurring theme in this family.

'Don't think I can't see that,' Lorcan said, leaning over my shoulder as he placed the cosy covered teapot in front of me on the table.

'Then perhaps you should listen to your mother more.'

A peal of laughter rang out from where Maria was removing a tray of something that smelled delicious from the oven. 'Oh, I like this one,' she said, pointing at me with an oven glove in the shape of a giraffe.

'You would,' he returned, but I could see the smile in his eyes, even if it didn't show on his lips.

'So, now,' his mum said, sitting opposite me as she buttered the warm scones. 'You'll like these, by the way. Scones, sort of, but with potato and cheese.'

'And a million carbs,' Lorcan added with more of a smile, earning him a sharp kick under the table.

'You're not watching your weight, are you, dear?'

'No, not really. I just tend not to eat a lot of carb-rich food and your son enjoys winding me up about it when I do.'

'Now that doesn't surprise me.'

'He thinks he's a lot funnier than he actually is.'

'Don't they always?'

'That's true.'

'I'm right here.'

His mother waved his protest away and served me up a plate. 'Have you ever been to Ireland before you were arranging Patrick's wedding?' she asked, pouring me a cup of tea as she did so.

'No. I'd always meant to visit as the photos I'd seen made Ireland look so beautiful, but it's actually getting round to these things, isn't it?'

'Now, there's a true word. Especially when you're running your own business. Lorcan here went through the same thing, didn't you, love?'

Lorcan remained silent, clearly realising this was a rhetorical question.

'It's lovely that you're here now though, especially with everything all revving up towards Christmas. Makes everywhere look extra cosy.'

'And twee.'

She flicked a tea towel at her son and his smile spread.

'Do you have more things to do for the wedding this afternoon, or have you got time to have a look around? Has our lad showed you the sights yet?'

'Ma, we're in the middle of nowhere. There are no sights. She's seen the sea. We flew over it. Even if she missed most of it the first time.' His blue eyes glinted mischievously as he said this and I raised my chin, ignoring the jibe and doing my best not to laugh. When he'd made a comment immediately after the incident weeks ago, I was still embarrassed at having thrown up at all, let alone in front of him. Now, though, I didn't mind so much. I wasn't the first person to ever get travel sick and I most definitely wouldn't be the last.

'Ah, you leave her alone, you big lump. No wonder she was sick, stuck next to you and the Beast of Bodmin for the entire flight.' We exchanged a conspiratorial grin as she slid another potato scone onto my plate and I didn't have the heart to refuse.

'Don't listen to them, Bod,' Lorcan said, leaning over and lifting the dog from my lap to immediately be greeted by a wriggly, cuddle-hungry dog who acted as if he hadn't had human contact for a week, despite having been resting content-edly with drowsy eyes since I'd sat down.

'Beast of Bodmin?' I repeated, laughing.

'That's how he got his name,' Lorcan explained. 'When I brought him home the first time, he was this tiny little ball of fluff. Ma took one look and said, "Not exactly the Beast of Bodmin, is he?" I hadn't settled on a name for him and it seemed to suit him so it stuck.'

'I love it. It's great that the name's got a story behind it too.'

'Thanks,' he replied, looking up at me through long dark lashes as he placed the little dog down on the floor to hoover up a crumb that had dropped from Maria's plate.

'It's such a shame he doesn't feed the poor animal,' Lorcan's mum said, laughing as the furry little vacuum wound himself round table and chair legs, ever hopeful.

'Some days I look for the zip – I'm sure I've been saddled with a micro pig in a dog outfit.'

'Or maybe he's just taking after his owner. You're hardly one to turn down a meal.'

'That's not the point.'

'No, love. Of course it isn't.'

I hid my smile behind my cup but not well enough. Lorcan caught me and raised his eyebrows, before emitting a small sigh, but there was a sense of calm behind it. His body was languid and relaxed, his expression soft. It was how he'd been with me when I was ill on the plane, when I was high as a kite on painkillers and lonely in my hotel room on my last visit and, despite the odd disagreement, how he was when we were together working on the wedding.

As time had gone on, Lorcan had spent more time at my place, especially once the sale of the schoolhouse had gone through and the renovation began. Quite often, he'd drop Bod at my house while he went across the village to oversee the project. I was always thrilled to see my fuzzy four-legged friend and I loved having his company in the office. He was so well mannered that several clients hadn't even noticed he was there until they got up to leave and saw him curled up cosily in his little bed. Lorcan never took it for granted that I would look after him, even though I was sure he knew that I was as excited at seeing Bod each time as he seemed to be at seeing me. I never got used to that adoration from the little dog and didn't think I ever wanted to. It felt like forever since someone had been that pleased to see me and I doubted any human would ever be able to match that enthusiasm again. Even if I'd let them.

'He's got himself a much better work-life balance now, haven't you, love?'

Lorcan smiled in return but didn't elaborate. 'I got so worried about him. Well, you would, wouldn't you? Even though he's that size, he's still my boy. I'm sure your mammy is the same with you.'

'I... unfortunately my mum died, but I'm sure she would have been, yes. It's natural, as you say.'

'Oh, darlin'. I'm so sorry. I didn't know. Lorcan, why didn't you tell me instead of letting me go and put my foot in my mouth?' she said, reaching out to take hold of my hand, which was resting on the table in front of me.

'No, really, it's fine. It was a long time ago.'

'Still, I'm sorry, love. Men! They don't tell you anything, do they?'

'If I'd known, Ma, I'd have told you.' His voice now was low and steady, and when I risked a glance his jawline was tense. He met my eyes, his own shuttered now, the warmth of earlier gone. A knot formed in my stomach, tightening as he looked away.

'You mustn't blame Lorcan. He didn't know. I don't really talk about it with anyone. As I said, it was a long time ago.'

Maria gave my hand another pat, a soft, understanding smile on her gentle face, her skin pale and unblemished, an almost youthful bloom on her cheeks. The easy, relaxed atmosphere of a few moments ago had shifted and I desperately wanted to get it back. I wanted the easy, relaxed Lorcan back too but I wasn't about to beg forgiveness for not sharing something personal when, judging by the arctic conditions that had blown in when Siobhan had entered the pub, there was a full-size skeleton lounging about in his own closet.

'So, have you had enough to eat?'

'More than enough, thank you. We ate lunch with Calum at the castle and your scones were delicious.'

'Good. Now, as you haven't seen much of the area, and there's still some light out there, Lorcan can take you out and show you around a bit. Give you a break from work before you dive back into it tomorrow, I'm sure. Bod can stay here and keep me company in the meantime.'

'Maddie might not want to see the sights,' Lorcan said from behind a local newspaper. I had the feeling it was more that *he* didn't want to, but Maria was right, it did seem a shame to miss out on a chance of exploring a little more.

'I would, actually, but it's fine, Maria. I have a hire car so can take myself. I'm sure Lorcan has plenty to do anyway.'

'Obviously,' she replied, the words spread with a thick layer of sarcasm.

Her son appeared from behind the paper and she met his eyes, not in the least intimidated, and clearly not expecting an argument either.

'Fine.' He glanced down at my feet. 'But you'll need better shoes than those.' I declined to point out that said shoes were bloody gorgeous and had cost me six hundred quid some years earlier, so clearly he and I had different views of what qualified as 'better' when it came to shoes. His mum followed his eyeline.

'Oh, my, I hadn't seen those. They're just beautiful,' she gushed. 'I don't think I could wear heels like that these days, but in my youth...' She patted her hair up and let that easy smile once more light up her face. 'But what the boy means is something a little more practical perhaps. Have you got anything? What size are you? I'm sure we can find you something if not.'

Ten minutes later I'd changed into jeans and was wearing an old pair of Maria's hiking boots and a thick, waterproof coat. 'It's dry out there now,' she said, as she held up a sleeve for me to feed my arm into, 'but you never know with Ireland. Now, have a lovely time, both of you, and I'll see you later for dinner.'

'What time do you want us back?' Lorcan asked, pulling the beanie from yesterday back on.

'Just take your time, love. It'll be dark before dinner's ready anyway so just come back when you're done,' she replied, reaching up and straightening the hat a little.

Lorcan bent and pecked her on the cheek, before opening the back door. 'After you.' He motioned to me. 'See you later, Mammy.'

'Bye, darlin'. Drive safe, now.'

He waved in response and pulled the door closed behind him.

'We'll go in this,' he said, pointing at a four-by-four vehicle, although thankfully not school-bus size like the hire company had reserved for me. 'If we get stuck somewhere, we've got a better chance of getting out again in this than yours.'

'I wasn't aware we were going off-roading,' I said, swinging myself up into the seat from the outside step of the vehicle. Lorcan, no doubt, wouldn't need the step with his long legs.

'Just in case,' he said, checking I had all my limbs inside the vehicle before closing the door and heading around to the driver's side.

'Is this yours?' I asked as he got in, hoping to make general conversation and prevent us from sitting in silence for the rest of the day.

'Mam's. We got it for her a couple of years ago after she'd got stuck late at night in some bad weather in her old car.'

'We?'

'My siblings and me.'

'That's so thoughtful.'

'More for our own peace of mind, to be honest. Phone

signal, as you know, isn't the best out here and she was in a black spot when she got stranded one evening. A bit of bank had slipped and made the road a mud bath. She'd left my sister's and normally texts to say she's home. Of course, when she didn't and nobody could get hold of her, it all got a bit tense. I'd just got home from a business trip and we had this mad phone chain going on as I was driving into the village.'

'So what happened? Did someone find her OK?'

'Yeah, I got one of the local farmer lads to get out his tractor and we set off towards my sister's, taking the road Ma would take. Found her about halfway along, still trying to get the damn car out of the mud.'

'Was she all right?'

'Ah, she kicked up a stink about everyone making such a fuss but we both saw the relief in her eyes when we jumped down from the tractor cab. She was frozen too, obviously having not planned to be spending time outside the car. I mean, she had a coat but not enough to protect her against driving snow and rain.'

'Oh, my goodness, you must have been worried sick.'

'I was,' he said, glancing across at me as he replied, the fear he'd clearly felt then resurfacing for a moment, shadowing his features. 'We all were. My eldest sister was almost hysterical, poor kid. Ma was coming home from her place so of course after a while she was imagining the worst and blaming herself for it, because she'd asked her to come over and help with something.'

'And she thought, if she hadn't then your mum would be home safe and sound.'

'Exactly,' he said, with another glance.

'Poor thing.'

'Yeah, Roísín was reluctant to ask her to do anything after

that, but at the time her husband was working away and some-times you just need a bit of help, don't you? Plus Ma was upset she wouldn't ask.'

'Which is when you came up with the idea of getting her a car that could handle any terrain.'

He nodded. 'Seemed like a good plan.'

'And how did your mum take to that? I may have only just met her, but she seems pretty independent and definitely has a mind of her own.'

Lorcan let out a huff of laughter. 'Oh, she's definitely got one of those.'

'Takes one to know one,' I said, an innocent expression on my face.

'I don't know what you're talking about. But to answer your question, yes, you're very astute. There was, initially, a bit of push-back from her. Firstly, because she didn't want the money spent on her. She'd rather we all spent our money on ourselves and our families, those of us that have them. But we managed to talk her round eventually and between five of us, and a brother-in-law in the business, we could get a good price.'

'That's good.'

'That's what we thought until we took her to show her this and then there was a lot of, "Oh, that's far too big for me. I'll never be able to drive that."'

'I take it she overcame that barrier as it's the only car parked outside the house.'

'Yeah. Took her about an hour and she was bombing around in it like a menace. Parallel parks better than I do.' He rolled his eyes in mock annoyance and I smiled, glad to see it momentarily reflected on his own face.

I'd been worried how this slightly enforced trip out was going to go, but thankfully the frosty moment of earlier seemed to have dissipated into the surrounding cold of the countryside, and, inside the cabin of the car, relations were definitely warmer. For the moment, at least.

We drove for a little while longer, with what sounded like a local radio station playing quietly in the background. Every so often, in between the traditional music would be a presenter, chattering away in what I could only assume was Gaelic.

'Do you understand what he's saying?' I asked after a short time.

'I do.'

'Do you all speak Gaelic?'

'All being whom?'

'In your family?' I shrugged. 'The village?'

'Yes to all in our family. Most of the people in the village do too, especially the older ones. Some of the younger ones don't so much but I guess that's to be expected these days, but we try and keep the language alive where we can.'

'Do you generally speak Gaelic at home?'

'A mix of both. Keeps your hand in. Plus if we have visitors that don't speak Gaelic, we can just shift into that when we want to talk about them.'

'How amusing.'

He didn't turn his head, but I saw the corners of his lips twitch as he restrained a smile.

* * *

'What is this place?' I puffed out, gripping onto Lorcan's hand as he hauled me up the steep grassy bank. He'd definitely been right about the shoes.

'Dunamayne Castle. Or what's left of it. A certain amount of it is down there now.' He pointed towards the edge of the cliff.

'So, it's unstable and yet we're still going up!' The sentence took three attempts to finish but he got the idea.

'It's grand. Safe as houses.'

I let go of his hand and bent over, resting my hands on my thighs for a second to catch my breath. 'Clearly you and I have very different ideas about what that phrase means.'

When I straightened up, he was staring out across the gunmetal-grey water, white horses charging across the surface.

'You want to see the sights or do you have some more whingeing to do?'

I pulled a face at him and mumbled that I would tell his mum on him. He leant back, took my hand and tugged me up the last section.

To give Lorcan his due, it truly was worth the effort. The view was spectacular, even though the cloud had come in now, and was sitting low on some of the hills further round the coastline. The mist of the sea and lowering cloud dampened my face, chilling the skin, but the magical atmosphere of the ruined building and its surroundings was a stronger force. I pulled my scarf further up in an attempt to keep my nose warm – assuming it was still there: I'd lost all feeling in that some time ago – then lifted the hood on my coat, wedging it over my woolly hat, and began exploring.

'Just be careful where you step.' Lorcan's voice drifted on the wind towards me and I turned.

'I thought you said it was "grand"?'

'It is. But we're still on a cliff edge on a damp day with a rising wind and I cannot face telling Peyton that I lost her wedding planner in the sea. Not this late in the game.'

'But earlier would have been fine?' I asked, hands on hips.

He actually took a moment to pretend to think this over so I turned away and ignored the soft echo of deep, rumbling laughter that followed me.

'Come here,' he said, catching up with me in a few steady strides as I navigated some fallen masonry. I took his hand, one, because it was definitely easier to manage with someone else balancing me, and two, I figured if I did slip, having some ballast on one side gave me a better chance of not going too far. Obviously, if he slipped first I'd be letting go.

'If I go, you're coming too.'

I snapped my head around. 'What?'

He cocked his head at the jagged edge of the cliff, about ten feet away from us now that we had moved inland a little.

'Well, that's not very gentlemanly.'

'And not very ladylike to plan to let go if I went.'

'How did you know what I was thinking? And for that matter,' I said, letting go of his hand and turning to face him, 'how do you always know what I'm thinking? You keep doing it and, frankly, it's quite unsettling. Brighid did it a few times when I was over but you keep doing it. Is it some trick you're born with here or something?'

'Maybe you're just easy to read.'

'I've told you before, I'm not.'

'And I say you are. Why do you think you aren't?'

'I've... been told.' Not always in the most flattering way either, but I wasn't about to mention that and just had to hope my companion's magical powers didn't pick up on that particular nugget.

'I see.'

'Seriously, if you carry on with the mind-reading stuff, I'm going to push you off this cliff myself!'

Movement close by made us turn to see an elderly gentleman watching us with a hesitant expression.

'She doesn't mean it,' Lorcan called, laughing, holding his hand up.

'I really don't. I mean, he can be super annoying but his mum's lovely and she'd be really upset.'

The man nodded, and called his spaniel, who had been rootling around, sniffing merrily away throughout the exchange. We stepped back onto the grass, allowing them more of the path on which to pass us. As they did, the man stopped level with Lorcan. 'Lesson one of marriage. Don't upset the wife when you're near a bloody great drop.' He patted him twice on the arm and then headed off inland and down what I now saw was a shallower climb.

'Probably good advice.'

'With age comes wisdom,' I replied, sitting on a large, square boulder, likely once part of a wall, its edges now softened by centuries of wind and rain. 'Even if he was wrong about us being married.'

'Understandable considering the conversation.' He grinned before taking a seat next to me on the rock. 'You all right? We can go back if you're cold. I noticed there's a flask of tea in the car. We were obviously going to be turfed out of the house whether we wanted to be or not.'

'I'm glad your mum suggested it,' I said, staring out past the faded pomp and glory of the castle to the ocean beyond, the wildness of it completely suited to this rugged, but somehow serene landscape.

'Me too.'

'I wouldn't really have let go.'

'You wouldn't have been much help.'

'I know. But I still wouldn't.'

'I know. But sometimes you have to save yourself.'

'Not always easy in the moment.'

'Nope.'

We sat in silence for a few moments, listening to the wind and the waves and sea birds I couldn't identify wheeling around above the ruins before disappearing back over the edge and swooping across the sea.

'My mum was killed in a car accident the night of my graduation from university.'

34

I felt Lorcan shift beside me. 'Maddie, you don't have to tell me this if you don't want to.'

'I want to,' I said, turning to face him. The scarf had already slipped but I tugged it down further so that he could see my face properly. Or read it, whatever it was he did.

'OK.'

I swallowed and studied my feet for a couple of minutes. Lorcan didn't hurry me, or say a word. He just sat there, as solid and as present as the stone boulder beneath us.

'They were so excited about the day and I was too. I'd worked hard on my degree and got a First and had all these dreams and plans. My parents were really supportive and always ready to listen to an idea, support me in it but also give me good, down-to-earth advice. We talked a lot. I knew some of the students didn't talk a lot to their parents, but I'd ring mine often, even if it was just for a few minutes to say hi, and speak to my little brother. He was a bit of an oops moment so there was quite an age gap between us. At twelve, he was still just on the cusp of wanting to chat to his big sister, which I loved. I had no idea what he was talking about sometimes but he was always full of enthusiasm for it, whatever it was.'

'Sounds like a family trait.'

I looked round briefly and smiled, feeling the overwhelming wave of sadness in it. 'Yes. We had a wonderful day. I didn't trip on my gown, so I'd called that a win, and then we went out for a lovely meal at this fancy restaurant Dad had booked as a surprise. We had champagne, although Dad only had a sip because he was driving. He'd put another bottle in the fridge for when we got home so that he could toast me properly. Even my little brother, Henry, tried a bit. Not that he liked it,' I said, laughing at the memory but feeling, and hearing, the fracture in my voice. 'So basically, Mum and I got to polish off a bottle, which we didn't complain about.'

Lorcan moved his gloved hand so that it butted up against my mittened one on the rock. It was the simplest gesture but I felt a wave of gratitude towards him. It was enough. Just enough to say, 'I'm here.'

'We weren't that far from home really. Just the last bit of the motorway. One minute I was tucking the blanket back over my brother, who'd fallen asleep, and the next all I remember is lights. Huge white lights beaming directly in front of us, then the most ungodly noise I ever heard for a fraction of a split second. Not even a blink of an eye.'

I looked back out over the dark ocean but, in my mind, all I could see was that night.

'You don't have to go on.'

'I'd like to.'

This time he gently lifted my hand and placed it within his own. I kept my focus on the water. If I looked at him now, I wouldn't be able to do it, and I really did want to. I didn't know why. Every time I came to Ireland, it had an effect on me, and

Lorcan was no exception. In fact he probably had the biggest effect of all. But watching and listening to him with his mum this afternoon had dredged up memories and feelings and now they were clamouring to be heard.

'I must have blacked out for a bit but when I came round, the car was on its side several hundred feet from where we'd started. It was crumpled around us and I could see the front was just...' I swallowed and Lorcan tightened his hold. He got the idea.

'I started calling my parents. Screaming for them, I suppose. I don't know. And then for my brother. Suddenly, he made a noise and I felt about for him. We were all folded into this tiny piece of metal although, from what I could make out in the dark, the door on my brother's side had gone. I felt around him and it was all wet. He was making these tiny little sounds and all I could say was how much I loved him and how he had to be strong for me and Mum and Dad and that we'd be out of here soon and back home.'

Lorcan let out the faintest of sighs.

'I don't know if I believed that or not at the time. I think it was the only thing my brain could cope with. Anything other than that was just impossible. I wouldn't let it be possible.'

I swiped at my eyes and nose with my mitten.

'It felt like forever but apparently it was only about ten minutes before the rescue services were on site. I was making the most noise so I was the one they were less worried about. Mum and Dad were silent but Henry was still making little sounds. I'd found his hand and was holding it but I could feel his grip getting weaker. I'm sure I was a nightmare for the poor rescue crews, screaming at them to help him. The helicopter landed for him and they managed to finally get him out. I wanted to go with him and initially they weren't going to let me because I was in a bit of a state. It was hard to tell whose blood was whose at that point but once he was out I calmed down and they let me accompany him, especially, I think, because he was a minor.'

I pushed myself up from the rock, sliding my hand from Lorcan's, suddenly feeling the need to be moving. Wrapping my arms around myself, I took a couple of steps to the left, no nearer to the edge and still close to Lorcan. 'I asked the fire and paramedic crews working on the car to look after my parents and tell them I'd talk to them soon, then got in with Henry.'

Breathing in the salty, biting air, I felt the chill of it down into my lungs and took another deep inhale.

'We lost Henry during the flight. His injuries were too traumatic to survive.'

'Oh, Maddie.' Lorcan was up and beside me, his hands cradling my face. 'I'm so, so sorry.'

'Thank you,' I said, a faint smile breaking through. 'He would have loved you. And Bod.'

'I'm sure the feeling would have been mutual.'

'Thank you,' I said again, not only because it was the most perfect thing he could have said, but because I knew he meant it.

'After I'd been checked out at the hospital myself, and had a broken shoulder set and various cuts patched up, they put me in a private room and a doctor came in to tell me that Mum and Dad were also gone. The lights I'd seen were a lorry. During the inquest, it came out that the driver was driving under the influence of drugs and lost control. The truck jackknifed and ploughed into our car. My parents were both killed on impact. The driver of the lorry was arrested and didn't have a mark on him.'

'Jesus, Maddie.' Lorcan's words were as soft as a breath as he wrapped his arms around me and all I felt, all I knew and wanted to know, was his warm, solid bulk as my tears soaked into his navy-blue padded jacket.

* * *

'Thanks,' I said, handing Lorcan back the travel mug as we sat cosily in the car, having walked back down from the ruins. Initially we'd just sat there together, Lorcan's arms tight around me as I rested my head against his solid chest and stared out at the ocean, watching the patterns on the surface change as the clouds played hide and seek with an elusive sun. We didn't speak. There was no need to. I knew he was there for me and that was enough.

'Did you want to go back to the house now? There's a bit of daylight left so we've still got time to have a general drive around and see a bit more countryside.' He sent me a half-grin. 'To be fair, most of it is just more fields and more sheep so don't be expecting a lot of variety.'

'I'll bear that in mind for my Tripadvisor review.'

'That'd be grand.'

I loved that he hadn't asked me how I was feeling now, or some other platitude. What could he say anyway? I wasn't sure I even knew how I was feeling. It was a long time since I'd spoken about my family, and the truth was I'd never really spoken about it in as much detail as I had sitting up on those rocks. Family had obviously come up in previous relationships but I'd always dealt with the subject in a slightly clinical, detached way. The only way I could. I'd say that they'd died when I was younger and wouldn't elaborate. I'd never spoken about Henry to anyone. Not until now. He'd been too special, too precious, too heartbreaking to talk about. But something about this place – and this man – had emptied my heart and I didn't regret it. I was glad I'd told him. And I'd meant what I said. Henry really would have adored him.

'I'd love to see a bit more of the area, if you have time?'

'All the time in the world,' he said, smiling as he turned the key, pushed the stick into gear and pulled back out onto the road. We wound around country lanes, got stuck in a cow-jam, which was so much more entertaining and relaxing than a regular traffic jam, and eventually turned back to head towards the village.

'Did you want to go via the castle on the way back? Not to stop, but just so you can see it lit up now the light's fading. I'm not sure you've ever seen that for yourself yet, have you?'

'No, I haven't. That'd be great. Thanks. We've planned for lanterns all the way along the entrance path so that'd give me a good opportunity to get a picture in my mind how that will look too.'

'Don't let that brain of yours go too hard into it though. This is supposed to be a day off, don't forget, and I'm sure you're pretty exhausted anyway.' He flicked his gaze from the road momentarily, the look in his eyes saying more than a whole raft of words could. And he was right.

'I promise.'

The smile spread on his face as he looked out of the front windscreen. 'I'm glad to hear it.'

35

Lorcan opened the back door of the kitchen for me, and suddenly I felt as if I'd entered an old saloon back in the Wild West. People crowded around the table chattering but the moment I stepped in, silence washed over the room as all faces turned to ours.

'Ah, there you are,' Maria said, immediately coming over and helping me off with my coat before I could object. 'Did you have yourselves a nice time? Oh my, your poor face is freezing. Come and sit down by the Aga and warm up. Cillian, move yourself and stop hogging the best seat.'

'No, really, I'm fine,' I said, before looking over to the man Maria had addressed. 'Please, do stay where you are.'

'Not at all,' Maria overruled. 'I've a job for him anyway. This is my youngest, by the way, Cillian. This is Lorcan's friend, Madeleine, the wedding planner.'

'Nice to meet you,' I said, waving in lieu of being able to actually reach across the table and shake his hand.

'And you.' He smiled that family smile. 'The youngest *and* best-looking, obviously.'

'Obviously,' Lorcan said drily from behind me.

'Now, come and sit down, Maddie. Here.' Maria stopped for a moment and peered at me. 'Are you feeling quite well? You look a little pale.' She touched her hand, its skin soft, to my cheek. 'Do you want to go and rest for a bit? Dinner won't be for a little while yet.'

'No, really, I'm fine, but thank you.' Unconsciously I'd stepped back towards Lorcan as his mum began fussing over me. The dams of emotion had already been busted once today and the last thing I wanted to do was burst into tears in front of a kitchen full of people I'd never met. As I moved, I felt the warmth of Lorcan's hand at my waist, the steady weight of it resting softly, just letting me know he was there and I was safe. The latter I certainly had no need to have worried about. After the initial lull in conversation, and introductions completed, I'd been made to feel part of the family almost at once, all of them wrapping me in a kindness that made me feel secure and relaxed. I spent time, money and energy every week attending yoga classes, all with varying names and claims, and yet not once had I ever felt as relaxed as I did now, sitting at this table, being absorbed into the heart of an Irish family.

* * *

'I hope that wasn't all a bit much,' Lorcan said later as he sat on a wicker chair in my room while I unpacked the rest of my things and put them into the wardrobe. 'The family can be a bit full on if you're not used to it. I didn't realise everyone was coming this evening. That particular message seems to have been left out of the family WhatsApp group chat.'

'Perhaps they thought you'd veto it on my, or your own, behalf if you were told.'

'It would have been on your behalf – and yes, you're probably right.'

'Then I'm glad they didn't tell you because I had a lovely evening. You have a wonderful family, Lorcan.'

'I do.' He nodded. 'Drive me round the bend some of the time, but I wouldn't swap them for the world.'

'And I can see why. As for the rest, I think that's just part of being a family, isn't it?'

He smiled, accepting the rhetorical question. 'I was concerned you might feel a little overwhelmed.'

'I know you were. And I appreciate that you were ready to bundle me out at my signal, but, once I was over the initial shock, it was good. Your mum is such a good cook, too,' I said, patting my tummy.

'She is that. I can always call you for a five a.m. run tomorrow to burn the stew off if you like.'

'Very funny,' I replied over my shoulder as I hung my last dress in the cupboard and closed the door. 'Somehow I think running around for this wedding is going to keep me pretty trim, especially chivvying that photographer. I have to say I'm still concerned about him.'

'I know you are. What are you going to do?'

'I've managed to pin him down for a longer meeting tomorrow and will be insisting he show me what his plans are. I've got a copy of the standard poses Peyton and Patrick are after, but I know they want a lot of candid ones to capture the day more naturally on top of those. He's charging enough and, from what I see, hasn't done an event on this scale before, but seems to be very full of himself about knowing "just what Peyton wants".' I raised a brow at my recollection of the exchange.

'He's the one thing Patrick hasn't been sold on from the

start, but Peyton was adamant, and we know that what Peyton wants, Peyton gets.'

'It sounds like this guy has been pretty persuasive and played on his existing friendship with Peyton. You know what she's like. Yes, she's used to getting her own way, but she's also quite naïve at times because she's had everything done for her. That's why I wanted to get this meeting booked tomorrow so that I can talk to him before Peyton gets here.' I plopped down on the bed and tucked my knees up, hugging them to me. 'Seriously, this element is usually already sorted ages ago.'

'But you'll fix it. He's not going to mess with you once he meets you.'

'What's that supposed to mean?'

'Let's just say you have a determined way about you, which belies your size.'

'I'm not sure how I'm supposed to take that.'

'OK, let me put it this way. You look like this petite, sylph-like waif but underneath that exterior is a backbone of steel and a woman who can kick arse. Clearer?'

'Yes. Thank you.'

'I'm not sure if any of that is politically incorrect – it's not meant to be.'

'I'm not offended. I rather like the description actually. It's always nice to have an advantage, and someone thinking they can get one over on you because of your size or gender is incredibly annoying and wonderfully satisfying when you prove them wrong.'

'I can imagine. By the way, the hot tap in there can be a bit temperamental so just shout if you're stuck.'

'If I'm stuck?' I asked, my voice pitching up. Lorcan and I had certainly taken another step closer today, but I wasn't about to invite him into my bathroom just yet.

'Running the bath, I mean,' he replied, the palest hint of pink on those cut-glass cheekbones.

'I see. Thanks.'

'It's on my list of things to do for Ma.' He took his phone out of his pocket. 'I'm going to make a note of it now before I forget again. What's the use of having a property developer son when he can't even fix a tap for her?' The question seemed more to himself than me but I picked up on it anyway.

'Quite a lot of the house looks like it's been modernised. That kitchen is beautiful and your mum clearly enjoys cooking and spending time in there. This room has obviously been redone as I doubt it came with an en suite originally, and I'm sure there's more. Who did all this?'

Lorcan levelled his deep blue gaze at me and stretched out his long legs. 'By the innocent look on your face, which I don't buy for a moment, you know the answer to that question.'

'Educated guess. And one stiff tap is not the end of the world.'

'It's not as it should be and that bothers me.'

'Lorcan, I promise you I will cope and if it bothers you, then fix it. Get one ordered or a chap in or whatever you have to do if it's getting to you that much, but don't ever think you haven't done enough for your mum. It's easy to see what you mean to her and, from what I heard tonight, there's plenty more you've done over the years, not just for her but for your whole family.'

'I knew I shouldn't have let Aoife switch places with me. My younger sister loves a gossip, true enough.'

'She wasn't gossiping. She was telling me about your family and I was interested.'

He pulled an unconvinced face.

'Too late now anyway. I know all your deepest secrets.' I

waggled my eyebrows, expecting Lorcan to make some comment, or quip or just roll his eyes. But he didn't.

'I'd better leave you to your bath. Been a long day. Like I said, shout if you need anything.' Pulling open the door, he gave a brief, fleeting smile that didn't quite reach his eyes and headed out, closing it behind him.

Why was it, just when you thought you knew someone, they did something that gave the rug you were standing on a good, hard yank, just in case you'd got too comfortable.

* * *

'It's OK, sweetheart. Peyton and I go way back. I know what I'm doing.'

Calum's face was fixed on a point just over the photographer's shoulder while I was staring straight at him, wondering if I could take him and thinking I probably could.

'First of all, Mr Benson, I would appreciate it if you didn't call me sweetheart. Madeleine, or Miss Hart, will suffice.'

He rolled his eyes.

'Secondly, I understand that you have known Peyton for a long time but, in this particular situation, that's irrelevant. The wedding is between two people, and obviously the photographs need to reflect both the bride and groom's wishes.'

'What groom has an input on the shots? Especially an Irish one.' He laughed at his own joke. 'I'm sure he'd much rather be in the pub anyway.'

'Mr Kelly does have views on both the style and particular photographs for the wedding. The bride and groom have been very much a unit in their decision making.'

Something about this man had my senses tingling, and definitely not in the good way.

'As for your other comment, perhaps it would be better to keep such opinions to yourself in order to avoid offending either Mr Kelly, his friends, family or really anyone, if we're honest. You are, don't forget, in Ireland and, as such, it would be best if you gave its people, including Mr O'Shea here, the respect they deserve.'

Vance Benson opened his mouth to either protest or make some other snide comment but I'd had enough by now and swept on. 'So now I think would be a good time to walk through the venue and decide exactly where the posed shots will be, then go over the plan to make sure you have all the ones that are required listed so that none are missed. Do you have an assistant to help you on the day?'

'I'm quite capable of doing this by myself.'

'I am sure you are.' Actually, I wasn't at all sure. My gut instinct was quite the opposite. 'I was merely asking as many photographers I work with have an assistant, especially when it is a function of this size.'

'Like I said, I'm good.'

Ugh.

'Calum, would you mind taking Mr Benson through to the main doors and we can start from there with the staircase? I just need to take this,' I said as my phone vibrated and the florist's name showed on the display.

'Of course, Maddie. This way, if you please.' Calum's back was up but his professionalism kept his attitude in check. I had no doubt we'd have a good old gossipy take-down later.

I stepped through a doorway to take the call from Fiadh, who wanted to double-check timings, pushing the door to as I did so. Just as I hung up, Lorcan came through another door hidden in the panelling that I hadn't even known was there, smiling as he saw me.

'Hi,' he said, then turned his head, the dark brows snapping together as he heard Vance speaking loudly to Calum outside the room. It had become obvious from the first meeting that Vance appeared to have no other volume. It was loud or nothing.

'Is she always that much of an uptight bitch?'

'She's lovely, actually,' Calum replied, loyally, and I made a mental note to give him a big hug.

Vance gave a sniff of derision. 'Strutting around like she owns the place, bossing people about.'

'She's the wedding planner. It's her job to make sure every-thing is as it should be for the bride and groom. And she's very good at it.'

'Yeah, well, she can back off me. I don't need to be told what to do by a—' His words faded as Lorcan yanked the door open and stepped out, his gaze focused like a laser on the photogra-pher. I'd tried to stop him but frankly it was like tying a bull in a field to a kebab stick.

36

'Is there a problem here?' Lorcan asked in a voice that was controlled but made no attempt to hide the fact he'd heard the conversation and wasn't best pleased.

Calum, God love him, merely looked at Vance, his brows raised as if interested to hear the answer himself. He certainly wasn't about to help this guy wriggle out of the hole.

Vance attempted to puff himself up, and I was thankful for the fact I'd always been good at keeping a straight face. Lorcan had about eight inches and several stone in muscle on him and it was clear to everyone in the room he was endeavouring to hold his temper.

'Who are you?'

'Lorcan O'Malley. The owner of this venue.'

Vance shrugged. 'Am I supposed to be impressed?'

Two things crossed my mind at this point. Firstly, how on earth was Peyton friends with this muppet, and two, how on earth had none of us yet punched him?

Lorcan shook his head. 'No. You asked a question and I answered it. Now perhaps you would do me the same courtesy.'

Vance looked confused.

'I asked if there was a problem.'

Vance shrugged but his eyes darted to me.

'I'm sorry,' Lorcan asked, 'is that a yes or a no? I'm not only the owner of this place, but I'm also the best man for the wedding so, as I'm sure you understand, I need to know immediately if there's a problem so that it can be rectified.'

The easiest way to rectify the problem would be to get this bloke on the first plane back to America but somehow I didn't see that happening.

'No problem.' Vance did another chest puff. 'I just don't need to be told what to do. I'm more than capable of getting the photographs Peyton wants.'

'I'm sure you are,' Lorcan said smoothly, and I tried not to giggle as he purposely let me see him crossing his fingers behind his back. 'But Peyton hired Miss Hart as her wedding planner in order to avoid more stress following their original plans falling through. As such, it's Miss Hart's job to tell you what to do, if needs be. Her requests are not to be taken personally, and, as such, it would be appropriate, and professional, if you showed her the respect she deserves.' Lorcan's words were delivered in his soft, lilting tones but there was a layer of unbending steel beneath them.

Vance had turned an interesting shade of purple, suggesting he clearly thought he was being unfairly attacked, but we were all beyond caring by then. Calum was staring down at his feet, but the tips of his ears were pink and I knew he was absolutely bursting with amusement. A thick atmosphere wrapped itself around our small group.

'Right!' I said, smiling brightly. 'Vance, shall we have a walk-through and perhaps we could exchange some ideas and see how they tie in with what Patrick and Peyton want?' Ideally, I'd have replaced this bloke in a heartbeat but Peyton was set on using him for some reason so right now it made my job easier if we could all get along. I didn't trust him an inch but, to paraphrase the saying, I'd decided it would be safer to keep my enemy close.

He took a deep breath, threw a glare at Lorcan, which was like throwing a marshmallow at Mount Everest, and condescended to accompany me.

'Let's go,' he said, smiling the fakest smile ever seen to man.

'Great.'

* * *

'You didn't need to do that,' I said as I returned to the little snug where Calum and Lorcan were sprawled, the open fire crackling enticingly. I'd just seen Vance off and had a short call with Peyton. I still had concerns about her choice of photographer but Peyton was so thrilled when I told her we'd done a walk-through that I didn't have the heart to steer her towards the possibility of hiring someone else. I'd pulled in a massive favour from a photographer I'd worked with a lot who was taking some time off but had agreed, in case of emergency, to get herself over to the castle if it got to Wedding DEFCON 1.

'Of course he did,' Calum said, pouring me a cup of tea. 'It was all terribly thrilling and ever so romantic!' He laid a hand on his chest. 'I loved it!'

'You would,' I said, plopping down next to Lorcan on the squashy sofa and toeing off my heels with the opposite foot. 'You live for drama.'

'This is true.'

'Has he gone?' Lorcan asked.

'Yes. I think we're more on the same page now though.'

'He needs to learn some manners,' Lorcan grouched into his mug.

'I don't disagree but I can look after myself.'

His gaze lifted to mine. 'That, I have no doubt of. But he'd already insulted Patrick and the men of Ireland in general. I'm afraid it was one step too far when he started the name-calling on you.' He gave a shrug. 'And I'd do it again. He's a cocky little eejit.'

It was hard to disagree with that so I sat back, lifted my feet towards the fire and wiggled my toes, warming them through and drawing a sense of comfort from the mellow setting.

* * *

Ballalee castle looked stunning. The twin stone staircases that greeted visitors as the main doors opened now had their carved balustrades swathed in deep green seasonal foliage, interspersed with white roses, lilies and froths of gypsophilia. Large silver lanterns lined each side of the path, ready to be lit as the light faded, with more floristry swathing the steps of the main entrance.

'It's definitely not subtle, is it?' Lorcan asked as Fiadh adjusted the two enormous, highly fragranced displays each side of the table where Peyton and Patrick would sign the register, one of the many photo ops.

'Subtle wasn't the brief,' I said, moving him out of Fiadh's way. 'Don't you have something to be doing?'

'Not really,' he replied, lifting a piece of ivy and studying it.

'Well, perhaps you could find something,' I suggested, removing the ivy from his hand and replacing it where Fiadh had initially, and carefully, trailed it.

'Like what?'

'Doesn't your mum need some help? She's got enough people coming to dinner for Christmas by the sound of it.'

'Why do you think I'm here? I already got ejected from there for getting under her feet.'

'Well, now you're under ours. Don't you have work to do or something?'

'Nope. I give all my employees and me a proper break at Christmas.'

'A cuppa would be grand, Lorcan,' Fiadh piped up from where she was pinning a beautifully woven garland that encompassed both the season and all of Peyton's choices for white, scented flowers along the front of the signature table.

'Oh, yes, perfect.'

'I can do that,' he said, shoving his hands in his pockets and strolling out, Bod toddling along behind him.

'Nicely done,' I said, grinning at her once he'd closed the door.

Fiadh looked across at me, winked and we both continued on our respective tasks.

* * *

'How'd it go, love?' Maria asked when we walked through the door later that evening. I'd told Lorcan he could go off and do his own thing – I had a hire car, after all – but he'd just shrugged and said he was happy to ferry me about. I had too much else on my mind to argue so just went with it.

'Good, thanks, Maria. Manic but good. I think everything is pretty much in place now for tomorrow.'

'Hi, Mammy, nice to see you too,' Lorcan said, walking up to her and giving her a kiss on the cheek, which she accepted, laughing, before turning back to me. 'Now take a seat. Aoife and her boyfriend are coming by for dinner too. It will be ready in a minute if you want to go and get ready.'

'Thanks, I'll just change quickly. My feet are killing me!'

'Why didn't you take them off earlier?' Lorcan said, watching as I gently massaged my toes.

'Because I was working. What am I supposed to do? Run around a castle's stone floors in December in bare feet?' Maria and I shared a 'men' look.

'Oh, ha ha, and I saw that, by the way. No ganging up. I meant take other shoes. Obviously.'

'It's not really my look, though, is it?'

'Whereas bunions are?'

'I'd make yourself scarce while you still can, my lad,' Maria said over her shoulder as she opened the oven, fogging the glasses she'd popped on to read the timer.

'Which boyfriend is this, anyway?' Lorcan said, once I'd returned to the room wearing a sweatshirt and jogging bottoms. I sat at the table next to him where he was pouring me a large glass of wine.

'That's enough, thanks. I need a super-clear head tomorrow.'

'Mark, the plumber lad.'

Lorcan did a little movement of his head, tipping his chin.

'Now, don't look like that,' his mum said, pointing at him with her wooden spoon. 'He seems very nice and Aoife likes him. You behave now.'

'I always behave.'

'You scared the daylights out of one and she never saw him again.'

'He was a little shit—'

'Lorcan.'

'Sorry, Mammy,' he said and I grinned.

'He spoke to her like she was stupid. She might be a bit flighty but she's not stupid. I just asked him to treat her with respect.'

Now I knew where the habit had come from. Being the eldest, and having three younger sisters, Lorcan had taken it upon himself to make sure they were all treated as they should be. His conversation with Vance had been along a similar line. Perhaps it was right that Lorcan should own a castle; he certainly had a chivalrous streak and, although I could look after myself, I wasn't objecting. Good manners and being made to feel special were never something to complain about, in my eyes.

Maria turned to me. 'The poor lad didn't say another word the rest of the meal. Every time he went to open his mouth, this one was watching him. It was like watching a guppy in a fish tank.'

'I can't imagine he'd have had anything intelligent to say. God knows what she saw in him anyway.'

'He was good-looking, Lorcan. Sometimes that's enough. She was only young.' Maria turned to me. 'Mad as anything she was with her brother. Didn't speak to him for a month after the bloke ghosted her – is that the right word? I'm sure that's what she said. I can't keep up with all these terms but anyway. He didn't call and she blamed Lorcan.'

'It does sound like he had a point.'

'Oh, sure he did. The boy was an eejit. Like Lorcan said, there wasn't a lot going for him other than his looks and you'd get better conversation out of Bod than that one. But my daughter had to have her time to flounce, which is fine. She saw sense in the end. From what I heard,' Maria added, her features creasing with concern now, 'it was just as well. Not long after, he got a girl in the next village pregnant and refused to have anything to do with the baby. Even bragged about it. Thought he was so clever. Nasty piece of work.'

'I didn't know that.'

'No. We decided not to tell you.'

'Who's we?' he said, straightening.

'The family,' Maria said, as though the answer was obvious.

'Why not?'

'Because Aoife said she couldn't bear to get a lecture on what a lucky escape she'd had and so on.'

'I wouldn't have done that.'

His mother fixed him with a look.

'I might have pointed out that circumstances had proved she was better off without him but other than that...'

'She already knew that.'

'What else haven't I been told? I thought we talked about everything. That was the point of having the WhatsApp group.'

'We do, my darling,' his mum said, bending to kiss his cheek as she passed. 'But you took on all the responsibility for everyone when your father died and sometimes we just keep the odd thing quiet so you don't have to worry.'

'If it's about my family, I want to worry.' The jovial tone had vanished now and his mum realised this too.

'I know. And I promise we'll tell you everything from now. OK?'

'Good. Thank you.'

'But don't you go scaring this lad away. I like him and he's good for Aoife.'

'Fine.' He looked up. 'What?' he asked as his mum peered at him.

'I mean it.'

'I said fine.'

'I know you did. Just make sure you mean it. Maddie, love.

Give him a kick for me, will you, if he starts on anything? I can't reach from my chair.'

'Will do.'

'Oi.'

'Behave yourself, then.'

Lorcan let out a long-suffering sigh.

* * *

As it turned out, the evening was fun and full of conversation and laughter. Aoife, of course, was interested in the wedding plans.

'I heard that photographer they hired is an old college boyfriend of Peyton's.'

Lorcan and I exchanged a look. I knew they went back a way but Peyton had omitted to mention that they'd dated.

'Really?'

'You shouldn't listen to gossip,' her brother cautioned.

'It's not gossip, actually,' Aoife said, pointedly. 'I saw them just this afternoon. Mark took me for lunch at the hotel. They were on a corner table cosied up together, giggling away.'

Lorcan's body was tensing beside me and, without thinking, I rested my hand on his leg. His hand slid to mine and covered it. OK, that was unexpected but, if it kept him calm, it wasn't the most unpleasant feeling in the world. If I'd had more time to think about anything other than the wedding, I might have thought it was a very pleasant feeling indeed.

'They're old friends and she hasn't seen him for a long time. I'm sure they were just catching up.'

'I guess.' Aoife's expression didn't match her words.

'Does Patrick know they dated in college?'

'Not that I'm aware of,' Lorcan replied, his brows lowered,

thoughts clearly running through his mind on behalf of his friend. 'I can ask.'

'No!' Aoife, Maria and I all replied.

'What?'

'It's not our place to ask questions like that.'

'I'm his best mate. I can ask what I like.'

'And say what?' I questioned him.

'I don't know. How about "Did you know that louse of a so-called photographer, who has seemed entirely unenthusiastic about this whole wedding from the start, used to date your fiancée and has been getting cosy with her?"'

'You do that and I will do something extremely unpleasant to parts of your anatomy I imagine you're very fond of. Do you understand?' My voice was calm but my words were sincere.

Silence drifted over the table for the first time.

'Oh my God, please marry him. You're the best.' Aoife shattered it, laughing as she spoke.

Lorcan flicked his gaze to her momentarily, which she returned without flinching.

'Fine. I won't say anything.'

'Everything's going to be fine. This time tomorrow, Patrick and Peyton will be married and partying and that little twit can disappear back from whence he came.'

'And what will you be doing then?' Maria asked me.

'Oh, I've got a morning flight back to London the following day. I think I might treat myself to a couple of days with my feet up.'

Lorcan gave a snort of disbelief so I kicked him. His mum hadn't actually specified booting him was only in particular circumstances, after all.

'After that it will be back to planning the next weddings on my books.'

'Are you spending Christmas with your family?' Maria asked and I felt Lorcan's hand, still resting on mine, tighten.

'Umm, no. I just have a quiet one at home. My next-door neighbours are very sweet and I sometimes pop in there for a couple of drinks, but I like it quiet.'

'That sounds peaceful.' Maria nodded, apparently sensing there was more to it but tactfully moving things along.

'Yes, it is.' I smiled and thankfully drifted into the next conversation.

37

I need to see you xx

Peyton's text sent my heart plummeting through the floor. This was not a good sign. I'd seen her message as I was just getting out of the shower and was already heading down to the car, calling her as I went.

'What's up?' I asked.

'I need to see you,' she repeated.

Oh, crap. 'Of course, I'm heading out of the door now. Where shall I meet you?'

'I'm about a mile or two away from the castle. I don't know where. I just turned right out of the entrance and drove until I found somewhere to pull into.'

'I'll find you. Sit tight.'

'OK. Thanks, Maddie.'

'Do you want some breakfast, love?' Maria asked, already at the stove as I hurried into the kitchen.

'Oh, thank you, Maria. That'd be lovely, but something's come up so I've got to shoot out. I'm really sorry.'

'That's OK, I hope everything's all right. Make sure you get yourself some food. You've a long and busy day ahead of you.'

'What's up?' Lorcan asked, his hair still damp and ruffled from the shower, the smell of the citrusy gel he used tickling my nose as he stepped through from the next room.

'I'm not sure yet. Peyton just messaged and asked to see me. That's all I know at the moment.'

'Do you want me to come? Should we tell Patrick?'

'No, and no. Not until I know what's going on. It might be nothing.'

'Your face doesn't look like you think it's nothing.'

'Stop reading me. It's very annoying!' His mouth briefly gave the flicker of a smile before setting back into a grim line. 'And I really don't know, but it definitely sounded like she'd been crying.'

'I bet this is down to that bloody Vance!' he said, his teeth gritted, voice low.

'We don't know that.'

'Yeah, but you think so too.'

I met his eyes. 'It wouldn't surprise me, but hopefully it's just a little bit of nerves and I'll be back shortly with everything on track.'

* * *

'And now I'm wondering if we really have rushed into things, like people said,' Peyton finished, inhaling a massive gulp of air to make up for not having done so for what seemed like several minutes as she'd poured out her worries and panic. We were sitting in a massive four-by-four like the one the hire company had tried to give me and looking out over a field of sheep. Well, we had been but a combination of our warm breath and

Peyton's hot tears had steamed the windows, so it felt as if we were stuck in a bubble.

'Everybody gets nervous, that's natural. But you and Patrick have been together for three years and you both wanted this. It's not exactly a two week whirlwind romance. Neither of you were pushing the other, which is just how it should be in a partnership that's right.' I started with reason and hoped that would be the only tool I'd need from my emotional toolbox to fix this.

'But what if I wanted to go back to the States to live? I mean, I do have my family and lots of friends over there.'

'Do you want to move back?'

'No. I love our house and where we live. I'm just thinking about the future.' She gave a sniff.

'But you travel back and forth now, don't you, when you want to see your family? And they're happy and able to travel too so that always makes things easier.'

'That's true.'

'And if that was something you did decide in the future, then you and Patrick would talk it over, like you do everything, and you'd find a solution.'

She nodded and worried a false nail. I sat on my hands in order not to try and move it away from her mouth. That was a minor problem compared to the bride getting cold feet.

'I suppose. Do you think Patrick loves me?' she asked, looking at me as if she was genuinely concerned.

'I do,' I replied without hesitation. 'And I know you think I probably say that to everyone, but the moment you two walked into my house that day it was obvious. I don't think he just loves you. That man absolutely adores you. He'd do anything for you. You were bouncing about at some godforsaken time when you video-called me while he was trying to sleep and he accepts that's you and adores you all the more for it because he loves you. Without question.'

'Why do you think he said about getting married over here? I mean, it's meant all my family and friends have had to travel whereas most of his are quite local.'

Peyton was lovely but there was no denying she was still rich and entitled and on the odd occasion that came across. From what I'd heard in the gossip vines from guests and her bridesmaids as we'd coordinated and double-checked details over the past few days, she'd actually been quite the diva back in the day. The perils of never having to wait for anything or be told no. But meeting Patrick had changed that. I meant what I'd said when I told her he adored her but his down-to-earth character and feet firmly set in reality seemed also to have balanced out the less desirable tendencies of her own nature.

'Peyton. You told me that you were the one that wanted to get married here. To connect with your ancestry. Remember?' I didn't let on that I knew there wasn't any, but I wasn't about to let Patrick get kicked for something he didn't do. 'On that first meeting you said that Patrick had told you he didn't care where you got married, so long as he got to marry you. Do you remember?'

She picked a different nail to fiddle with. 'I suppose.'

'So Ireland was your idea.'

'Yes... but don't you think he should have insisted we get married in America. Where my friends are? I mean, the wedding is supposed to be about the bride, isn't it? I mean, it's supposed to be my day.'

I wasn't sure I liked this side of Peyton.

'It's both your days, Peyton. It's a day about showing those you care about how much you mean to each other, making that commitment. Yes, it's also the opportunity to wear a beautiful dress and have a magnificent party, but that's all just window dressing. The main thing, the most important thing, is that you love Patrick, and he loves you and today you show each other that.'

She nodded quietly.

'Can I ask something?'

'Hmm?' Peyton looked up.

'Where has all this come from? A couple of days ago on the phone, you were saying you wished the wedding were happening that day. And now you're hesitating.'

'Nowhere really,' she said, two spots of high colour appearing on her make up free face.

'It must have been something?' I pushed gently.

'Well, Vance and I were just talking over old times yesterday and, well, about all sorts really, and I suppose it just got me thinking.'

I was going to kill him.

'And what do you think now?'

She shrugged. 'I suppose it just all feels a bit overwhelming.' Her eyes began to fill. 'And then Vance was saying it was a shame that I'd been persuaded to get married here, where it's cold and grey, and how a Californian wedding would have been so much prettier and...'

Warning bells began clanging in my head as red siren lights whirled round.

'And?' I asked, keeping my tone steady and light.

She looked up. 'He told me he still loves me. That he always has.'

I was going to kill him, bury him, dig him up, use a defibrillator, then kill him again.

'I see. And how do you feel about him?'

'I... well, I hadn't really thought about him in that way since we split up back in college. But I suppose seeing him again now, and he does have a point about me getting married over here—'

'Although you have already confirmed that that was your request and not Patrick's.'

'Yes, well, I suppose so.'

'Do you have feelings for Vance?'

She looked down at her lap, then back at me, and shook her head. 'I don't think so.' The tears bubbled through and her nose began to run. 'But it all made sense when he said it and now I don't know what to do and it all feels too much and I...' She continued to speak and, although I'd practically earned a degree in 'crying speak' through my years as a planner, even I was having trouble translating this time. 'What am I going to do?' she wailed at the end.

'Do you want to speak to your parents?'

Her mouth formed a horrified o. 'No!'

'I'm sure they'd understand and would want to help.'

'Yes, but they'll take over and the next thing I know, I'll be back on a plane to California!' She looked genuinely upset at this prospect, which buoyed my hopes.

'Have you eaten?' I asked.

'I had a macrobiotic plant smoothie jello shot this morning.'

'So that's a no. OK, do you trust me?'

Peyton raised her eyes to me, suddenly looking young and vulnerable. There was a nine-year age gap between her and Patrick but right now, unsure and insecure, she looked even younger than her years. 'Yes.'

'Good. Then come with me.'

'Where are we going?' she asked, following me out of her

car and towards mine parked behind, which looked even tinier in comparison to Peyton's.

'This is your car?' she asked, distracted for a moment.

'Yep. Isn't it lovely?'

She smiled. 'It's cute but I asked them to get you one like mine.'

'Yeah. I have a confession about that,' I said as we belted up and I pulled back onto the road, executing a U-turn on the narrow road courtesy of the excellent turning circle of my little car. 'I asked them to find me something smaller.'

Peyton looked at me and then began to laugh. 'Well, they sure did that!'

'Hi. You OK? Have you found Peyton?' Lorcan's deep, concerned voice came through the speaker on the car.

'Yes. She's here in the car with me now. Are you still at home?'

'Yep.'

'Does your mum have space for another one for breakfast?'

'Yep,' he said, without missing a beat.

'OK, we'll see you shortly.'

Peyton had been making hand-waving gestures the entire time I'd been on the phone.

'I can't go to Lorcan's. What will he think of me? He's Patrick's best friend. Please, Maddie, I can't. He'll hate me if he knows I've been having second thoughts.'

'No, Peyton. I promise you. He won't. He wants the best for both of you. If you were having second thoughts, or are, he wouldn't want you to go ahead and marry his friend, making both of you miserable, would he?'

'No, I don't suppose so. I never thought about it like that.'

'We just need somewhere that's not full of wedding guests

and that's a little hard to find in the village at the moment. Maria's place is as neutral as we can get right now.'

'Is that Lorcan's mom?'

'Yes. She's lovely. Here we are.'

'What a beautiful house,' Peyton said, looking out of the window at the large farmhouse.

'It is, isn't it? Come on. Let's get you inside and warm. You're frozen.'

38

'Oh, my dears!' Maria said, bustling up behind Lorcan, who opened the door to us and stepped out into the cold towards Peyton, wrapping her in a huge hug before walking them both back inside. I could have kissed him. If I was honest, it wasn't the first time that face had inspired such a thought but his action at that moment had been exactly what the bride-to-be – something I hoped she still was – needed.

'Here you go, sit here and warm yourselves up and I'll get some breakfast on.' Maria busied herself as we sat around the table.

'I'm so sorry,' Peyton said, looking from me to Lorcan and back to me. I'd filled him in briefly while she nipped to the loo and freshened up her face so he was now up to speed and it was time to decide what our next move was. Or more accurately, Peyton had to decide.

'There's nothing to apologise for, Peyton,' Lorcan began softly. 'It's a big step you're taking and you need to be sure you're doing the right thing, and for the right reasons.'

She sniffed through her smile. 'Maddie said you'd say that.'

He turned his head briefly, locking gazes with me for a long moment. 'Our Maddie knows me pretty well, then, I'd say.'

'I guess she does.'

'So, how are you feeling now?'

'Better, I think.'

'About the wedding?'

She paused and he reached out across the table, wrapping her fidgeting hands within his own. 'Forget about the castle, and the flowers and the guests and everything. Just think about you and Patrick. None of the other stuff matters. Maddie mentioned something about Vance?'

Both of us saw her tense.

'It's OK,' Lorcan soothed. 'I'm just asking. Do you feel the same way he does?'

She shook her head. 'No. No, I don't. I think he just got me all confused and wondering if I was doing the right thing. I wish I'd never agreed to let him do the photography. We stayed friends after we broke up and he was always so keen to be around my family and talking about his business plans. Our parties were pretty well attended by influential people and he was always trying to hand his card over and stuff. It got kind of embarrassing sometimes. And I guess when he asked about the wedding and how much it would mean to him to be able to do this for me, I was flattered. But I don't think it's really about me at all. For a start, he's charging more than some of the professionals we spoke to.'

Lorcan gave a small headshake.

'I've been a real sucker, haven't I?'

'No, not at all. You're kind and sweet and sometimes less moral people manipulate qualities like those for their own ends.'

'I feel so stupid. I don't even know if I can go through with it all now. When Patrick finds out, he's going to be so mad and my parents are going to be talking about what a waste all this effort was.'

'Forget all that,' Lorcan said. 'And I can guarantee Patrick won't be mad. He's just going nuts with worry. Unfortunately, word's gone round that the bride is MIA and he's been ringing every two minutes asking me if we've found you. I've told him everything's in hand and you're safe with us, but he's been worried sick.'

Peyton's blue eyes filled with tears again. 'I never meant to hurt or worry him. I... I just love him so much,' she said and burst into another fresh round of tears. Without a word between us, Lorcan and I swapped jobs as I wrapped my arms around Peyton and rocked her gently, glancing over the top of her head to where Maria was watching, worry and care creasing her face. Lorcan, in the meantime, slipped quietly out of the back door, shucking on his coat as he did so.

* * *

Ten minutes later, Maria and I had combined to calm Peyton back down and I'd taken her up to my room to let her use my bathroom to freshen up and brush her hair before returning to the kitchen. As we entered from one door, Lorcan came in through the back door, Patrick following him in. His brow was furrowed with distress and his hair was sticking up at odd angles from, I imagined, several hours of running his hands through it.

'Patrick!' Peyton's voice cracked. 'But you're not supposed to see me the day of the wedding. It's bad luck.'

He was already hurrying past us to her side, taking her

hands in his. 'I wasn't sure if there was even going to be a wedding, and, right now, I don't care about superstitions. I just had to see you.'

'I wanted to see you too.' Peyton smiled, tears beginning to flow.

'Peyton, my darling. If you're not ready for this, that's OK. If you don't want to marry me, that's OK too.'

Her perfectly sculpted brows shot up as far as the Botox would allow.

'Now, don't interpret that as meaning that I don't want to marry you. I've wanted that from about a week after I met you, but if you've changed your mind, then I would never try and force you. This has to be your choice and your choice alone. If you want to wait, I will wait for you. If you don't want to be...' he swallowed audibly '... us any more, then I will accept that but—'

'I do want us!' Peyton broke in, almost wailing. 'I do, I do, I promise. I just got all confused and overwhelmed and then Vance...' She looked up through her wet lashes, cheeks flaring.

Patrick's jaw hardened. 'Yes, Lorcan filled me in about Vance. Don't worry. Although, assuming you want to go ahead...'

'I do! More than anything!' Her voice had shot up several octaves and there was a hint of panic in it now as the tears began once more in full flow as she clung onto him.

'OK, darlin'. It's OK,' he said, his voice gentle as he stroked her hair. 'God, I love you.'

'I love you too!' she wailed. Lorcan winced and, over at the stove, Maria chuckled to herself at his reaction.

'Well, that all works out well now, doesn't it?'

'I can't guarantee I'm going to want to smile for the photos with this Vance bloke the other side of the camera, though,' Patrick commented.

'Not a problem,' I interjected. 'Back-up is on the way. She'll be here within the next half an hour.'

'Really?' Patrick and Peyton's heads both swivelled towards me.

'Yes. I hope that was OK. She's excellent. I've worked with her a lot and... well, Vance wasn't really being terribly co-operative so I pulled in a favour and had Ellise on standby.'

'What about Vance?' Peyton asked.

'If you want to use him still, then that's up to you.'

Patrick's face suggested he most definitely didn't want to. 'No, no, I don't,' Peyton said, still clinging to Patrick's hand but beginning to regain some of her normal poise. 'I thought he was a friend, but I don't really think he is. I don't think he loves me either. All he's interested in, ever has been interested in, is what my family's name and money can do for him.'

'Do you want to tell him that his services are no longer required, or would you prefer me to?' I asked.

Pick me! Pick me!

Peyton looked at Patrick, then me. 'I'm happy to do it,' Patrick interjected.

'We need to start getting you into a fit state to be seen to marry this woman, mate,' Lorcan said. 'That could take a while so I'm not sure you'll have time.' He'd been standing behind the two of them, leaning back on the work surface, quietly taking it all in. When Patrick made the suggestion, he gave the smallest headshake to me and I sent him a look of agreement. Probably best not to have the man whose fiancée you just tried to steal deliver the news. There was every chance, something Lorcan's mini gesture had confirmed, that Patrick might well deliver something else.

Especially to someone as smug and underhand as Vance Benson.

'Very funny,' Patrick replied, glancing over his shoulder at his old friend.

'I'm happy to do it,' I said. Ecstatic, to be truthful.

'Right!' Maria said, brushing her hands on her apron. 'Now that's sorted, everyone sit down for breakfast.' She began dishing out the plates, full to the brim with sizzling bacon, eggs, fried bread, beans, fried tomatoes, fresh local sausages and a pile of mushrooms.

I glanced up at the clock. It was only just coming up to seven and it already felt as if it had been a long day.

'I can't possibly eat all this!' Peyton was now sitting and staring at the plate.

'Just eat what you can, then, lovey,' Maria encouraged her.

'But I never eat this sort of thing.' She was still staring at the food.

'If I'm honest, Peyton, neither do I, but I can guarantee you don't want to miss out on this. You've already had a tiring morning and it's only seven o'clock. You're going to need a lot of energy today. This is the best fuel.'

Maria looked over the heads of the others and gave me a wink and I knew then where Lorcan got it from.

'But my dress...'

'One meal isn't going to make a difference, sweetheart,' Patrick said, already tucking in. 'Come on, you need some energy for all that dancing we're going to be doing later.'

Peyton tried a piece of fried bread, clearly a new experience, and it was as if she'd seen God. Butter could do that to you.

'You're not even supposed to see me before the ceremony!' she reminded him again, tapping him on the arm with her fork.

'I know. But for a while there I thought I wasn't going to see you at all, so let's just enjoy this delicious breakfast and we'll get back to the plan after that. Deal?'

'Deal,' she said, grinning at him with that wide Californian smile, enhanced just a little by a thin layer of tomato sauce, courtesy of the beans.

39

Vance did not take the news well, but I rather enjoyed myself. Lorcan was desperate to come with me to pass on the message because the bloke had irritated him from the start, but I persuaded him to deliver Peyton to the castle, where she was staying, and take Patrick back to his parents' and begin getting ready. As a compromise, I promised to get Calum to surreptitiously record our conversation so Lorcan could enjoy it at a later date. To say Vance wasn't exactly complimentary about me was an understatement, but, then again, most of the wedding party came in for it from him. Bearing in mind how Lorcan had reacted last time Vance had been rude, it was probably just as well he wasn't there as I didn't have time to clean up blood or bury a body.

* * *

'You look like you need this.' Lorcan handed me a large brandy and I just about found the energy to lift my arm to take it. I was flopped on the sofa in the snug, the door locked behind us, the wedding party having all finally made their way back to their respective abodes for the night. Calum had looked fit to drop and Lorcan had sent him home and made sure he'd messaged when he was back so we knew he was safe.

'I really do. What a day.'

'Are you pleased?'

'I am. Peyton looked stunning and they both looked so happy, I couldn't have asked for more.'

'I think you'd be forgiven for asking for a little less drama at six o'clock this morning, but I know what you mean.' He sat down heavily next to me, his bow tie hanging loosely around his neck and the first few buttons of his shirt open, exposing a few dark hairs against his skin. When I'd headed out with Ellise to meet him and Patrick approaching the castle, I'd hoped the bolt of electricity that shot through me at seeing Lorcan all dressed up had been calmly covered by my professionalism.

'This is the guy you've been working with?' Ellise had asked. 'The taller one?'

'Umm, yes. That's him. The owner.'

She'd turned her head and met my eyes deliberately. 'Lucky you.'

I'd given a wave of my hand. 'It's all business.'

'Sure it is,' she'd said, taking some candid shots as they'd approached. 'Don't forget once the wedding is over, those rules of yours can be tossed out. For God's sake, take him to bed, woman, otherwise you're both going to waste.'

'Ellise!' I'd hissed. 'He'll hear you.'

'Even better.'

'I'm regretting getting you down here.'

She'd laughed, throwing her head back. 'Liar.' She'd had a point.

* * *

'You look pretty done for too.'

'Yep. Been a long day, but, unlike you, I wasn't working.'

'I know. But it can still be tiring. Thanks for helping this morning. I can't even remember if I said that now or not. If not, sorry.'

Lorcan shook his head and rested one large warm hand over mine. 'Not a problem. Comes with the territory of best man anyway. I'm just glad it all worked out.'

'So am I.'

'So, are your duties as a planner for this wedding officially over?'

'They are,' I replied, sighing languidly as I warmed the golden liquid in my glass with the palm of my hand.

'Good,' Lorcan said, shifting on the sofa, taking the glass from my hand and placing it on the coffee table in front of us. 'Then that means I finally get to do this.' His hands cupped my face as his lips tentatively brushed mine, sending thrills and sparks of electricity racing through my body. He pulled away, his gaze meeting mine, almost as if waiting for permission, which I willingly gave.

This time the kiss began softly but quickly grew into something more raw, more urgent, the pent-up frustration of our time together bursting through as his hands slid back from my face. A low, guttural moan escaped from him as they met the confines of the clips securing my hair. With a couple of swift moves, they were gone and Lorcan was entangling his fingers in my curls, one hand winding a length around his fist and tightening as he pulled me towards him. The sense of pleasure combined with a hint of pain set my senses spinning as we explored each other's mouths and then further. One hand dropped to my waist, impatiently pulling at the blouse before sliding up my skin to cup my breast, his kisses moving down my neck as now his hands moved to the hem of my skirt and pushed it up. His fingers found the fastenings of my suspenders and Lorcan momentarily pulled away, my skin suddenly chilled from the loss of his lips. The heavy-lidded gaze dropped to my thighs, straddled as I was across him, stockings on show, and the deep appreciative sound growled again in his throat as he slid his hands around my backside and pulled me closer.

* * *

We crept back into the house in the early hours, hoping not to wake Maria, and Lorcan left me at the door to my room. As much as I wanted to be close to him, he'd been right when we'd lain on the sofa earlier. Both of us exhausted and spent, cuddled close together. He'd cupped my face in one large hand and told me we ought to get back so I could rest properly. I'd protested but now, having said goodnight, I knew he was right. I cleaned my teeth, stripped off, climbed into bed and was asleep within seconds of my head touching the soft Irish linen of the pillow.

* * *

'So it went well, then?' Maria asked as we sat at the table the next morning, watching as she dished up yet another hearty breakfast. Her family clearly had good metabolisms. I was less hesitant to wolf my own portion down. Yesterday had been exhausting, emotionally and mentally, but thankfully had turned out well – and I hadn't expected to have to find more energy in the early hours closed away in the snug of the castle with Lorcan. My body definitely needed replenishing – not to mention more of Lorcan O'Malley. He sat beside me, his hand slipping to mine beneath the table as we all shuffled in to make room for each other. The whole family had descended this morning, ready for the gossip, it would seem.

'She looked so beautiful, though,' Roísín, Lorcan's eldest sister, was saying. 'That dress was just stunning.'

'I'll pass on the compliment to the designer. Thanks.' I smiled, my body and mind properly relaxed for the first time in what felt like years.

'And Patrick looked like the cat that had got the cream, bless his heart,' Grace, the next sister down, added.

'He's just married a hot heiress. Of course he did!' Cillian said, laughing as he grabbed a piece of thick, hot buttered toast from the large plate in the centre of the table.

'That's not why he married her,' Lorcan reminded him.

'Nah, I know. Bonus though.'

Lorcan looked at me, rolled his eyes and grinned before tucking into another thick rasher of bacon.

'Even you looked relaxed and happy,' Roísín said, pointing her toast at her brother. 'About time you let go of that rigid belief about weddings and marriage being a bad idea at last.'

'Just because I enjoyed seeing my friend happy doesn't change my opinion on any of it. Look at all the drama it caused yesterday morning. That could all have been avoided if they weren't actually getting married. That Vance bloke wouldn't have even been in the picture to start with.'

'That's a bad example.'

'Not at all. It's a good example. It just goes to show, no matter how much you plan, it can still all go wrong. So why take the risk?' He took a bite of fried bread to punctuate the sentence.

'To be happy?' his sister shot back. 'To have someone else to enjoy life with?'

'I enjoy life plenty. And I don't need a shindig or a piece of paper to tell me I'm allowed to.'

'Of course you don't, but it's another level of commitment.'

'Or another level of pain.'

The conversation had taken on an unexpected intensity as the words bounced back and forth like a high-stakes tennis match across the scrubbed pine of the family dinner table.

'Not everyone is Siobhan, Lorcan. You know that,' she said, her eyes momentarily flicking to me.

'No, that's true. She's definitely one of a kind.' His usually warm, soft voice was suddenly cold and hard-edged, laced through with bitterness.

'Don't you think it's time you let it go?'

'You're on her side now?'

'Don't be an eejit. Of course I'm not. But it was a long time ago and you're giving something that should be in the past too much power over your future. Your happiness.'

'I'm plenty happy, thank you very much.'

'Are you now?'

'Yep. And all without a bit of paper.'

'Or a steady woman by your side.'

'Again, I don't need a piece of paper for that either. Not everyone's as set on traditional relationships as you are, Roísín.' His hand reached for mine beneath the table but I moved it to my lap, lacing them together. The food I'd eaten was now sitting leaden in my stomach and I was concentrating on ensuring that it didn't pay a second visit. From the corner of my eye, I saw his head turn towards me before looking back at his plate.

'No, I know that,' Roísín agreed.

I could feel other eyes on me but I kept my own lowered. This was not how I had expected, how I had wanted, today to begin. Lorcan knew my views, and the words he had whispered last night, the longings he'd confessed to, the wishes he'd spoken about, promises he'd made while exploring my body and after, as we'd lain together in the snug, limbs still entwined... Had they all been just words? Just a way to get me into bed? I'd seen similar tactics used at weddings over and over and yet I'd fallen for the same lines. I remembered the comments about Lorcan being a heartbreaker, but the more time we'd spent together, the more I thought my first impressions had been wrong. I thought I'd discovered the real Lorcan. But, as it turned out, it wasn't the bridesmaids I'd needed to warn – it had been myself. With all my experience as a planner, not once had I let any possible attraction cloud my judgement. Until now. But this time it hadn't just clouded it, it had been a full-on white-out.

'But some people are,' Roísín continued. 'You used to be once as well. You need to let it go now, Lorcan.'

'Just like that, eh?' His voice still had that hard edge of steel but his sister wasn't backing down. Everyone else was silent. Listening. Watching. Waiting.

'No, not just like that, but it was a long time ago and you have to take back your life. I know you were devastated and if I could have got away with it, I'd have shoved her off the bloody cliff for cheating on you and lying about that child but—'

'Child?' I said, my head snapping up.

Lorcan's eyes blazed then looked away.

'What child, Lorcan?' I asked.

He remained silent.

'I said, what child?'

'I'll tell you later,' he snapped.

'No, you will tell me now.'

'Oh, I will, will I? Don't forget you're not in charge of me any more.'

'I'm very well aware of that. But I'm asking you to tell me of your own free will.'

'Funny how once marriage and weddings come into the conversation, free will seems to make a swift exit.'

I glared at him, hot tears burning in my eyes, everyone else just a little bit out of focus as I struggled to keep them from escaping and pouring down my cheeks.

'Excuse me,' I said, attempting to retain as much dignity as I could, and pushed my chair back from the table.

'Are you going to tell the girl?' Maria spoke for the first time.

'It's fine, Maria. I don't think any of it matters now.'

Lorcan let out an icy huff. 'Pleased with yourself now, are you, Roísín?'

'Don't you dare blame her, Lorcan. This is all on you.' And with that I walked out of the kitchen, ran up to my room and grabbed the suitcase I'd thankfully mostly packed the day before the wedding and headed back downstairs. Nobody had moved, except for Lorcan, who was nowhere to be seen.

'Ah, love,' his mum said, wrapping her arms around me. 'I'm so sorry. I thought this was different. He was like his old self again once he met you.'

I swallowed hard, trying not to cry, trying not to wish that I could go home now and be wrapped in my own mum's embrace as my heart sat broken in little pieces on the floor of my chest. One by one the family each gave me a big hug. Not many words were spoken, for which I was glad. They and I knew there was little more to be said.

'Drive carefully now, won't you?'

'I will, I promise. And thank you again for all your kindness and hospitality.'

'It was truly my pleasure, darling,' Maria said, taking my hands within her own and bringing them to her heart. 'You're a special girl, so you are.'

My throat had closed, raw and painful with emotion, so I merely nodded and she did the same.

'I'll take that for you,' Cillian said, grabbing the handle of my case and leading me out to the front of the house where he loaded it in the back of the car for me before wrapping me in another big hug. 'Sorry about the big eejit,' he said softly. 'Doesn't know a good thing when he sees it.' I hugged him back, giving a squeeze of acknowledgement before letting go and opening the driver's side door.

'That's it, then?' We both turned at the deep voice. Cillian looked at me, a silent question in his eyes. I nodded and he headed back inside, but not before shooting his brother a dirty look.

'So it would seem.'

'Not going to give me a chance to explain?'

'I offered you a chance. In fact, if you recall I asked you a direct question and you refused to answer so yes, Lorcan, that's it. I'm just sorry I was stupid enough to fall for your lies. I mean,' I slapped my hand against my forehead, 'sleeping with the best man? What a bloody cliché! I can't believe I fell for that after all these years.'

'You think that's all it was? Sex?'

'I didn't yesterday but right now, yes. I do.'

'Well, it's not.'

'It doesn't really matter now, does it?' I said, turning away towards the car.

'Not to you, it seems.'

'Don't you dare!' I said, spinning back to face him. 'Don't you dare try and twist this so you're the injured party.'

'What do you want me to say? What did you think? That I was going to propose to you?'

'Of course not, but you told me you wanted more. That I meant more to you! That things had changed for you since we met and you trusted me. The stupid thing is, I never once questioned whether I could trust you! But clearly the answer to that is no!'

'You can trust me,' he said, close now. 'Of course you can, but that doesn't mean I'm about to dive into marriage with you or anyone.'

'If your ego can stand it, I hate to break it to you that I don't want to either. That's not the point. The point is that you know that's what I'm looking for. What I've always been looking for and you made me believe that you were thinking the same way.'

'I never meant to mislead you.'

'It doesn't matter,' I said, shoving at his broad chest. 'I can't even look at you right now.'

'You're overreacting, Maddie.'

Amazingly the thump I landed actually caused him to make a sound of not only surprise but, if not pain, then certainly discomfort.

'Overreacting! You have a child you never told me about and you think I'm overreacting?' I screamed at him, completely losing the poise and restraint I prided myself on. 'I stood on that cliff edge and poured my entire soul out to you. Things I've never told anyone! I shared my baby brother's last moments with you – moments I keep locked in my heart because they're too precious to share with just anyone, but I thought you were different. I thought you were the one, Lorcan. And you let me believe it. But you're not, are you? You're just another chancer. You didn't deserve to hear those memories and you sure as hell don't deserve me!' With that, I shoved him out of the way of the car door, got in and floored the pedal, joining the road towards the airport without looking back.

40

Spring had finally arrived. You could feel and smell it in the air, even here in the city. I was on my way to another potential booking, meeting at a coffee shop near the Shard. I'd put Lorcan O'Malley out of my mind, as much as I could. Occasionally his face would drift into my dreams but I'd learned to ignore it as best I could. I knew it would be a while before I'd be able to fix my heart entirely and I had a feeling the traces of the damage would remain, like when you glued a pot back together – the crack could still be seen, even if it was faint. But I'd faced worse than Lorcan O'Malley in my life and survived and I would do so again.

In contrast to my personal life, work had gone from strength to strength. Peyton had done a deal to do a feature on her wedding on a well-known socialite's blog, which linked to the hundreds of thousands of followers on the woman's socials. Apparently the two had gone to school together so as far as Peyton was concerned it was just a chat between friends, and an opportunity for thousands more people to see how beautiful she'd looked on their special day. Patrick hadn't been so keen but she'd sweet-talked him and he'd gone along with it on the proviso that hardly any of the pictures featured him. As this gave Peyton even more chance to shine and be the centre of the attention, it wasn't a hard ask.

Although it had been merely a chat for Peyton, the outcome for my planning business, Izzy's atelier and the venue (according to Calum, with whom I'd kept in touch), as well as Fiadh's florists and all the other businesses involved, had been impactful in the best way – something we were all grateful for after the previous couple of years. My books were almost full and I was only meeting the couple today because Peyton had asked me to as a favour and I, like most people, was rubbish at saying no to her.

I took my coffee and grabbed a table near the window, pulling out my notebook ready before checking my email and messages while I waited for my clients.

'Hi.'

I didn't need to look up. That voice would be forever etched into my memories – and my heart.

Slowly I lifted my head and met his eyes.

'Hello,' I said, my voice cool and professional as I tried not to show my surprise at his appearance. There were dark circles under his eyes, he'd lost a little weight and his hair was several weeks past needing a cut.

'You look well,' he said, having apparently ascertained I wasn't about to jump up into his arms, begging him to let us try again.

'Thank you. So do you.'

'Liar.' The smile I'd loved spread across his face. 'I look like crap and we both know it.'

I gave a small smile in return but said nothing. He'd already seen straight through my words and I wasn't about to expend energy on something that no longer mattered. That was what I told myself anyway, but the truth was my heart was now hammering against my ribs and it felt as if the only reason the entire café couldn't hear it was due to the soft jazz playing in the background.

'Do you mind if I sit?' he asked.

'I'm sorry, Lorcan,' I said, meeting his eyes again, determined not to let the rush of emotions currently flooding through me show on my face. He'd always been able to read me from the first moment we met, but I needed all my barriers up now. 'I don't think we have anything to talk about and I'm meeting a potential client.'

'I'm the client.'

'But...' I looked down at my notes. 'I have a different name.'

'Keane. It's Mam's maiden name. I knew if I booked it in my name, you wouldn't agree to see me.'

'Right. Well, honesty doesn't seem to be your strong suit so I suppose I shouldn't be surprised.'

For a moment he looked as if I'd slapped him, but he kept his focus on me. 'I guess I deserve that.'

There was no 'guess' in my opinion but I kept my thoughts to myself. Looking up, I saw that tactic didn't seem to have made a difference. As usual, he knew exactly what I was thinking, but right now I didn't care. I couldn't be here with Lorcan and certainly not to help him plan a wedding when even the thought of such a step with me had been anathema to him. My coffee only half drunk, I picked up my notebook and dropped it back into my tote bag.

'Look, I'm pleased that you've found someone with whom you want to build a life, but I'm afraid I won't have time to be your planner. Please do pass on my apologies to your fiancée.'

I made to stand but he reached out and touched his fingertips to mine, not stopping me. At least, not physically. The shock cracked through me as though I'd touched an electric fence.

'Lorcan, I—'

'There is no fiancée.'

'What?'

'There is no fiancée,' he repeated. 'At least not yet.'

I shook my head, pulling my hand away from him and gathering my things. 'I don't have time for this, Lorcan. My calendar is rammed and I only agreed to this meeting because Peyton asked me to...' Great. So Peyton was in on this too. After all I'd done for her, I thought, suddenly mad with everybody. 'Unbelievable,' I snapped, pushing the chair out quickly and standing. Lorcan mimicked my movements.

'Maddie. Wait. Please.'

'No! And please tell Peyton I don't appreciate her—'

'I love you.'

My mouth snapped closed like a turtle.

'Please, just hear me out. I know it was a sneaky way of getting to see you but I couldn't get hold of you any other way. Please? I appreciate I don't have the right to ask any of this, but I needed to tell you some things. Things you deserve to know.'

'It's a little late now, Lorcan.'

'You're right. But you deserve to hear them anyway.' He waited to see what I would do. My mind was running in circles but eventually both it and my body tired and I lowered myself back down.

'Thank you.'

I remained silent.

'I'm not really sure where to start. I made such a giant cock-up of it all.'

My only reply was a slight quirk of one eyebrow acknowledging that he'd at least got that bit right.

'I don't have a child.'

'But your sister said...' I couldn't help myself interrupting.

'I know. And I can see now how it must have sounded. And I can also see now how it must have felt when you realised I'd kept something from you when you'd bared your soul to me. It was unforgivable – although I'm of course hoping you might find a way, but my whole family think I'm an eejit and told me not to get my hopes up.'

I tried to smother the beginning of the smile that wanted to play on my face, easily imagining them saying those exact words.

'Siobhan and I were engaged, and she got pregnant. I was over the moon. I mean, I couldn't have been more thrilled. She seemed less so but, when I questioned her about it, she said she'd just been nervous about telling me because that hadn't been our plan so soon into the marriage.'

'That's understandable.'

'Yep. That's what I thought too. Until a couple of weeks before the wedding when she told me that the baby wasn't mine.'

'Oh... Lorcan.'

Even now I could see the pain of that revelation on his face.

'She'd known it wasn't all along. I'd been surprised because we'd always used protection but, you know, accidents happen and I had no reason to think anything else.' He took a deep breath and I gave him a moment as I caught a passing waiter and asked him for a black coffee, which came moments later and Lorcan took a sip. In truth, I always thought tea was better for crises but right now he looked as if he could do with the caffeine. Either that or a fortnight's sleep.

'It turned out she'd been seeing an old boyfriend. They'd connected on Facebook and got chatting and then, one thing led to another. And that another led to a baby.'

'I'm so sorry.'

He shook his head. 'She told me she was in love with him and, as painful as that was to hear, I could cope with that. The thing I couldn't cope with was that she'd known from the beginning the baby wasn't mine. And yet she let me carry on thinking it was, attending scans, shopping for baby things, reading bloody baby books.' He drew a hand across his brow.

I didn't know what to say. I could understand Siobhan being caught in a difficult situation but to let this man believe she was carrying his child when she'd known all along he wasn't the father just seemed cruel.

'After that I went a bit over the top against the whole relationship thing. Long term seemed pointless. So far as I could see – wanted to see – it just led to disappointment and heartache. Mam hadn't been happy in her marriage either, but divorce wasn't a thing in Ireland and then Siobhan. I chose to ignore the fact that my sisters had had beautiful wedding days and happy marriages. I was wounded and didn't want to see anything that might challenge that view.'

'I can understand that.'

'Then you came along and you were this beautiful, bright, funny woman with a wonderful heart but your big thing was weddings. I knew it couldn't work. There was no way I was going to change my mind but I knew you wouldn't either. Your parents had been happy and you made no secret of the fact you wanted marriage eventually. And it's obvious to anyone how much you love your job and how skilled you are at it. It was only right that you wanted a partner who respected and understood your career. I couldn't be any of those things. I didn't think I even wanted to be. But I couldn't stop thinking about you. I wanted to be with you all the opportunities I could.'

'I thought Peyton and Patrick wanted you on hand all the time with the arrangements?'

His expression was sheepish. 'Their actual instruction was just to keep an eye on things but that they had full faith in you. After our first meeting I knew I was in trouble and tried to stay away. But once I'd met you again at the restaurant, I used every excuse I could to see you.'

'I see,' I said, not sure what else to say. My mind was whirling, trying to make sense of everything, but what it kept coming back to were the words Lorcan had spoken when I was about to leave.

'I love you, Maddie. I think I've loved you from the moment you told me there had only been the one murder at the model village. Which I thoroughly deserved, by the way. My first words to you came out wrong and I was cringing the rest of the time and trying to think of a way to apologise but then it just got too far and I felt it would be even weirder to bring it up.'

'I can understand that.'

'I love you, Madeleine. I love your strength, your determination, your sense of fun and intelligence. Your planning to the nth degree drives me nuts but I love it anyway, not to mention your beautiful face, how sexy your hair is when you let it tumble down and, of course, that great arse of yours.'

'Romantic.' I grinned.

'I'm determined to be honest with you about everything now and your arse is amazing.'

'Shooosh!' I said, waving my hands, my brain currently swinging between wanting to laugh and cry.

'I know I don't deserve another chance, but I would spend every moment of my life grateful for it if you would grant me one. You make me a better man, Maddie. I want you in my life now and forever. I want to marry you. I want to stand up in front of family and friends and look a right eejit when you walk in and I burst into tears because I know I'm the luckiest man that ever trod God's green earth. But most of all, I need you. I thought I was living the life I wanted but now I know what was missing. It was you.'

EPILOGUE

Ballalee Castle was the only possible choice of venue for our wedding, and although it was a far smaller affair than Peyton and Patrick's, it was everything I'd ever wanted. Izzy had designed me the most beautiful dress I'd ever seen – which was saying something in my line of work – and Calum arranged everything there to perfection. Lorcan's family had claimed me as one of their own and I didn't have words for how much that meant.

Lorcan, true to his word, cried when I walked in, which of course set me off. To be fair, I'm not sure there was a dry eye in the place by the time we finished. I was probably biased, but it really was the most perfect wedding I'd ever planned.

My business was once again thriving, but now I'd found a better balance for my life. Now I had a reason, and help, to find that balance. Lorcan had changed too – but only for the better. He still teased me relentlessly, but I loved it. I think, deep down, I always had. But now that stillness within him, the calm he'd radiated when we'd spent time together in my office, in my home, on the cliffs of Ballalee, was with him all the time. He'd let the hurt that had been eating at him for over a decade go. It was always something he'd carry, that memory, but the agony was no longer in his heart. The space it had left had been replaced with happiness and joy, and love.

Lorcan had moved into my cottage and now only occasionally forgot to duck under the low beams. We'd thought about moving, perhaps into the newly completed Victorian schoolhouse conversion, but decided against it. Both of us loved the cottage, its cosiness, its feeling of home. My husband, especially, was a fan of the open fire. And, after one particular night on a new sheepskin rug he'd brought home, so was I. I'd even taken up gardening. I'd kept things neat before but hadn't had a clue what I was doing. Now I took a proper interest and we could often be found nosing around the local garden centre together on a weekend, along with Bod, of course, – something I didn't think either of us had envisioned. But I loved it. And I loved Lorcan. He'd taught me to slow down, to literally smell our newly planted roses. My life was so much more now, thanks to him. I'd said yes to him that day, and yes to taking the time to enjoy life and all that it had to offer, and the rewards were wonderful.

ACKNOWLEDGMENTS

As usual, thanks to the fabulous team at Boldwood Books for helping me get yet another book out into the world. I'm constantly grateful for their enthusiasm, support and determination to get my books in front of more readers. It's wonderful.

Also, thanks to copy editor, Sue and proof reader, Rose who are both brilliant and patiently help improve things and fix all the oddities.

I'd also like to thank Gloria Sanders, something I should have done before this, for the fabulous audio versions she creates of my books. She's so thorough in her preparation, and hugely talented. And I'm sorry, Gloria, I've thrown yet another accent your way with this book but I know you will be absolutely brilliant, as always.

Thanks to all my writing pals who understand that this bonkers writing life isn't all about laying back, being fed grapes and dictating the odd sentence. In fact, sadly it's not about that at all. It's more about abandoning the laundry/housework/hair-washing as a deadline looms!

And with that in mind, I'd also like to thank James for being totally accepting of this and making sure we eat when I'm buried in the words.

And, of course, thank you to you, the reader, for choosing this book and hopefully enjoying it. Without you, I wouldn't be able to do this so thank you so much. Happy reading!

ABOUT THE AUTHOR

Maxine Morrey is a bestselling romantic comedy author with twelve books to her name including *#NoFilter* and *Things Are Looking Up*. She lives in Dorset. Maxine lives on the south coast of England, and when not wrangling with words loves to read, sew and listen to podcasts and audio books.

Sign up to Maxine Morrey's mailing list for news, competitions and updates on future books.

Follow Maxine on social media here:

f facebook.com/scribblermaxi.co.uk

🐦 twitter.com/Scribbler_Maxi

📷 instagram.com/scribbler_maxi

BB bookbub.com/authors/MaxineMorrey

ALSO BY MAXINE MORREY

#No Filter

My Year of Saying No

Winter at Wishington Bay

Things Are Looking Up

Living Your Best Life

You Only Live Once

Just Say Yes

You've Got This